Annabel French is a bestselling author of several contemporary romantic fiction stories for HarperCollins, including her chateau series. Based in southeast England with her husband and teenage children, when she's not writing, she can be found running around after her three-legged rescue dog, Skips. She's also Vice Chair of the Romantic Novelists' Association because she firmly believes romance is the best genre in the world and nothing beats a good love story!

Also by Annabel French:

Summer at the Chateau
Christmas at the Chateau
Wedding at the Chateau
The Floating Amsterdam Flower Shop

The Floating Venice Bookshop

ANNABEL FRENCH

avon.

Published by AVON
A division of HarperCollins*Publishers* Ltd
1 London Bridge Street
London SE1 9GF

www.harpercollins.co.uk

HarperCollins*Publishers*
Macken House, 39/40 Mayor Street Upper
Dublin 1, D01 C9W8, Ireland

A Paperback Original 2026
1

First published in Great Britain by HarperCollinsPublishers 2026

Copyright © Katie Ginger 2026

Katie Ginger asserts the moral right to be identified as the author of this work.

A catalogue record for this book is available from the British Library.

ISBN: 978-0-00-873647-7

This novel is entirely a work of fiction. The names, characters and incidents portrayed in it are the work of the author's imagination. Any resemblance to actual persons, living or dead, events or localities is entirely coincidental.

Set in Sabon LT Pro by HarperCollins*Publishers* India

Printed and bound in the UK using 100% Renewable
Electricity at CPI Group (UK) Ltd

All rights reserved. No part of this publication may be reproduced, stored in a retrieval system, or transmitted, in any form or by any means, electronic, mechanical, photocopying, recording or otherwise, without the prior written permission of the publishers.

Without limiting the exclusive rights of any author, contributor or the publisher of this publication, any unauthorised use of this publication to train generative artificial intelligence (AI) technologies is expressly prohibited. HarperCollins also exercise their rights under Article 4(3) of the Digital Single Market Directive 2019/790 and expressly reserve this publication from the text and data mining exception.

To my best friend Jen, who is one of the most amazing, supportive and brilliant people I know. I'm so blessed to have you in my life!

PRAISE FOR *ANNABEL FRENCH*

'A charming and evocative read that
will have you wishing you were there.'
Rebecca Raisin

'Swoony and romantic!'
Leonie Mack

'Oh la la! This is the perfect escape.'
Bella Osborne

'A sun drenched read that conjures up the scent of summer.'
Julie Caplin

'A gorgeous escapist read, with a wonderful love story
about healing and the power of taking chances.'
Holly Martin

'This beautifully written romance set against the backdrop
of the canals of Amsterdam was a delight to read.
A much needed and joyful respite from the world.'
Rachel Burton

'Beautifully crafted and uplifting. I loved this story!'
Samantha Tonge

'We've never needed hopeful books more, and I recommend
this to anyone who wants to feel their heart lifted.'
Kate Storey

'What a blooming lovely story!'
Kate Frost

'The kind of romance that ticks all my boxes.
The perfect, escapist holiday read.'
Sarah Bennett

'Beautifully written – a real gem of a read!'
Lucy Coleman

Chapter 1

The air in Venice was cold as it whipped around the Gothic buildings that looked like they belonged on a movie set. The typical Venetian architecture, a mix of Byzantine and Renaissance with Islamic influence, appeared in the crowded streets, houses and shops all around her. And everywhere there was the smell of the water: the deep salty sea of the lagoon and the winding rivers of the canals that snaked and wound through the city. The bracing air bit at Beth's cheeks as she moved through the empty streets towards work, contemplating not just her day, but her life. She tucked her latest book underneath her arm and thrust her fingers deep into her pockets.

Some people hated the new year. The dull January weather, the winter stretching out before them, bringing what, at times, felt like never-ending cold. That was certainly how it had felt in England, but Beth had always loved the new year. It was a time for organising. For setting goals. For deciding and planning how she would improve herself and her life. What did she want to achieve in the year to come? How would she get there? SMART goals. That old business acronym: Specific. Measurable. Achievable. Relevant. Timebound. She would beat her PB in rowing one thousand metres; she might even set a higher reading target. This approach had served her well so far, getting her to exactly where she'd always wanted to be. Here. In Venice. Living her best life.

Venice had had some grey, rainy days, but today the sky was a bright, vibrant blue, the clouds pale and fluffy. Nothing compared to the beauty of Venice. Not in Beth's mind, anyway. She walked into the *Gallerie dell'Accademia* and inhaled. The air was different in here, softer somehow, and the quiet of the gallery wrapped around her like a blanket as soon as she turned off the increasingly busy Venice streets and in through the giant wooden door.

Even after almost a year's secondment, she still couldn't quite believe that she lived and worked in Venice. That she got to walk the city streets and stay here like a local. She loved the way the city smelled of salt water, sometimes even a little like seaweed, and of course, there were the scents of the gorgeous food and drink Italy was famous for. But for Beth, nothing compared to the smell of centuries-old oil paintings and the slight dustiness that all museums and galleries seemed to have. It was the air of history, and Venice was an art history lover's dream.

Years of planning and determination had got her here: a degree, a master's and then a doctorate landing her a job at the National Gallery in London and finally, her secondment here. Her term was soon coming to an end but Signor Sanna, the gallery director, was confident it would be renewed. There was no reason it shouldn't be, and Beth had been more than a little relieved. She didn't want to return to England yet. It wasn't that she hated her home city. Not at all. It was just that it had always felt like a stopgap to getting somewhere else. England was full of history, but nothing had excited her more than Italy and particularly the island of Venice with its unique, interesting past. That was why she'd applied for as many secondments here as she could, and though she'd been so busy she'd barely seen all the beautiful city had to offer, it had already become more like home than her now rented-out two-bedroom house in a quiet London suburb ever had.

'*Buongiorno*, Antonia,' Beth said with a wave, greeting one of the visitor assistants who was readying the gallery for opening.

Beth was pretty much fluent now. She'd noticed on first arriving how quickly Italians spoke and had found the pace of speech somewhat challenging, but combining history of art with Italian back at university had been a genius move, and her language skills had improved to the point that she now spoke like a local.

'*Buongiorno*, Beth,' the older lady responded in a sing-song voice, and then practising her English: 'What are you reading today?'

'Another book on the de Medicis.'

'I'm surprised you haven't read them all! Oh, Signor Sanna wants to see you straight away. He said to ask you to go to his office.'

'Oh! Sure, okay.'

Beth frowned a little. They'd only caught up the day before and he was aware of everything she was working on at the moment. What could he need to see her about? Perhaps it was to do with moving one of the more important paintings. She'd noted a couple of frames were needing repair and a few of the ridiculously precious paintings needed conservation. Maybe he'd finally got around to checking for himself and agreed they should swap them with something from the stores and get the conservators in.

Her low heels echoed on the tiles as she walked the stairs to the first floor, savouring the brilliant works of art from the thirteenth to seventeenth centuries that adorned the walls: the rich reds and blues of Titian and the paler colours of Tiepolo. The talent and skill that had gone into every painting made the hair on her arms stand up and goose bumps flush her skin, even though she was still wearing her coat. She pulled it tighter around her, over her normal uniform of plain black or grey trousers and a smart jumper. Old buildings like this were known for being draughty and the *Gallerie dell'Accademia* dated back to 1343, which meant there were numerous nooks and crannies the winter wind could sweep in, but it did mean it was nice and cool during the hot summer months when Venice was at its best and chock-a-block with tourists.

Beth knocked and opened Signor Sanna's door, the heat from his small portable heater hitting her face. Finally feeling warm enough, she shrugged off her coat and hooked it over the back of the chair.

'Signor,' she said in Italian, with a smile. 'Is everything okay?'

His shock of grey hair was even more unruly today, as if he hadn't even bothered combing it, and the way his eyes darted to her face then back down to his papers told her things definitely were not okay. He spoke in English, his thick salt and pepper eyebrows pulling together as he grimaced, and the lines on his face deepened. He'd always enjoyed practising her native language and in turn he'd helped with her Italian pronunciation, the nuances and inflections that made her sound like she belonged there.

The temperature in the room seemed to drop despite the heater and his downturned mouth meant this wasn't going to be a pleasant conversation. She wondered again what could be wrong. She'd never seen him like this before. He was always cheerful. He could be a little uptight sometimes, but lots of curators and academics were. It was part of the laser focus required to study a subject to the depths they often did. That was why the walls of his room were covered in shelves full of academic tomes and hefty reference books, spiral-bound papers covering every surface. She resisted the urge to run her fingers over the solid leather bindings on the nearest bookshelf, open one to sniff its pages or simply hold it for comfort.

'Please, sit down,' he said kindly. 'It is better that you sit.'

She did as he advised and dropped her book to the floor by the leg of her chair. Her stomach knotted uncomfortably, like her ribs were trying to push their way up and out of her body.

'What's going on?' Beth asked nervously. She suddenly didn't know what to do with her hands, and her fingers felt too long as she clasped them together. She pushed her long, plain brown hair back from her face. She had a band on her wrist but had worn it down on her walk into work to keep her warm. She wasn't cold now though and wished it would stop tickling her cheek. 'Are you okay?'

'Me? Yes, yes, I'm all right. It's just . . . oh, Beth, I'm so sorry.' He rubbed his hand over his forehead, settling his thumb and forefinger at each temple and squeezing. 'The funding for your post . . . it's . . . it's not going to be renewed after all.'

She froze, a wave of icy panic washing over her. As it moved slowly downwards from the top of her head, she could feel the colour draining from her face. Her heartbeat pounded in her ears like a drum.

'Wh – what? Sorry, I don't understand.' She squeezed her clasped hands even tighter. 'You said you were sure – that there was no reason to think—'

'I know.' He shook his head as if he wished he'd never

made such promises. 'I had an email late last night.' His fingers finally dropped from his forehead, and he looked her in the eye. The sorrow there almost made her cry, but she bit the inside of her cheek to stop the tears forming. She was at work. A professional. She wouldn't cry in a work setting. 'The society funding your position have said unfortunately they're going to have to withdraw it for the coming year. They've had unexpected costs and don't have the money anymore.'

'But why? What costs?'

'They haven't specified but you know this job. This industry. It could be anything. Perhaps an important work needs renovation. Maybe a building needs repair. Funding is difficult at the best of times.'

'But they can't! That means . . .'

'I know it's a shock,' he said gently. 'It was a shock to me too.'

'But without their funding my job's . . .' She couldn't finish the sentence.

'I wish there was something more I could do,' he said quietly, in barely more than a whisper. 'I really am so sorry.'

'But – but—' She tried to focus and make sense of the frantic thoughts running through her head. She took a deep breath, trying to calm her brain. She needed to think logically. 'Can't the gallery do something? Can you argue with them that my position is needed? I was planning that amazing Giorgione exhibition.'

Giorgione was a Venetian painter well known in academic

circles but not so much by the public. Beth had hoped to shine a light on him and his work during the height of the summer season.

'Believe me I've already tried. I answered the email as soon as I read it, and they've come back this morning to say no. There's nothing they can do, and we don't have the money to pay you. We barely have enough to pay the essential staff and run the building or do the conservation we need. You know the paintings have to come first. I wish there was something more I could do.'

Essential staff. That was the problem with a career in the arts. It was never seen as important enough and people who worked in it were never considered 'essential' even though museums and galleries taught people so much about the world and its history and protected important artefacts for future generations to enjoy.

Beth's teeth were in danger of chattering as cold shivered through her bones. Her nerves roiled like she'd been picked up and tipped upside down. She felt discombobulated, her brain struggling to process what Signor Sanna had said. It was like when you stepped off a roller coaster and your legs, arms, brain and torso couldn't connect or work together. She tried to think logically, to make a plan, but her synapses were working too slowly. After a second, her brain began to pick snippets of information from the jumble and the stark facts floated to the surface just enough for her to focus on one thing.

'So I'm out of a job?' She'd thought the secondment

would lead on to something more – a permanent position here or at a different Venetian gallery. Now she wasn't just out of a job, but her future prospects had also disappeared.

Signor Sanna sighed heavily. 'I'm afraid so.'

'So what happens now?'

Her apartment was paid for as part of the secondment but that too would be rescinded. She'd have to move out and while a change of job would have necessitated that anyway, she now only had weeks rather than months. As panic rose, it seemed her options were to find somewhere else to live or return home to England. And when? When would she have to move?

As if pre-empting her question, Signor Sanna said, 'I've told them they can't expect you to leave straight away. They've agreed to give you four weeks to make arrangements.'

'Four weeks?' It came out in a high-pitched squeak. And what did arrangements mean?

To them it meant packing up her things and arranging a flight home, but to her it meant the end of her dream. The end of the life she was building for herself here. It wasn't a perfect life, far from it. She still preferred books to people and hadn't really dated any of the gorgeous Italian men all around her. And she hadn't explored the city fully or its beautiful surrounding islands, but she had friends. She'd only just summoned up the courage to join her local rowing club and she didn't want to let that go. There was still so much for her to see and do here. She wished she'd prioritised herself and her life, instead of putting her career first all the time.

Signor Sanna reached his hand out, and like a robot she moved hers from her lap and slipped it into his. 'I am so sorry, Beth. I wish there was something more I could do.' He patted her hand in a fatherly fashion, and she gave a pathetic smile, his face blurring as tears sprang to her eyes. She stared at the ceiling, forcing them back, her jaw aching with the effort. 'You will still come to the masquerade ball though, won't you? Even if you have to come back for it. You enjoyed it so much last year and it seems only fair given the work you've done this last year.'

The grand event, held at the galleria, was part of Carnevale and she'd loved wearing a fancy dress and sipping champagne. She'd felt like she'd made it. A soirée in a famous Venetian gallery, in the most historic, beautiful city in the world. And now her career had halted and her time here ended.

'Umm . . . yes, probably. I . . .' Her words faded, unable to form a sentence or think that far ahead.

'Why don't you take the rest of the day off? This is a lot to think about, and I cannot ask you to work today.'

Part of her wanted to work, to stay and stare at the paintings and surround herself with the art she loved so much for as long as she was able to. The worst part of her job was giving tours – she much preferred to be behind the scenes – and she definitely couldn't face standing in front of people, citing the genius and craftsmanship that went into every painting knowing that she'd soon be forced to return to England. If anyone asked her a question, she'd probably just cry.

As if reading her mind, Signor Sanna said, 'I can do your tour this afternoon. It's no problem.'

'Are you sure?' Her voice wavered as she struggled to keep her emotions in check and Signor Sanna nodded.

'Go and have a strong coffee at Giambattista's. You will feel better. I'm so sorry, Beth. I wish there was more I could do.'

'I know there isn't. And this isn't your fault. You've been lovely, Signor. You've taught me so much and I'm so grateful for your help. I appreciate you getting me four more weeks.'

'If I could make them change their minds, I would. We will all miss you very much. Now go. This is a big shock. Take some time. Take as much time as you need. I will help you in any way I can.'

His grip loosened and she slid her hand away as she stood, gathering her coat and trying not to look at him. Her legs were like jelly as she moved, and she worried she might actually fall. When she got to the door, she held it tightly and she flashed him a weak smile before closing it behind her.

Her heart pounded, blood thudding in her ears as she tried to deal with what had just happened. Queasiness reached up from her stomach into her throat and after a few unstable steps, she leaned against the wall, tears beginning to escape. She quickly brushed them away. Beth didn't like anyone to see her cry. She only did it in front of people she really knew and who knew her in return. She focused on her breathing and took a deep, shaky breath in, held it for a second and squeezed her eyes shut as she let it out slowly. After a few more breaths, the tears had dried, and she was able to move again.

Now open to the public, the gallery was growing busier. Members of staff chatted with tourists eager to learn about the treasures inside. Treasures she'd be guardian of no more. She was being sent home like a naughty schoolgirl. Deep down she knew it wasn't a reflection on her or her abilities, that it was all to do with money and other people's choices, but it didn't stop it hurting and in some ways, the feeling of helplessness made it even worse. There was nothing she could do to affect this decision. It was made and confirmed. A done deal.

Fumbling, she threw on her coat, felt her wallet and keys in the pocket and headed back downstairs. Her book, she realised, was still in Signor Sanna's room where she'd left it by her chair.

'Ah,' Antonia said, 'there you are. I was— Beth! Is everything—'

'Sorry, I need to go home.' She carried on rushing past her, keeping her head down as her nose stung. Her long hair still irritatingly tickled her cheek but at least it hid some of her face and the tears once more threatening to overtake her. 'Signor Sanna's covering my tour. I'll see you tomorrow.'

The heavy, dark wooden doors had been pinned open,

and the chill air hit her as she made her way outside. This time, she didn't look at the buildings on the familiar route or enjoy the sights around her. Dodging through the crowd, she didn't stop walking until she was more than a few streets away. That familiar smell of salt water filled her nose and, as she stared at the uneven, paved streets, her heart burned with pain.

It was over.
This job.
This city.
This life.
It was all over.

Chapter 2

Beth thought about going home, but unable to think straight, she simply followed Signor Sanna's instruction and made her way to Giambattista's, the café they regularly visited for mid-morning takeaways and after-work debriefs.

Her brain was frazzled and though her pulse was no longer thudding in her ears, it had been replaced by a sort of buzzing, like a bee had taken up residence in her head. She approached the canal-side café, her legs still shaking, and suddenly noticed all the things she'd missed before, too busy with life and rushing to and from work to have taken them in. The green awning that ran the length of the building was the same colour as the algae just visible above the waterline on the houses opposite. The shutters on the higher windows needed a lick of paint and the pale greyish-cream Istrian stone was darker in some places due to damp or water damage. But still, even on this wintry day, the café was bright and cheerful, the fake flowers on the tables welcoming and adding even more colour. They'd be changed for real flowers when the tourist season started, but she wouldn't be here for that now.

Even though it was cold enough to see her breath, she chose to sit outside. She needed the icy, fresh air on her cheeks to get her brain moving again. She had to find a way to process what had just happened, what it meant, and what her next steps were. She'd loved the challenges of a new year but this wasn't exactly what she'd had in mind.

Evalina, a waitress, came over and greeted Beth by name. Thankfully, the chill breeze always turned Beth's nose and cheeks pink, and now it hid the fact she'd been crying.

'Are you sure you'd like to sit outside?' the waitress asked in Italian.

With her brain in such a muddle, Beth replied in English. 'Definitely. I need some air.'

Evalina nodded, clearly thinking it was odd, and waited. After a second, Beth realised she hadn't actually asked for anything to drink. 'Oh, sorry. Can I have a large latte, please?'

Really, she should have ordered an espresso or *caffe*, but she just couldn't manage such a strong flavour right now. Evalina clearly recognised how much she needed the comfort of the more milky coffee as she frowned and said: 'Of course. It is not traditional, but I will let you have it as you look so stressed.'

Beth managed a weak smile, but Evalina couldn't help her brows pulling together as Beth acted so differently to usual. She hesitated as if she was about to say something but then thought better of it. Beth tried to flash her a smile, but from the narrowing of her eyes, it didn't convince her, and she moved away slowly, glancing back as she went.

The outside wooden tables sat right next to the canal bank with a straight drop into the water. It lapped gently against the side, making a gentle splashing sound. Beth's eyes wandered to a small iron bridge at the end of the road that linked two streets. She'd been here a year, and she hadn't taken the time to go in either direction to see where they led. She hadn't explored the city at all. Not properly. She'd never just taken a coffee and wandered through the alleyways, soaking up the vibes. Of course she'd visited St Mark's Square, the famous main public square, and she'd taken in the beauty of the Doge's Palace and St Mark's Basilica. But she'd never explored the nooks and crannies and funny little side streets of the famous floating city. There were so many restaurants she'd never eaten at, bars she'd never visited, cafés she'd never drunk at. Not to mention shops and markets she'd never seen. The thought of the bookshops she was yet to visit almost made her cry again.

Seeing a gondola tied to a set of steps further down the canal, she realised she'd never even had a gondola ride. She hadn't wanted to do it alone, as un-feminist as that was. It was such an iconic romantic gesture. Her dating history was nowhere near as impressive as her résumé. Dates were few and far between, and despite setting a goal when she moved here to find a tall, dark and handsome Italian to enjoy the city with, it hadn't happened. She'd been consumed by her job and the beautiful artwork at the galleria, and now it was all too late.

It was Giambattista himself who brought out the coffee, pulling her out of her thoughts. He placed it on the table along with a small plate piled high with *baicoli*, a hard but delicious biscuit, and a small dish of *zabaglione*, a sweet cream she could dip them into. She'd never been more grateful in her life.

'I didn't order these,' Beth said, looking up into his kind face.

'I could tell you needed them. Free, of course.' Giambattista grinned, showing the gaps in his teeth. He was pushing eighty now, though following the Mediterranean diet he didn't look it. His face was tanned and wrinkled from the long, hot Venetian summers and his hair looked dark grey where the once black met the encroaching white. He'd been handsome in his youth; she could tell that from his bone structure. He slipped into the seat opposite her, speaking in Italian. 'Something's happened, hasn't it?'

Beth's lip began to wobble and through sheer willpower alone she managed to hold back the tears. 'I've just found out my job's over,' she replied, and he immediately broke into English.

'You've been fired?'

'No!' She hadn't meant to shout but the idea was preposterous. She was barely ever told off. Her best friends still called her a goody two-shoes sometimes when they were teasing her, and they weren't wrong. 'The funding's been removed. It's just a whole thing in academia.'

'So what does that mean?' he asked gently.

'It means I don't have a job anymore and I have to go home in four weeks' time. Maybe even earlier.'

The tears threatened once more, and she grabbed a *baicoli*, dipping it into the cream and ramming it into her mouth, partly to stop the tears falling and partly to try and cheer herself up. Nothing did that like delicious Italian treats. The hit of sugar made her feel slightly better for a moment. If only she could eat them continually, or at least until this initial hurt faded.

'Slow down,' Giambattista said gently, smiling, as she tucked into another. 'You'll make yourself sick.'

'I can't help it. They're delicious.'

'*Grazie*. Now, do you *want* to go home?'

She shook her head, another *baicoli* heading into her mouth. She wouldn't have got the words out anyway. She liked her life here. She should have done more by now, but really she felt like she was only just getting started. She looked up at the bright blue sky. It was probably raining again in the UK, the sky dense with dark grey cloud. Even those sorts of days hadn't seemed so bad here. She loved the sound of the rain on the gallery windows, on the apartment roof as she slept. And Venice was as beautiful in the winter as in summer. Better even, as it felt like it belonged to the locals, the tourists departed until the sun brought them back again.

Giambattista stood up. 'It's too cold out here for my old bones. Let's go inside.'

Her fingers were like ice and the warmth of the coffee cup wasn't doing anything to help. Still eating a *baicoli*, she stood up and he carried the plate of biscuits as they headed inside. The change in temperature brought a flush to her skin, turning her cheeks even pinker. He placed the plate down on a small table and she settled on the large deep red bench next to him. The walls were adorned with traditional frescoes, most of them religious – replicas or takes on the religious art Venice was famous for. She sent a silent prayer to heaven that some sort of answer would present itself to her soon, though she didn't have much hope it actually would.

'So,' Giambattista said, helping himself to a biscuit but not bothering with the *zabaglione*. 'What will you do, if you don't want to go home?'

'I don't know. All I've ever done is work in museums and galleries. It took me so long to train for, I've never had time for anything else.'

'Forget all that.' He waved his hand dramatically, brushing her worries aside as though she were concentrating on the wrong thing. 'What would you do if you could? Your dream job. And I don't mean eating *baicoli* all day.'

A hint of a smile played on her lips but was soon replaced

with a frown. She didn't quite understand his question. 'What do you mean? I *am* doing my dream job.'

'Are you? Or are you doing something you like? Maybe even love. They're two different things, you know.'

It was true she loved her job but was it her dream job? She'd never thought they could be two different things. She'd always focused on the next step on the career path she'd chosen at twelve years old when she'd visited the British Museum and the National Gallery on the same day. Her mind had been made up then and with parents who'd drifted from job to job, causing money worries and giving her more responsibility than a child that age should have taken on, her mind had never had the chance to wander from that path.

She felt like the earth was shifting under her feet again, just like it had in Signor Sanna's office, and the biscuits threatened to rise up. She could feel them churning in her stomach amongst bitter bile, fear and panic.

'So you're not sure what job you would like to do next, but you know it is here?'

'Yes,' she said, suddenly certain of that one thing. 'I do know that. Maybe I can see if any other museums are hiring. There are one or two here,' she said with a smile. A historic city like Venice had them everywhere.

Giambattista chuckled. 'Yes, we have a few you could try. But . . . is this not a chance to do something else? Something you would love even more? I know you love your job, but do you not get lonely working all by yourself all the time?

You could turn this into an opportunity. It doesn't have to mean the end. When you come in, you aren't always smiling. Only when you are reading do you smile.'

She hadn't thought of it like that. To be honest, at this moment she wasn't sure she'd ever be able to think of it like that. The pain was too raw, and she was too angry. She'd worked so hard to get where she was. She couldn't just throw all that away, could she? What would she even do? Nothing particular came to mind, though, if this was make-believe, she'd probably want to do something with books or reading. Could she switch to being a librarian?

A few more customers came in. Regulars, old friends of Giambattista's, and as they settled at their usual table, Giambattista placed his large, warm hands over hers.

'I'll leave you to think, but try to think . . .' He searched for the word, his English failing him. 'Wider,' he said eventually, his hands a foot apart as though he were showing her the dimensions of a box.

Beth settled into the seat, warm enough now to remove her coat. There were two *baicoli* left but only half a coffee. She ordered another one and got to work on her phone, searching for any job opportunities in Venice that would suit her and her training. As she selected filters and amended searches, the opportunities dwindled in front of her eyes. Maybe she *should* be thinking wider. Giambattista's advice rang in her ears but with no idea what she'd ever dream of doing, she couldn't search for anything in particular.

Unfortunately, by the time she'd drained her second coffee

and finished the sweet treats, she hadn't found anything suitable and her shoulders were slumped, her spirits lower than the Venice waterline. She knew from experience there might be some visitor assistant posts available nearer the summer, but right now there was nothing. She was just about to leave when Giambattista rushed to the door excitedly, opening it widely, and in came an army of young men carrying tables.

'*Mi scusi, signora*,' one of them said, trying to remove her table while a colleague replaced it with the one he was holding.

'Oh, what—' She turned to Giambattista, picking up her cup and plate. 'What's going on?'

'I'm changing the tables. These are too boring.' He patted the top of the plain wooden table in front of him. 'The same as every other café and restaurant in Venezia. But look at these; aren't they beautiful?'

'Gorgeous!' She put her plate and cup back down, admiring the unusual design.

The base was made of a stack of old books that reminded her of the academic tomes in Signor Sanna's office. They were set in a spiral and varnished so they had a slight sheen and were firm enough not to buckle under the weight of the tabletop which was reinforced glass so you could see the cover of the topmost book. She tilted her head to read it.

'*L'Arte Di Venezia*. *The Art of Venice*. Where did these come from?'

'You remember my friend who owns the book barge?'

She nodded. She'd visited it a few times, loving all bookshops. It had stocked mostly non-fiction, which she herself enjoyed, but recently she'd found her tastes wandering more to novels. She loved the escapism they provided, particularly if she could find something set in Renaissance Venice.

'I had the brilliant idea to turn some of his stock into table bases – I saw it on Pinterest.'

For the first time since her meeting with Signor Sanna that morning, Beth chuckled, knowing Giambattista wasn't exactly tech savvy, and at the image of him on his phone, flicking through Pinterest for inspiration. 'An artist friend I know offered to do it. I am so pleased with them!' He stood back admiring the new tables the small army of men were still putting in place. 'Do you like them?'

'I do. Very much.'

'Stay and see once they're all in.'

Feeling in the way, and with her mind so full of the day's events, Beth gave her apologies. 'I'll come and see them tomorrow. I just . . . I think I better go. I'm not very good company right now.'

'Think about what I said,' Giambattista added and Beth nodded.

What would she do for the rest of the day? Where would she go? Before she reached the door, she knew there was only one thing to do: go to her happy place.

Chapter 3

Beth's heartbeat began to rise as she pulled back the handle of the rowing machine. Her abs tightened and her legs were already burning from the effort, sweat trickling down her temples.

She used the handles of the rowing machine to propel herself forwards, her knees up near her chest, inhaling as she drew closer and watching the counter on the console. Thoughts of galleries and flats fell from her head as her mind calmed and she focused entirely on the task at hand: her own steady breathing, the feeling of strength.

Through the large gym window that looked out into the Venetian lagoon, she could see the pale January sun, the shimmery golden light reflecting on the water. Gosh it was beautiful. She ignored the fire in her lungs and the slight panic that came with it each and every time she worked out, knowing it was a normal part of the process as her body pushed harder and harder. She told herself to breathe, to keep going.

Breathe.

Keep going.

The endorphins were beginning to kick in, sending positive thoughts into her head. She was doing this. Pushing herself and achieving. She loved this moment, edging her limits further and further away. Improving. Getting stronger. Not that it was easy. There was always a constant battle between the voice screaming, *Stop it! You're going to die!* And the one telling her to pull one more time, to hit another fifty yards.

'Your fitness has improved so much,' Francesca said, her long dark hair tied back into a high, bouncy ponytail. Even without make-up she was stunning, with her olive skin and Italian colouring. Her deep brown eyes crinkled as she smiled. 'You should start rowing on the water now.'

'Maybe,' Beth replied in a sharp exhalation, working harder than she ever had before.

Francesca had befriended her as soon as she'd joined the gym attached to the rowing club. She'd planned to row on the water, but seeing the fitness and ability of the others, she hadn't felt confident enough to, sticking to the gym. The tall, pretty Italian woman had spied her across the gym floor on her first nervous day when she'd arrived and started using one of the treadmills. To be honest, Beth hated running and had found a natural affinity with the rowing machine. But before she'd had the chance to move to a different piece of equipment, Cesca had landed next to her, welcoming her with lots of chatty conversation and cheering encouragement. The two had hit it off instantly and become fast friends. Cesca was always giving her top tips for making the most of Venice. Not that Beth had followed many of them and she deeply regretted that now.

Beth gritted her teeth and kept going. There was only a short distance left. She was nearly there. With a flood of relief, and a final endorphin hit, she hit her distance. Allowing the handles to slide back into place, she relaxed, stretching her legs and pushing the seat back so she could ease the burning tightness in her quads. 'Oh, thank God.'

Cesca giggled. 'Why do we put ourselves through this, hey?'

'I have no idea.' Beth's breath began to slow, letting her heart rate drop and her muscles recover. Instantly, thoughts of the day returned, and disappointment hit Beth again.

Cesca handed her a water bottle, and she took it gratefully, gulping mouthfuls of cold, refreshing water. She normally felt better after a good row, and though her muscles didn't feel tight with tension and sadness, it had been too much to expect today. She unhooked her feet from the foot plates and stood, her legs like jelly as she precariously balanced and shook them out one at a time, stretching her quads and hamstrings.

'Are you all right?' Cesca asked. 'I don't normally see you at this time of day.'

They moved to the weight rack and Beth picked up some medium dumbbells, beginning her usual routine. Her arms were already protesting, but she ignored them, knowing she was growing stronger with every rep. In between breaths, Beth told Cesca about the morning.

'Oh no! That's terrible. I'm so sorry, Beth. What are you going to do?'

'Honestly, right now, I have no idea.' She put the weight down and placed her hands on her hips, taking in a deep breath. 'To be honest, I'm still in shock. I – I don't think it's quite sunk in yet.'

'Let's go to the café downstairs and talk. Are you nearly done?'

'Nearly.' Beth's body felt deliciously tired. Though she wasn't anywhere near all right, she felt calmer somehow. That physical feeling of achieving was filtering through to her mind, telling her that if she could do that, she could do anything and would somehow figure a way through the next few weeks, no matter what they looked like. 'But if you're busy, I understand. Please don't—'

'I'll meet you in the café.'

'Thank you. I – I could really use a friend right now.'

'I'm just going to do some core work while you shower, but Beth . . . it will be all right.' Cesca made her way over to the corner of the gym and began holding a plank, her muscles lean from working out and from her day job.

Francesca was a carpenter with a talent for interior design. She'd done some work around the rowing club, fixing odd things here and there and from the type of person she was, Beth knew that her standards would be exacting. She was something of a perfectionist when it came to her rowing form, and Beth could see that would extend to her work too.

Her friend's kind words sent a lump into Beth's throat as she moved away. She'd connected with Cesca immediately and they'd enjoyed some great evenings out together. Beth had loved hearing about her family and what it was like being the only girl with seven brothers. As an only child, and not a particularly valued one, Beth had found it hard to comprehend. But Cesca's family sounded close, and Beth could imagine that could be both a good and bad thing.

After showering, Beth wandered to the small café situated on the floor between the gym above and the clubhouse below. Like the gym, it had large floor-to-ceiling windows where they could watch the Venetian waters, rowers gliding through the calm surface. The sunlight shone through the windows, warming the café, and tiny dust motes danced in the beams of light. The actual boathouse, which housed the different-sized rowing boats and oars, was next door.

Beth rubbed her face, ensuring her moisturiser was soaking in, and grabbed them a table. She'd already bought them both a chocolate and banana protein smoothie (their favourite post-workout snack) and she resisted the urge to tuck into hers. She was starving now, even though she'd eaten that whole plate of *baicoli* at Giambattista's.

Cesca joined her a few minutes later in jeans and a tight

jumper that landed at her waist, revealing her flat stomach. Beth looked down at her tracksuit bottoms and tattered hoodie, thinking she should have embraced Italian style by now. If she wasn't in her uniform of black trousers and a jumper, she was in workout gear or this. Not exactly tantalising.

'*Grazie*,' Cesca said as she sat down. 'Now, what can I do to help?'

'To be honest, I wish I knew,' Beth replied. Though she'd felt a little better earlier, and the lingering endorphins were still softening the blow of the morning, she still had no idea what to do next. 'But thank you for being here. I appreciate it.'

'You're a friend. We make time for friends and family here.'

'How're all yours?'

Most of Cesca's brothers were married, and she had numerous nieces and nephews of various ages. Her whole family lived in Murano, a small island not far from Venice, famous for glass-blowing. Cesca was immensely proud of her family's business and its heritage and, as a history fan herself, Beth could easily understand it.

Just as Cesca was telling her about sickness bugs, family dinners and one particular sister-in-law she wasn't overly keen on, Beth's eyes fell on the most handsome man she'd ever seen, and she almost choked on her smoothie as she did a comedy double take. He was tall and broad-shouldered with floppy dark hair, a clean-shaven, chiselled jaw and ice-blue eyes. They were so pale and yet so bright; Beth couldn't stop looking at them. Her heart almost matched the speed it had been when she had been rowing, and she checked her fitness watch, disturbed to see it was inching towards the red zone. He was wearing shorts revealing bronzed skin, the perfect amount of dark hair on his legs and lots and lots of muscles. She tried to stop her eyes wandering up over his toned torso, but she couldn't, and when his eyes met hers he smiled and, embarrassed, she looked away. He was like a character from the latest historical fiction she'd read: another book set in Venice with a swoon-worthy hero. It was a welcome distraction after the morning.

'I've not seen him before,' Beth whispered to Cesca. 'Is he new here? He must be because I would definitely have remembered him.'

'Him?' Cesca asked, astounded, pointing right at him. Beth immediately pushed her hand down, making Cesca giggle.

'Stop it! He'll know we're talking about him. Do you recognise him?'

Before she could answer, he changed direction and started walking over to them. Beth grabbed her smoothie and stuck the straw into her mouth so quickly she jabbed her gum. Wincing, she took a mouthful, but when he paused right in front of their table and she tried to swallow, it went down the wrong way and she coughed, her cheeks turning even redder than they had been before. Her eyes began to water and she wished she could dissolve into the floor, never to be seen again.

'Are you all right?' he asked in Italian, as Cesca hit her forcefully on the back, but before Beth could speak, her friend answered for her.

'She's English, Marco.'

Marco? So she did know him.

'I do speak Italian though,' Beth answered, still coughing between words, not wanting him to think badly of her. 'Pretty fluently.'

'Oh,' he replied. '*Spero che il tuo frullato sia delizioso?*'

'My smoothie is very delicious, thank you for asking.' She prickled slightly at being tested and his eyes glittered. She added, '*Vuoi prenderti un frullato o resti lì a sorridermi tutto il girno?*'

He and Cesca both burst out laughing. After a second, he composed himself and answered. 'I don't plan to smirk at you all day, no. And I prefer a coffee to a smoothie, especially before I train.'

Cesca cleared her throat while the two of them locked eyes, Beth trying to figure out what to make of him. She didn't know whether to be charmed or offended. She did realise what a rarity it was to find an English person fluent in another language.

'Marco, this is Beth, and Beth this is my brother Marco.'

'Your brother!' Beth's cheeks grew instantly hotter, the warmth spreading down her neck and back. She was almost afraid to touch them in case the fabric of her hoodie caught fire. She'd been ogling and lusting after Cesca's brother! Great. That wasn't something to be embarrassed about at all. Could today get any worse?

'It's a pleasure to meet you,' he said in English, sliding out a chair and joining them.

'And you,' she replied, trying to salvage some dignity after choking and now embarrassing herself in front of Cesca's brother. Today was, without doubt, turning into the worst day of her life. She switched into professional mode, as though she were meeting him at a work event. She could feel her posture changing despite her slouchy outfit, and she sat taller in her seat, her chin slightly lifted. She tried to ignore the fact she wasn't exactly looking her best. 'I've heard a lot about you.'

Cesca had mentioned her brother a few times, generally with regard to family arguments and tensions surrounding the family business. She wasn't sure what Marco did, she just knew he didn't blow the glass and make the art. He was connected to their family business, but more on the corporate side, and his modern ideas sometimes caused him and his far more traditional father to fall out. But the relationship between brother and sister seemed easy enough. Cesca was obviously fond of her black-sheep brother.

'Marco's the difficult middle child,' Cesca said with a grin and Marco rolled his eyes.

'And you probably already know Cesca's the baby of the family. The princess who always gets her own way. *Mi scusi.*' He stood up. 'I need a caffé.'

The way he said it made the regular coffee drink sound exotic and utterly delicious, and Beth cleared her throat, but she couldn't help her eyes following him.

'Eww,' Cesca said, drawing Beth's attention straight back. 'Do you *like* my brother?'

'Shhhh! No! Not like that. I'm just being polite.'

'Really? So your eyes following him and saying that he's—'

'He is handsome,' she interrupted, feeling the need to clarify and put an end to the conversation. 'But no more than a lot of Italian men. No offence.'

'None taken.'

'You have a different quality here than we do back home. It's all that sunshine and a healthy diet.'

Cesca giggled before sipping her smoothie. 'Don't worry, I won't say anything.'

Marco returned, sliding into his seat and wiping the foam from his upper lip after drinking his coffee. He had the most perfect Cupid's bow, and she could just imagine it running kisses down her neck. She shivered and hoped the blast of cold air was cooling her cheeks a little.

'Beth thinks you're handsome,' Cesca announced, and Beth's head whipped round so fast it was a wonder she hadn't hurt herself.

'Cesca!' She could have died. Right there, on the spot, she could have happily let her life slip away just so she didn't have to look at him ever again.

'At least I made you laugh. You needed it.'

'Thank you.' Marco smiled, catching her eye. 'Do you say that to every man you meet?'

'No. Yes. Well—'

A year in Venice and the very few dates she'd had had been like pulling teeth. She much preferred book boyfriends. The most flirting she'd done was with a painting of a particularly handsome cardinal from 1475.

Beth narrowed her eyes at Cesca, who pretended she hadn't noticed. Her cheeks were on fire, but she lifted her head to meet his eye, refusing to show how awkward and embarrassed she felt. Cesca was due some payback and she'd enjoy every minute of it when the time came.

'I haven't seen you here before, Beth. Have you only just joined?'

'No, I've been coming here for about ten months, but I've stayed in the gym.'

'You haven't been out on the water?'

She shook her head.

'Why not?'

'She didn't think she was up to it,' Cesca said. 'But she definitely is now. Hey, why don't you come out with me tomorrow?'

'Tomorrow?' Beth squeaked.

'Yes! You don't have to go back to work, do you? That's not fair.'

'Oh, I, umm . . . maybe another time. I need to figure out what to do now.' She turned to Marco, eager to change the subject. 'I don't remember seeing you around either.' *And I would have remembered,* she thought, trying not to watch the way his thigh muscles moved as he adjusted his position.

'No, I—' He glanced at Cesca and there was a moment of discomfort between them. Cesca smiled down at her smoothie and took a drink. 'I travel a lot for work.'

There it was again, that flash of something remaining unsaid between brother and sister. Was this the cause of the family arguments? Something to do with the family business? Cesca hadn't ever gone into specifics, but she'd definitely grown uncomfortable now. Beth wondered what it could be. If she'd learned anything about Italians since living here, it was that they were a passionate, fiery bunch. As the word *passionate* played in her head, her eyes drew up to Marco and, at the same moment, his gaze went from his sister to her. That killer smile with bright white, beautifully even teeth flashed again, and she was in danger of overheating once more. But the atmosphere had grown heavy. Marco seemed to have suddenly closed in and Cesca, always relaxed and open, had crossed her arms over her chest. Awkward was an understatement.

'Right,' Beth said, standing up. 'I better go.' *And figure out what I'm doing with the rest of my life.* 'See you later, Cesca. Nice to meet you, Marco.'

'You too.'

She had only just made it outside, the cool air refreshing after her flaming embarrassment, when her phone rang. Strangely, it was Giambattista who could only have got her number from Signor Sanna. What could he possibly want?

'I have good news!' he announced after she greeted him. 'You know my friend who gave me the books for the tables?'

'Yes,' she answered tentatively.

'Well, he is old – even older than me—' He chuckled. 'Too old to look after his bookshop, so he's selling it along with all his stock.'

'Right.' Beth stood blinking in the wintry sunshine as the words he'd just said filtered into her brain.

'*You* should buy his book barge!'

'Me?' she squeaked. No! It was preposterous. She couldn't. Could she . . . ? Should she . . . ? Was this a terrible idea?

'This is exactly the solution you were looking for.'

'But . . . but . . .'

She stood still, thinking. She wasn't an impetuous person. She didn't make rash decisions. Every life choice had been carefully considered, mapped out and thought through. Last-minute coffee dates and unexpected invitations always threw her and, more often than not, she'd say no because she just couldn't handle the stress of being unprepared. But the information Giambattista had just given her was connecting with his advice of earlier. She loved books. She read all the time. Her small flat was full of all her latest reads, novels filling the bookcase and piled high next to it because there just wasn't enough room.

'What do you think?' She could hear him smiling down the phone.

'I think – I think I'd love to run a book barge, if I could, but—'

'Exactly! You always have a book in your hands. Always.'

Words were tumbling around her brain. Could she do this? A part of her told her no, she didn't have the training. She preferred being behind the scenes, not talking to customers. She knew about art and paintings, not the latest fiction releases. But she was a true bookworm, and she knew how to cash up; she'd done it to help out at the galleria often enough. She could market exhibitions and marketing a book barge couldn't be that different. It would allow her to stay in Venice and, with no museums taking on, what else was she going to do?

But was this all too much caffeine? The shock of the morning catching up with her?

Her stomach churned but with something that felt like excitement rather than blind panic.

Giambattista was so excited he spoke in Italian and as her brain fought with itself, she had to work hard to pay attention. 'He'll be so happy! He was so worried no one would want it!'

Worry and fear began to take over. What had she done? What had she said? She hadn't thought through costs or implications; she'd done no research . . . nothing.

Did she really, actually want to run a floating bookshop? On a barge? In Venice?

A strong voice inside her replied with a resounding yes, quietening her doubts.

'I've told him you will see him tomorrow at ten o'clock,' Giambattista said.

Suddenly, a thought crystallised in her head. It wasn't the galleria that was right for her. It was Venice. And the possibility of running her own small, perfect bookshop on one of Venice's beautiful canals seemed like a dream. Her chest tightened and she knew she couldn't let this opportunity go or let her own need to plan and be in control hold her back.

'I'll send you the address now. I am so happy, Beth! This is fate!'

He rang off and Beth stared ahead, blinking in the sunlight. Cold air brought her back to life, blowing hair into her face. Yet, her brain had frozen, too many thoughts tumbling around in a whirlwind. Without thinking, she turned around and marched straight back into the café, plonking into the seat she'd only recently vacated. Cesca and Marco's conversation halted.

'Oh,' Cesca said, her voice high with surprise. 'I thought . . . Beth . . . Are you okay?'

Vaguely, Beth was aware of Cesca and Marco glancing at each other, then her, their eyes widening in concern.

Was this a good idea or had the shock sent her off the deep end?

'I've just had a very odd phone call.'

'Right . . . ?' Cesca said.

'I – I think . . . I think there might be a solution to my staying in Venice.'

'Staying?' Marco asked and Cesca quickly and quietly gave him a rundown of the day's events.

In disjointed sentences, as though she was only just learning to talk, Beth explained about the phone call she'd just received and Giambattista's excitement.

'This is brilliant,' Cesca said, clapping her hands together. 'It's such a perfect solution.'

'But – I can't! It's – it's such a big change. A big risk. I don't know if I can do it.'

'Of course you can! Can't she, Marco?'

'If she wants to,' Marco said, his tone a mixture of question and concern. 'Do you want to?' He looked at Beth, their eyes meeting, and the intense kindness made her stomach flip.

'I – I think so . . . ?'

Cesca clapped. 'Then you should do it! I can help with any repairs and design work. But how often does a chance like this come along?' She leaned forwards and grabbed Beth's hands.

'Not very often I suppose.'

'Then you should do it? What's the worst that can happen?'

Her mind almost listed too many options to count, but then Marco's deep voice cut through them.

'You cannot predict what will or won't go wrong, but even if it doesn't work out, you won't be any worse off than you are now. And who doesn't like bookshops?'

Who indeed, she thought. Could he become any more attractive? Who didn't love a man who loved a bookshop!

'Taking chances,' Cesca added excitedly, 'can be good for the soul. That's what our mamma says.'

Beth's soul was here in Venice. She knew that more than anything.

'Would you like me to come with you?' Cesca asked gently, and Beth felt a surge of love for her friend.

'Would you?'

'Of course! I would love to.'

Excitement began to build, and a smile lifted Beth's face. With Cesca there to let her know what needed doing, she'd be in a much better position to make a decision. Not to mention she'd love the moral support. She glanced at Cesca, whose smile was familiar and comforting, and to Marco, who she'd only just met, but whose kindness in this moment had helped settle her nerves and stop her automatically saying no. She felt a blaze of attraction cut through the panicky thoughts swirling in her mind as he smiled.

A floating bookshop. It did sound wonderful. And there was no harm in at least taking a look, was there?

Chapter 4

Beth spent the rest of the afternoon in her small apartment. As she'd suspected there would be seasonal front-of-house vacancies soon, but nothing on the curatorial side. A quick look at vacancies further afield showed exactly what she'd been expecting: reduced opportunities due to budget cuts. If she went home, she'd be looking at working in a different field and if she was going to do that back home in England, somewhere she didn't particularly want to be, why shouldn't she do it here, in Venice? A city she'd loved from the moment she'd arrived. Soon, she'd gone on to making budget spreadsheets. She could afford to make a change if she wanted, thanks to some money her grandparents had given her after downsizing. She'd tried to refuse it, but they'd insisted and instead she'd promised she would use it for something special.

The question now had to be: did she really want to do this? This was an unplanned, totally different route that she hadn't prepared for. It would mean a new lifestyle, a new routine. She also much preferred to be behind the scenes, but while she loved talking about books, would she be any good at it? She'd also be throwing away years of study and hard work she'd put in to reach her current career level, and regardless of how much she loved books and liked the idea of running a bookshop, that left a nasty taste in her mouth.

The next morning, the sky was a bright cornflower blue, the clouds banking like bundles of cotton wool. Beth left to walk to the book barge, feeling surer of her financial situation, if not her emotional one, and wrapped her smart camel-coloured coat around her, tightening the belt against the wind, but enjoying the way it brushed her skin as if it were blowing the doubts away.

She'd already let Signor Sanna know she was going to be late as she explored a new possible opportunity, and he was only too happy to give her another day off, telling her again how sorry he was and that she was to do whatever she needed.

The route she'd decided to take to the book barge took her through parts of Venice she hadn't made the time to explore. This time, she let herself be guided by some unknown force, a part of herself that she'd never tapped into before, that led her in whatever direction looked the most appealing. It was freeing. She had plenty of time to get to the book barge and there was no more perfect time to explore the city than out of tourist season. Once the spring hit, Venice became a go-to destination for city breaks and honeymoons, and it grew harder to move around so easily. It was even busier in summer when the streets were packed so full of tourists, it was difficult to change direction, and you were swept along in whatever direction the traffic was moving. But she loved the way the city felt alive when it was full.

Right now, the city was quiet, and she studied the historic red-brick houses, the pinks and creams of the buildings and the random sets of stone steps that led you up and down the different levels of the city. Venice really was a wonder of the world, a tiny island of such cultural importance and utter beauty.

Veering down another strange alleyway she'd never seen before and which was only just wide enough for her to fit through, she ran her fingers over the rough stone walls on either side, the coarse brick dragging against her fingertips as she inhaled the chill salty air. There were beautiful medieval doorways, Juliet balconies, window boxes that would bloom again soon once the spring came. Some houses were adorned with crosses, others rustic, and all the time the water snaked its way through the city like veins through a body. They were the lifeblood of Venice, even now, when they were quiet and empty.

Before long Beth was canal-side, nearing the book barge, and nerves coiled in her stomach. As she approached, she noticed a few gondolas tied up either side, as they weren't in use at this time of year. It wouldn't be long before the owners would be cleaning them out, beating the small rugs and cushions they put inside to make them more comfortable, ready for couples to snuggle together as they toured the city via its famous waterways.

Looking up, Beth's eyes landed on the book barge and a spark of excitement pushed through the lingering anxiety. Giambattista had described the owner as being too old to look after it, but she knew from her own visits that, on the surface at least, it wasn't in too bad a condition. It was a busy sight to see with books everywhere, stacked and shoved into every available space. There was something homely about it, but Beth's mind was already crying out to give the books some order. The barge itself, though, just needed a bit of jazzing up. It didn't look like it was falling apart, but who knew what lurked underneath the piles of books.

Her breath hitched, worry tightening her chest and pressing down on her lungs. Was she really considering doing this? The idea had only been mentioned yesterday morning and now, twenty-four hours later, here she was about to talk to the owner. Cesca appeared at her side as she'd promised she would, and Beth almost stumbled as she also spotted Marco.

'I like it,' Cesca replied nodding. 'It looks in good shape too. Nothing major to do.'

'You could make this a good business,' Marco added, his eyes meeting Beth's and sending a shock down her spine.

'Yeah, I . . .' She took a deep breath. She hadn't known he was coming and wondered what had made him. 'I do like it, but . . .'

'But?' Cesca asked.

The simple fact remained that Beth Thorpe didn't do spontaneous things. It simply wasn't how she was made. As far as she was concerned, impulsiveness led to mistakes and mistakes led to regret. So far, thanks to reasoning and calculation, she'd avoided those feelings. Sometimes it made her feel boring, but other times she was grateful. She'd seen friends all through her life make rash decisions and then deal with the consequences. Buying a book barge was a random, mad idea, and she almost turned on her heel and walked back to her flat. But then, it wouldn't be her flat for much longer, would it? Because everything was changing whether she wanted it to or not, and here she was, staring at a boat filled with books, and she had to admit, she did quite like the look of the place.

'But what?' Cesca asked again.

Beth shook her head. 'Nothing.'

The barge was moored close to the path and a small gangplank at one end led to an open door. Running the entire length of the barge were open cabinets, the type that you see books sold from along the Seine in Paris. She scanned the titles: a mixture of English and Italian, classics and modern, battered, second-hand fiction. A few heavier reference books and non-fiction were mixed in along with children's books and coffee table reads. It was a mess, but an appealing one. An urge to tidy and organise niggled inside. It always did when she visited this particular bookshop. She knew it could look better and be easier for people to find what they were looking for. As much as she loved shops where old books were stacked on one another, in corners and in piles, she loved things to be neat and tidy.

Just as she was reaching out, unable to stop herself touching a battered but beautiful copy of *Jane Eyre*, the owner popped his head out of the open door.

'Signora Thorpe?'

He pronounced it Torp, and she greeted him in Italian.

'Very good,' he replied, referring to her language skills, and she smiled proudly as he introduced himself. 'I am Signor Balbo.'

Though she'd seen him when she stopped by, she hadn't ever really spoken to him before. 'It's lovely to meet you.' She shook his hand, surprised at his firm grip. He wasn't even wearing a coat or gloves, just a jumper and shirt with the sleeves rolled up. 'These are my friends Marco and Francesca.'

'Welcome all. Giambattista told me you'd be coming. What do you think? Do you like it?' He widened his arms, taking in the boat.

'It's lovely,' she replied, unsure what else to say. In many ways it was, and it felt rude to mention the chaos and less than efficient design, but her brain was already noting ways to improve it to show more stock and therefore make more profit. Not to mention she wanted to single-handedly search through the books, categorising them, finding the hidden gems that were undoubtedly there somewhere.

'Come inside. Come! Come!'

Stooped with age, he didn't have to duck to fit through the low doorway, whereas Beth who wasn't unusually tall, still had to bend to avoid banging her head. Cesca and Marco followed and they all manoeuvred down a small flight of steep stairs. On the lower deck, she was able to stand fully upright, and as she did, the excitement built inside her. This could be hers if she wanted. If she was willing to take a leap of faith. To try something new. Something she hadn't planned for.

The lower deck was as higgledy-piggledy as the upper, with books crammed into every corner, stacked in piles, but there was also a small seating area at the opposite end, and a wood-burning fire halfway along the hull. Its orangey light gave the whole place a cosy glow, as did the numerous table lamps scattered along the shelves. As the warmth from the fire wrapped around her, she felt instantly at home. A sense of peace washed over her, the same thing she felt in the galleria when she was working on an exhibition or researching something. The same way she felt when she walked into those sacred spaces, and history and culture surrounded her.

Now she came to think of it, it was the same with all bookshops. She'd always felt at home in them, protected from the world outside. As though the worries of the world or her life couldn't follow her. She could continue to have this every day if she wanted to, and she did, she realised with a grin. She really did want this. She grinned at Cesca and Marco. He and Signor Balbo were chatting but when their eyes met and he smiled widely at her, something surged inside her just as it had the day before.

Why was he here? Had Cesca dragged him along?

After a moment, Signor Balbo broke away and turned to her.

'What do you think?' he asked tentatively, moving down to the armchairs at the end and lowering himself into one.

Before she could answer, Cesca and Marco stepped forward.

'We'll leave you to it,' Cesca said, leaning into Beth and whispering, 'But there is only surface-level work to do. Nothing major.'

'This is a great spot,' Marco added. 'Very popular. Most people would love a barge on this canal.'

So that was why he was there. Cesca had asked him to come along to consult on the business side of things. 'There's definitely a lot going in its favour,' Beth replied.

Cesca held her arm. 'I'm biased because I want you to stay, but I think this is a good chance. And Marco thinks so too, don't you?'

'It is your choice what you do, but as a business proposition, it is a good one.'

'Call us when you're done,' Cesca said.

With that, they left.

Signor Balbo signalled to the seat opposite him and Beth edged through the chaos. A small cat wandered in through the doorway, leaping from the ledge to a stack of books and then walking along in that wonderfully elegant way cats did. It hopped down, crossed the barge and then jumped up into Signor Balbo's lap. 'This is Polo, after Marco Polo because he likes to go off and explore but he always comes back.'

'He's lovely.' She watched as the cat curled into a ball in Signor Balbo's lap but pushed his head into the man's hand to enjoy the scratching behind his ears. His fur was a beautiful dark grey and his whiskers a dark black.

'And the bookshop?' Signor Balbo asked.

'It's very cosy,' she replied, revelling in the warmth from the fire. She hadn't realised how chilly she'd grown wandering around that morning, or how in need of another coffee she was. She could have dozed off in the comfortable chair with the fire on and the sense of peace and calm floating around her.

'Do you want to buy it?'

The direct question threw her, pulling her from the reverie she'd been enjoying, even though that was the only reason she was there. Panic and doubt gripped her and she found herself saying, 'Well, I – I think I need to—'

'My children don't want it,' he said sadly, speaking in Italian. Polo dipped his head and Signor Balbo's old hands stroked the cat's back instead. 'They have careers in Padua.'

'That's a shame. I'm sorry.' She didn't know what else to say, but the man continued.

'This was my life's work.' He looked around, taking in the book barge, the overcrowded shelves, scanning each title. 'It was tidier when I could look after it properly, before my wife died and I got old.' He gave a sad smile. 'It didn't always look like this. And now it needs to go to someone who will take better care of it.'

'Does this place have a name?' she asked gently. She'd never seen one outside and had only ever known it as the floating bookshop as most of the ones in Venice were in brick-and-mortar stores.

'*La Libreria delle Parole.*'

Immediately after he said it, her nerves began to tingle. 'The Library of Words,' she said in English. 'Beautiful.'

'Exactly,' he replied, a small smile lighting his tired, pale grey eyes. Polo looked up when he stopped stroking, and he smiled down at the cat as he began again. A soft purring sound filled the barge.

Her heart seemed to warm in her chest at hearing the name, radiating out through her body. She could imagine herself here, instead of the galleria office, in the warm glow, tidying books and rearranging displays. In the summer, with the sun streaming in through the windows, queues of people would wait for her to serve them. And when she thought of herself doing all those things, to her surprise, the worry and fear of an unplanned choice faded, and she pictured herself smiling and happy, contented.

Beth's mind began to race. She'd stock the latest commercial fiction – stuff people on holiday wanted to buy, and maybe she'd keep some of the more beautiful older books for decoration. There might even be some rare finds here, in amongst all this mess. She'd have to sort through carefully rather than just chuck the old stuff out and start again. And she could run events, sell beautiful, hand-picked pieces of art, maybe other bookish gifts too. And if money got tight, she could freelance, giving tours of the museums. Signor Sanna wouldn't mind that, and she knew every piece of art in that place, could recite the bios of every artist in there. This could work, she thought excitedly. This could actually work.

The image of her with a queue of customers, everyone chatting happily over books, sat with her and a calmness settled inside. As it was only January, she'd have plenty of time to get everything ready for the spring and the hordes of tourists who would hopefully visit the floating bookshop and buy something from her.

Was it finally time to take a chance instead of spending all her time thinking and planning? Was this a sign from the universe that this year, she should do something different? Live a little differently? She had to move forwards somehow and all she knew at that moment was that moving forwards did not mean returning to England, it meant forging on with her life here, and the book barge felt right. It felt like home in the same way the galleria had. The same way every museum she'd ever visited had. Excitement won out, and doubt and fear faded.

Signor Balbo looked at her in expectant silence, hope clear in his eyes. 'So . . . ?' he asked. 'Do you want to buy her?'

For the first time, Beth let the impulsive voice she'd always buried come to the fore, and it drowned out every other thought in her head. In a loud, confident voice she said, 'Yes. Yes, I do.'

Chapter 5

That evening, Beth moved around her tiny apartment, preparing her dinner as she informed her best friends from back home of her rather sudden career change.

'You've done what?' Elsa was so shocked her voice had risen by about three octaves and Beth instinctively moved her phone further away from her face. Not that Beth really knew what three octaves were. She was tone-deaf and the type of person who always stayed silent during karaoke - she'd learned that lesson the hard way. But Elsa's reaction wasn't at all surprising. If Beth were honest, it was still a thought echoing through her mind, though one that hadn't been as loud as she'd thought it would be, especially after meeting Marco and Cesca afterwards. They'd shared in her excitement and had taken Beth for a coffee to celebrate. She had hoped she and Marco might get a chance to talk more, but Cesca had been so full of plans, they'd barely got a word in, though her excitement was catching and Beth was soon thinking of the hows, whens, and wheres, of improving the floating bookshop. Now, Beth wondered – hoped even – that she'd see Marco again soon, though she had no idea when.

'When?' Elsa asked. 'When did you do this?'

'Today,' Beth replied, trying to keep her voice calm and shoving her hair behind her ear. 'This morning.'

Earlier on, when she'd been sat with Signor Balbo and Polo at the book barge and with Marco and Cesca at the café, she'd felt certain this was the right choice, but she couldn't deny the dread and regret starting to creep in. She'd acted so against her nature she was unsettled, unable to sit still and even an afternoon row at the gym hadn't fixed her anxiety. She'd bought a book barge! Or more accurately, was in the process of buying a book barge, and she swung so wildly between excitement and terror it was impossible to sit still.

'Can you pull out? Was it just a verbal agreement?'

'Elsa, calm down,' Daisy, Beth's other best friend, said. Elsa re-angled the phone so the two of them were fully on camera, but not before Beth caught Elsa's disbelieving headshake. 'Beth knows what she's doing, don't you? I'm sure she's thought this through. She never does anything without thinking it through and figuring it all out ahead of time. But I have to admit, it is a bit of a surprise.'

Beth stayed quiet. How did she tell them she'd done the craziest thing she'd ever done in her entire life?

The three of them had met at university and been

instantly inseparable through years of hard work (Beth), hijinks (Elsa), and the perfect work/fun balance (Daisy). They'd basically grown up together and so far had relied on each other through all the stages of life ever since, from first tentative steps into love, careers and mortgages.

Daisy and Elsa were also a couple, having discovered their love for one another when uni ended and the idea of going their separate ways, heading out into the big wide world apart, had forced them to admit their true feelings for one another. Beth had always known those feelings were there and had been over the moon when they finally got together. Years later, they were still as in love as ever and living an almost perfect life in a sweet little semi-detached property in Kent.

A year ago, they'd been particularly excited for Beth's move to Venice, especially as it was to work in one of the most prestigious galleries (and cities) in the world, but she had to admit, losing her job and randomly buying a book barge was something of a sideways move that would have surprised even the most understanding of friends.

Beth cleared her throat. 'I know it's a bit . . . unexpected but—'

'Unexpected!' Elsa screeched, brushing a hand through her stylish hair (short on one side and longer on the other, styled to spiky perfection) in frustration. It revealed the enormous earring joined by a chain that ran from the top of her ear to the bottom. 'Honey, you've lost your job, you're about to lose your home – you're emotionally untethered, and instead of coming home and crying into a bottle of wine like any normal person would do, you've bought a bookshop . . . on a barge! I mean—' She sat back against the sofa cushions and huffed out a breath. 'I just didn't see that coming when we started this call.'

'Neither did I,' Beth replied with a nervous giggle. A part of her was beginning to feel slightly proud of the mad thing she'd done. People were always offering clichéd sayings like 'seize the moment', and she had! The least likely person in the world to do that! And that was why Elsa's reaction was exactly what she'd expected. This was the type of thing Elsa herself would have done – but Beth? No. And knowing Elsa had her own regrets from impulsive actions, she didn't want Beth to have them either.

'What Elsa means,' Daisy interjected with an accusatory side-eye at her wife, 'is why didn't you call us as soon as you found out about your job? You know we'd have been there for you. You must have been upset and shocked. You should have called, and we could have talked everything through with you.'

Her friend's kindness sent a lump into Beth's throat, but she wasn't going to cry. Things were looking up and when she remembered the sense of calm she'd experienced in the book barge, the feeling of the rightness of her decision returned. She just had to hold on to that. She was making a new future for herself and, if she were honest, they'd both reacted exactly as she thought they would. Elsa was always more direct while Daisy was kinder, softer, and both approaches had their merits. Daisy could be relied upon for good hugs and tissues, while Elsa would say the things you didn't always want to hear but knew you had to listen to.

'I know you would, sweetie,' Beth replied, 'but it was just such a shock. I didn't really know what to do with myself. My brain literally couldn't contemplate it all. I ended up just wandering around for a bit and then having a coffee and eating a whole plate of *baicoli*.'

'So you went and bought a boat instead?' This time Elsa's comment earned her a jab in the ribs and Beth smothered a laugh. 'What did I say this time?' she asked Daisy before turning back to the screen, rubbing her side. 'I'm sorry, Bethy, you know I love you, but it's just . . . you never do anything impulsive. That's just not . . . you!'

'I know.' A half-laugh escaped her mouth, sounding more like a puff of air. The maelstrom of feelings she'd been swept up in clarified for a moment, like the clouds clearing after a storm and the images that had played in her mind that morning – happy and contented scenes that left a strange feeling of fulfilment inside her – sprung up again. 'But you know what? I don't think I regret it. Not yet at least. And you should see it, El, it's gorgeous. I mean, it needs a little bit of work, because it's kind of a mess and the space isn't used as efficiently as it could be, but that doesn't matter, I've got someone who can help with that. But when I was sat inside, it just felt so homey. So . . . sweet. I could totally see myself finishing work for the day, content and happy, and closing the door with a smile on my face. Is that mad?'

'A bit,' Elsa replied with a teasing smile. 'But there's a look in your eye I like. I haven't seen it for a while. It's challenge mixed with certainty. You used to get it when you were talking about your next course or career move.'

Daisy smiled at her wife, but as she turned to the phone, the smile faded. 'But where will you live once your flat's revoked?'

'I'll find somewhere. I've a few weeks here yet—' Beth signalled to the small living room she was currently sitting in.

As the property was rented by the society who funded her post, she hadn't been allowed to hang anything on the boring, pale cream walls or really personalise it any way. Stacks of books were the only real decoration. She found she was drawn to history books and historical fiction, but she couldn't deny she loved a bit of historical crime and romance. She went through phases where she'd read a lot of history books, her attention caught by a certain subject but then she'd need the engrossing writing of fiction. Something to grab her and help her escape to another life, another time.

Perhaps it was time for her to think about setting up a permanent home here in Venice and buying instead of renting a flat. She could have book prints on the walls, bookshelves lined with books, maybe even some specially chosen pieces of art. After all, she'd kind of decided this was it from now on anyway, what with buying the book barge. It made more sense to pay a mortgage rather than rental fees if she could find somewhere she could afford.

'Don't worry.' Beth popped a crostini into her mouth. She'd bought herself a picky tea on the way back from the meeting with Signor Balbo, knowing she'd be too lazy to cook and the array of tiny, tasty crostini, olives, artichokes and cured meats was the perfect thing to eat while she talked.

'Tomorrow I'm going to find a new place to live. I've got some money saved for a deposit as I haven't had to pay rent on this place. The money from Granny and Gramps has paid for the barge so it's all good financially. My budget will be tight, but it is doable.'

Elsa added, 'Until you need a regular monthly income to pay for bills and food.'

This time, Daisy stared daggers. 'Can you not be so . . . so—'

'So what?'

'So you! I get you're a practical person, but this is not the time for negativity. It's the time for support and excitement.'

'It's fine,' Beth replied, not wanting them to argue over her. 'Honestly! And Elsa's right. I will need to start making a living. I can't rely on my savings forever, but I'm okay with that. That, I can do. I've already started thinking about stock and expanding from just books.'

'See!' Daisy said to her wife.

Beth hid her smile behind her wine glass. After taking a sip, she knew it was time to open up. Her friends knew her too well and would only ask if she didn't volunteer the information. 'It's just the . . .' She swallowed heavily. 'The emotional side that's the worst. Like you said, I've never done anything like this before and I'm . . . I'm a bit scared if I'm honest.'

'Do you need us to fly out?' Daisy asked, concern wrinkling her smooth brow. Where Elsa's hair was cool and edgy, Daisy's was long and soft. Her dark blonde, tight-spiral curls reached down to her shoulders, untameable, and she had a peaches-and-cream complexion. 'Because you know we will. We can be there tomorrow if need be.'

Beth shook her head. 'No! Absolutely not. It'll screw up all your IVF stuff, not to mention you don't need the extra costs right now.'

'But we want to be there for you.'

'You are! Right now. And I tell you what, we can have regular catch-ups, and I can update you on how things are going with the bookshop, and I promise that if I need even the slightest bit of moral support, I'll call you straight away. Is that okay?'

'I suppose so.' Daisy looked so sad, Beth wanted to reach out and hug her friend through the phone screen.

'Good.'

Silence fell for a moment, and needing to distract herself from the unpleasant feelings prickling her, Beth picked up her phone and moved to the kitchen to top up her glass of wine. The small galley kitchen was as unwelcoming and boring as the living room. She'd actually love to have her own place, she thought, with elegant wallpaper, maybe some framed pictures on the wall.

She wanted to ask about the IVF treatment and as difficult as the subject was for her because her own body, with its PCOS, had caused her more problems than she could count, she really did want to know how things were going and to support her friends. After a fortifying sip, Beth finally asked. 'So how is the IVF stuff going?'

Daisy and Elsa had been desperate for a baby for a while and had finally taken the leap to start the process. They'd chosen a donor and had opted for reciprocal IVF with Daisy carrying the baby while Elsa donated the eggs. This meant they could both be biologically connected to the baby, but they were still at the early stages of the process. Beth found it all a little confusing but there seemed to be a lot of things to consider, a lot of medication, and a hell of a lot of hoping and waiting. Just getting to this point had been emotionally exhausting for her friends and their families, and the stakes were rising considerably now everything was becoming more and more real. It was emotionally exhausting for her too, given her own body's limitations, but she tried not to talk about it because she hated bringing the mood down, and as they'd begun to mention starting a family, Beth hadn't wanted them to feel the need to tread gently.

As a teenager, when she'd been diagnosed with PCOS, polycystic ovary syndrome, it had been hard to hear. It brought with it a wealth of unpleasant symptoms and, as she'd grown, the realisation that her chances of getting pregnant were slimmer than most people's. Lately, as her friends had explored different options for having children, this had brought on a whole existential crisis about whether she even wanted children or not. At times she was undecided as the question of partners and futures popped up. So far she hadn't had any relationships get that far, her work giving her far more pleasure than any mediocre dates ever had. But it often led her to wonder, what if things were different? What if she met someone and fell in love, and they wanted kids and she didn't? Would it be easy to meet someone who felt the way she did? Someone who was still as unsure as she was. It was a minefield. And, if she were honest, that was probably why she hadn't dated much here, even though she was surrounded by gorgeous Italian men. Deep down, she'd always had a feeling inside that motherhood wasn't really for her. She hadn't had the same hankering for it Daisy, Elsa and some of her other friends had. Would that ever change?

She pushed the thought aside. The last two days had been difficult enough without her thinking about things she couldn't change and weren't actually a problem right now, and might never be. Right now, Daisy and Elsa needed her full attention.

As Daisy launched into an excited update on specialist appointments and their hopes for the future, Beth poured herself some more wine, smiling at the love radiating through the phone screen. After a while, when conversation turned to their jobs and the mundane bits of life, Elsa asked: 'So what are your next steps? When does the sale complete?'

'It should be fairly quick as it's a private sale. Apparently it's all very straightforward. Which works out nicely. I can get out of here into somewhere new, and by the time I've moved, I'll be ready to start my new business.'

Beth suddenly realised she hadn't told her parents what was going on. They'd never been particularly close, and the gulf had only grown since they'd both retired and started cruising around the world. They'd always been impulsive and had urged Beth to be more like them, but as she'd been the one to sort out the messes they'd got themselves into (especially financially) it wasn't any wonder she was how she was. She'd send them an email. Later.

'What are you going to call this bookshop then?' Daisy asked.

'I think I'll keep the original name to be honest. I was so touched by Signor Balbo, and I love the one he chose all those years ago. I think it'll be nice to carry it on, especially as his children aren't interested. It's called *La Libreria delle Parole* which means *The Library of Words*.'

Both Elsa and Daisy said 'Aww!' at the same time and it was like another stamp of approval on her crazy move.

'I love it!' Daisy announced with a clap.

'Me too,' Elsa replied. 'And if you need any help advertising the place, let me know straight away.' She was a media executive and had worked in advertising since leaving uni. Her skills would definitely come in handy, but first, Beth needed to decide what she really wanted the Library of Words to actually be. She had ideas, but she needed to turn those into firm plans.

She had to know exactly what it would stock, who would

it appeal to and if she wanted to attract mostly tourists or locals. She knew from working in *Gallerie dell'Accademia* that to attract the locals they had to change things up – host touring exhibitions, change displays, host events – and they made up a good, stable part of their income, especially in the winter when Venice wasn't the most sought-after destination. Would she be able to do that?

Feeling suddenly inspired, that need to organise her thoughts and to plan grabbing her stronger than ever, Beth signed off her call and grabbed her e-notebook and began making a list. She'd also need to set up a business bank account, a business email address and lay the groundwork before she did anything else. There was a lot to do before she took possession of the barge, not least of which was finding somewhere to live. She clasped her wine and moved back to the sofa, phone in hand. Switching on the TV for some background noise, she began searching the local estate agents and researching the best business bank accounts. Impulsive or not, her decision had been made – she was here and here to stay – and it was time to put her organisational skills to good use. First she'd see what flats she could find and second, she'd plan the first step for the book barge. There was work to do!

Chapter 6

Beth arrived at the first apartment she was viewing with only a few minutes to spare.

Located near the main train station, the small flat she was due to look at would be useful for hopping over to mainland Italy, but the further she got from the centre of Venice, the canals and the book barge, the less happy she felt. Her spirits fell further when she saw the small, squat, unattractive building. The cream walls had faded to a tobacco brown, and the dark shutters made it look ominous rather than inviting. The flat itself was an end-of-terrace and spread over two floors, and she reserved judgement, deciding she wouldn't make a decision until she'd seen inside. All she knew was that unlike London, she wanted to be in the centre of the city. To feel it hum with life and be part of its heartbeat. As she was starting a new life, she might as well aim high and go for exactly what she wanted.

Beth had just enough time to catch her breath when the estate agent arrived to show her around. After exchanging pleasantries, she unlocked the door and Beth went through first. The building was so dark, she almost had to turn on the torch on her phone to guide her way. The small windows let in hardly any light and the décor was incredibly old-fashioned with peeling wallpaper. She tried to look past, thinking she could decorate, but something about the place just didn't feel right. Buying or renting a flat was a big commitment and she wasn't about to lay down money unless she knew it was right. After giving a polite no, she made her way to the next appointment.

This time, Beth had a few minutes to grab a takeaway coffee and a pastry on her way. A smoothie had done a good job of reviving her after another morning workout, but it was heading towards lunchtime, and her stomach was beginning to feel empty. She walked past a number of cafés and single tables lined up outside close to the buildings, so there was just enough room to walk the narrow streets. She chose to stop at one she'd never been in before with a deep red awning, matching seats and tablecloths and gold writing on the windows giving the name of the place. Though disappointed the first apartment hadn't been up to scratch, she was hopeful for the next one, which had beautiful views over the city. Or at least it had from the pictures they'd shown on the website.

The estate agent who arrived at the next apartment carried a leather folder and held out his hand for her to shake.

'*Buon pomeriggio.*'

Beth bid him good afternoon in Italian, thanking him for meeting her. He seemed surprised she could say more than just a greeting in his native language and smiled kindly as he told her about the building, its history and the apartment they were about to see. As expected, he told her it was highly in demand and that he had a number of showings there this week. Beth wasn't sure she believed him but nodded along all the same. This building was much prettier. Well kept, with pale pink exterior walls typical of Venice and wooden shutters painted in dark blue. Beth's hopes rose and a slight hint of nerves tingled her stomach at the idea that he was telling the truth and it might be snapped up before she had a chance to make an offer.

They climbed the three flights of steep, narrow stairs to the top-floor apartment, Beth's legs burning after her workout that morning. It took her a moment to catch her breath when she got to the top and she loosened the collar of her coat as Signor Ajello opened the door. Immediately, her hopes faded, the nerves vanishing as she was hit was the smell of dampness. Damp was a problem many buildings in Venice had. It was quite common in the floating city, but this smell was so strong it was clear the apartment hadn't been looked after at all. Just as bad was how small it was. She hadn't expected a mansion or anything bigger than the flat she had now, but it took all of a minute to see every tiny room in the tiny apartment. She'd go mad if she lived here, and where would she put all her books? Not to mention how long would it take to get rid of that smell, if she even could. When Signor Ajello turned and smiled, asking her what she thought. She mumbled, 'It's umm, it's very nice, but I'm not sure it's quite what I'm looking for.'

'No matter,' he replied. 'Like I say, is very popular. It will be gone quickly, I think.'

'It's just not for me,' she repeated, making her escape.

Several more followed all in different parts of the city, but nothing had felt right. They'd either been too cramped or in disrepair. There'd been several problems from a leak that needed fixing ('But that's why the price is so low!') to a room so small she had to walk sideways like a crab. She'd get a crick in her neck living like that.

Beth knew her budget wasn't particularly large, but now she worried she was going to have to think of something else or save for even longer to be able to afford somewhere decent. Venice was an expensive city – she knew that already – but she hadn't thought she wouldn't be able to find a place to live somewhere within its boundaries.

That afternoon, after a final viewing where she'd been on the verge of saying yes until the man who would be her neighbour walked out of his house stark naked, smiling and waving a greeting as though it was all perfectly normal he went about in all his natural glory, she stopped in for a coffee at Giambattista's.

Beth fell into her chair, huffing out a breath as her bum hit the seat.

'Why are you so miserable?' Giambattista asked in his usual direct fashion. 'You've just bought a bookshop; you should be happy!'

'I am,' she responded, spooning the foam from the top of her cappuccino and eating it. He tutted in disapproval, not just because she was eating the foam 'like a savage' but because cappuccinos were considered a morning drink and not for afternoons, but she needed the strong coffee hit and she couldn't stand espressos. They made her eyes water. Beth put down her teaspoon and told him about the day she'd spent apartment hunting. 'Venice is so beautiful; I thought it'd be easy.'

'Venice is like any other city. It has good parts and not so good parts. And it can be hard to keep the buildings in good condition. The water is hard on them. How many weeks do you have left to find somewhere?'

'Three.'

He waved a hand. 'I'm sure something will come up.'

Three weeks and she was going to have to move out of the society's flat. Maybe Cesca could put her up? Her mind flew to Marco. She knew she shouldn't still be thinking about Cesca's brother, but his smile had played in her head all day. She'd liked what she'd seen, and unfortunately, had made that clear to Cesca, who'd made that abundantly clear to Marco. Her muscles tensed as the cringe factor spread through her body.

She shook the thought of him from her head, returning to the matter at hand, and scooped more foam from the top of her drink. Maybe she'd have to take one of the terrible apartments she'd seen today, covered in mould and smelling of old socks, or so small she'd be able to go from the bed to the kitchen in two strides. She hadn't expected anything extravagant. None of the apartments in Venice were overly huge, but she did have to live there. Forever. She had to feel comfortable.

'Signor Balbo isn't selling his apartment as well as his barge?'

He shook his head. 'Unfortunately not.'

'No, I'm not surprised.'

Giambattista sat with her and sipped his espresso. 'Nothing will make him leave Venice. He is a true Venetian through and through. There will be somewhere though. I'm sure of it.'

'I suppose as it's out of holiday season, I can always stay in a holiday let for a while if need be.'

'Good idea! I'm sure we must know someone who can help.'

'No, it's fine! Don't worry, I can handle it.'

He stood to greet a customer, waving at them before turning back to her. 'No, no, no! I will ask around, see if anyone knows of anything.'

Beth smiled. There was no point in arguing with Giambattista, but she was grateful for his support. She just hoped he was right that something would come up. Until then, she'd have to keep looking. At least she had a plan, Beth reminded herself, and it wasn't like she had a lot of stuff to pack up. She only really had her books, her clothes and a few knick-knacks. She'd find somewhere, she told herself. She was sure she would.

Chapter 7

Beth approached *La Libreria delle Parole* – the Library of Words – excitement mixing with nerves in her stomach, the keys jangling in her fingertips.

The paperwork was done, and the book barge was now hers, stock included. Thanks to Signor Balbo, it had been a quick and easy process, though saying goodbye to her colleagues at the galleria (and some of the paintings too, if she were honest) had been harder than expected. Signor Sanna had given her a beautiful book about Venetian art and Antonia had baked her some *frittelle* (fried doughnuts filled with cream), which had been delicious. They'd devoured them with the rest of the team, drinking warm white wine after the doors had closed for the day, and Beth had felt a mixture of sadness and joy at the old chapter she was leaving behind and the new one she was about to begin.

After a morning gym session, where she'd secretly looked out for Marco, as she had for the past couple of weeks, she'd changed and hurried to the estate agent's office to collect the keys to her new book barge. Marco hadn't been at the gym and the disappointment had hit her unusually hard.

Now, as she approached the book barge, ready to start her first day as a self-employed, floating bookshop owner, the feeling of home she'd experienced the first time she'd visited filled her once more, and a smile spread over her face.

This was it!

She'd done it! For the first time in her life she'd made a rash decision and with any luck it would turn out to be the best decision she ever made. What she was loving more than anything, though, was that she had no one else to answer to. The cold January wind snuck under the collar of her coat, chilling the back of her neck, and she hurried closer. The first month of the year would soon be over and February brought Carnevale, life and excitement, brightening the winter months. Everyone loved Carnevale and the way it filled every street on the city one way or another, with music and song, dancing and performance.

Later, she needed to take the last of her stuff from the apartment the society had rented for her, to a holiday let she'd found that wasn't too far away from the barge. It wasn't ideal and it had that strange feel of somewhere several hundred people had slept before, but it was clean and tidy, and it would do until she found an actual apartment she liked. She wouldn't worry about that now though and would instead focus on the excitement of the new opportunity in front of her.

The cabinets lining the outside with their flip-down lids needed varnishing, the wood pale and cracking. She studied them for a moment, deciding if she'd keep them or get rid of them altogether and have Cesca design something new. Something a little fancier. She might even do what the gondoliers did and have a carpet along the canal side on sunny days, maybe hang some lights outside to cast a soft orange light over the place and make it look more welcoming. The keys jangled in her fingers. First she needed to get inside.

It took a moment to figure out which key fitted each lock, but eventually she had it open and the smell of leather book binding and aged paper greeted her as she walked inside. She pulled a cord and a light, covered in an old-fashioned shade, flickered into life. It cast a warm orange glow over the room, but cold air seeped under her coat. It had felt so cosy the first time she'd visited and on the few times she'd come since then, but without the fire lit the barge was freezing. She moved to the fireplace and stared at it, unsure what to do. She'd never lit a fire like this before.

A small basket of various-sized pieces of wood sat next to it, as well as a blackened metal dustpan and threadbare brush. She quickly grabbed her phone and searched for how to light a fire, following the instructions, cleaning out the ashes. She laid a new fire and took the box of matches that were sat on top of a pile of books and lit it. Slowly, it came to life and when it was roaring, kicking out heat that wove through the book barge, she pushed the glass door on the front of the fire too. On the armchair, there was a note from Signor Balbo wishing her many happy years, just as he'd had. Warmth and gratitude spread through her and she promised herself to make the most of this opportunity.

'So what should I do first?' she asked herself.

She had asked Signor Balbo for a list of his stock, and he'd laughed in her face, albeit kindly, but still. It hadn't been the response she was hoping for. She'd have liked an inventory like they had in the galleria, though everything they had was on an object management system so she could just type something in the search box and find where it was in the stores. She needed something like that for this place, so maybe her first job was to start sorting the books into genres. Warmer now, she shook off her coat, unpacked the kettle, tea, milk and cup she'd brought with her and got to work. She needed to start earning money soon, so she'd stay open while she sorted out stock, just in case someone popped by, but on the next market day she'd make a big push, selling whatever it was she had.

With a cup of tea made, Beth started outside, opening the cabinets one by and one and making piles on the canal side. Luckily it wasn't raining and the pale white clouds ahead were like dots of cotton wool in the sky. There were second-hand fiction books from the last fifty years and various non-fiction titles covering every subject from history and politics to gardening and drawing. None of them were priced at more than a few euros and even then, the small yellowing price labels had fallen off most of them. She really needed to clear as much of this older, less attractive stock as she could before she bought anything new or she'd end up with nowhere to move, and she couldn't bin them. Books, in her opinion, should never, ever be binned.

She then moved inside and began doing the same. After another hour and eager to stretch the crick in her back, Beth stood, saw a face at the window and screamed.

'It's all right,' came a voice she recognised.

'You frightened me!' she said as Marco walked inside. She pressed a hand to her heart, willing it to calm down, but his gorgeous eyes and playful smile weren't helping it slow at all. In fact, they were probably making it worse. To her surprise, he was holding some flowers.

Shyly, he dipped his head. 'Sorry to scare you. I brought you these as it's your first day.' He held them out.

'How did you—'

'Cesca told me.'

The book barge suddenly seemed tiny, like the stacks of books had all shifted a couple of inches closer. Beth moved forward to take the bouquet. The flowers were beautiful in sweet pinks and rich reds. 'Thank you. They're gorgeous.'

He shuffled a little, looking around. 'You have a lot of tidying to do.'

She laughed. 'Yes, I do. But I'm excited to get started.'

He nodded. 'Of course. I shouldn't have disturbed you.

Perhaps I should—' He pointed towards the door and turned to walk away.

'No, I—'

Just then, her phone rang and Beth pulled it from her pocket, seeing it was Daisy and Elsa.

As much as she wanted to speak to them, she didn't want Marco to go either. 'Sorry, it's my friends, I—'

Marco shook his head. 'I have a meeting anyway.' He checked the large silver watch on his wrist. 'I really should go. Congratulations again.'

Before she could respond, he was gone. With her hands full of flowers and her mind racing as to what she should have said and done to make him stay longer, she accepted the video call and smiled in return at her friends' happy faces.

'Hey, you two! I wasn't expecting to speak to you today.'

'We weren't going to miss you barging it up for the first time,' Elsa said.

'Barging it up? Is that what we're calling this?'

'I think so. So, show us it then!'

Beth had sent a few photos before, but it was difficult to take a video with Signor Balbo standing over her, trying to make her sit and chat. She'd grown quite fond of him, though, and was hoping to invite him over for coffee sometime. She had the feeling he was quite lonely. She put the flowers down without them seeing – she didn't need the questions right now – and turned the camera around.

'Ready? Welcome to my new place of work!' As she walked

through the space, everything lit by the soft orange lighting, her friends cooed.

'It's gorgeous, Bethy,' Elsa said, and Daisy added: 'I can see why you fell in love with it.'

'So what do you plan to do?'

Beth turned the camera back around and snuggled into the armchair Signor Balbo had left. 'So much! I mean first of all, it needs organising and then I'm going to get that friend of mine I told you about, Francesca, to come and build me some storage. Stuff specially designed to fit the spaces to make the most of the nooks and crannies.'

Daisy wiped a tear from her cheek and concern stopped Beth in her tracks. 'What is it? Is everything okay?'

'I'm just so proud of you,' she sniffed, taking a tissue from Elsa. 'You're being so brave taking this chance. Doing something new. I'm really, really proud of you!'

Beth chuckled. 'Well I'm really proud of you too. And me – I'm really proud of me, as well. Look at me being impulsive!' She looked around the mess. 'I kind of wish I had a better plan for all this stock though, but hey, I can't sort it all out today, can I? One step at a time.'

'Yes, just take each day as it comes. You'll get there. You're always so focused. If anyone can do this you can.'

'Right,' Elsa said authoritatively. 'We better let you get back to work. No slacking, even if you are your own boss now!'

Beth laughed. 'I promise I won't. I'm going to open as usual because it's going to take time to sort everything out properly and I still might make some money but I want to be refurbished and have a new set-up by Easter, when the tourist season starts again. I'm hoping with Carnevale in February I might shift a lot of this older stuff, with Venice being a bit busier.'

'That sounds like a great plan. You can do this, Bethy! We know you can!'

She hung up, buzzing from her friends' reaction and their faith in her. The feeling of being surrounded by books matched that of being surrounded by paintings and history. But if she was going to hit her target, she really needed to get on. Beginning again, the time passed quickly. She was head down, sorting another pile of books when a crash jolted her head up and she screamed.

'What the—'

She turned to see that Polo, Signor Balbo's grey cat, had jumped in through an open window, onto a pile of books that had then toppled to the floor. Beth placed a hand to her racing heart.

'What are you doing here? Signor Balbo should have taken you with him.'

'There is no point in me doing that,' an old voice said and Signor Balbo magically appeared at the open doorway. The heat had grown so strong as she started moving around that she'd opened the door, not wanting to put the fire out in case it grew colder again.

'Signor Balbo! Come in, come in! Can I help you?'

After getting down the steps, he held out his arm and she

helped him manoeuvre through the piles of books she was making to the armchair. He carefully lowered himself into it and Polo jumped straight onto his lap, curling into a ball.

'This is his home. Here. He always comes back here.'

'But I – I can't look after a cat! I've never had one before.' She tried to keep the panic from her voice. A cat had definitely not been part of the deal.

'They are great pets. Independent, but there when you need them.' Signor Balbo stroked behind Polo's ears and the cat straightened his neck, pushing against his fingers.

'Don't you want to take him with you?' she asked, hoping he would. 'I can bring him back to you every time he comes here.'

Signor Balbo shook his head. 'I will be travelling a lot. I plan to see my children more. My son has already invited me to stay. My daughter too. I am a very happy old man.' He sat back, smiling at her, and seemed to have de-aged since the last time she saw him. 'So he is yours now.'

'Mine?' The word came out as a high-pitched squeak, so high-pitched that Polo's head jerked around, looking for whatever creature had made it. 'Signor Balbo, I appreciate it but . . . isn't there a cat sanctuary around here somewhere he could go? A kid who wants a pet that you know of?'

Signor Balbo looked horrified at the suggestion, as though he'd sold his beloved bookshop to the evilest person in history and Beth had to admit that a stab of shame hit her. She glanced at Polo. His bright eyes were watching her, and she was sure they were pleading.

Don't be impetuous, she told herself. *Not again*. Once was enough. Once was more than enough for someone who never, ever did outlandish, spur-of-the-moment things.

'This is his home,' he said again, half to the cat and half to her.

She opened her mouth to protest again, and as the cat's eyes met hers, Signor Balbo was also watching on with a sad, puppy dog expression, and when they both tilted their heads in that pleading way cats did, she found different words coming from her mouth. 'All right then.'

What?! Where did that come from?

Beth rolled her eyes at herself as Signor Balbo turned to the cat and smiled. 'Signora Torp will look after you now, Polo. Be a good boy.'

'Does he sleep here?' she asked.

He shook his head. 'You'll need to take him home with you. He has a basket here.' He went to a low cupboard behind the armchair she hadn't had a chance to look in and pulled out a small carrier. 'But I let him roam all through the day. He will come back at six o'clock for his dinner. That's when I grab him and put him in here.'

So now she was the sole owner of a cat as well as a book barge. Stupidly, out of the two decisions, the cat was the one causing her the most worry at the moment.

'Goodbye, my friend,' Signor Balbo said, kissing the cat on the top of the head. His eyes were glassy, his voice shaking a little, and Beth bit the inside of her cheek to stop herself from crying. It was such a sweet and moving scene.

'Stop by anytime to visit him, won't you?' she said as he moved past her. He didn't speak in response, but simply took hold of her hand in both of his and kissed it gently before shuffling out.

After he'd left, Beth turned back to the cat who was curled in the seat he'd vacated. What was she going to do now? She'd have to take him to the holiday let with her; there was nothing else for it. And she'd have to buy cat food, a litter tray, a water bowl, toys. She really had to stop with the impetuous decisions.

Her eyes fell on the flowers Marco had given her. She should put them in water. Had he just been passing? The idea that he hadn't sent a thrill down her spine. She had a rowing club social coming up, and the little black dress she'd barely ever worn had been dry-cleaned and was already hanging on her wardrobe. It was about time she wore it.

With a grin she turned back to the shop, surveying every pile of books, the old-fashioned till and the odd knick-knacks Signor Balbo had left. Polo's soft purring filled the air and Beth smiled. This was her domain. Her floating bookshop. And her cat now, it seemed. A small chuckle escaped her mouth. The first stage of building a life in Venice started now.

But no more rash decisions. Definitely none.

Chapter 8

A couple of days later, Beth's feet ached as she finished another day of owning a bookshop. Not only that, despite her fitness, her back also throbbed, her shoulders were tight and even her neck seemed to be struggling with the weight of her head. A part of her just wanted to fall into a hot bath and then bed, but she'd agreed to go to a stupid rowing club party. She picked up her phone, about to message Cesca and cancel, but her finger hovered over the screen.

Was she going to let herself go back to her old ways already? She looked at Polo, having trapped him inside and about to force him into the cat carrier. Instead of swiping to message Cesca, she put the phone down and found some treats to tempt him inside it. He wasn't convinced and refused to move.

'I know, my little friend. I wouldn't want to get into that little prison either,' she said out loud. 'But it's not for long. You'll have the whole apartment to play in soon.' Still the cat wouldn't move. 'Please? I need to get ready! I haven't got time for this.'

This was why you shouldn't have said yes, said a mean part of her brain, but she quietened it. When she got back tonight the cat would sleep on her bed again, and she found she was quite looking forward to it.

After she threw most of the packet into the back of the carrier, Polo drew close enough to sniff and, with a gentle shove from behind, a tactic she'd picked up after several disastrous attempts, he was soon in the carrier, and she closed the latches on the grate. A sad meow came from inside.

'Oh shush, it's not for long.'

Fastening her coat and grabbing her bag, and now the cat, she made her way home. She unlocked Spotify and put on a party playlist to cheer herself up. As the music filled the small apartment, she danced to the kitchen, poured herself a glass of beautiful Italian wine (she was sure they kept all the best stuff for themselves) and made her way to the bathroom. Polo was now curled up on the sofa, sleeping. She quite liked having him there, stopping to stroke him every time she moved near enough, hearing his gentle purrs of contentment. Maybe she should have considered a pet before now.

An hour later, Beth slipped on her most comfortable black

heels and headed out feeling good. The skater-style black dress showed off her toned arms and though she wasn't that keen on her legs, the length was just right, sitting just on her knees. With a spritz of her favourite perfume she felt elegant and pretty for the first time in ages. She'd remembered the diffuser on her hairdryer and had styled her long hair into gentle waves that fell around her face. Daisy and Elsa had sent her two thumbs-up emojis and a short video of them wolf-whistling to show their approval. They'd been wowed by Polo, cooing that she'd done the right thing, but also slightly disappointed she'd ever considered, even for a nanosecond, taking him to a sanctuary.

Venice was such a small city it didn't take long to get to the clubhouse. The outside had been decorated in bunting in the colours of the Italian flag and light spilled from the large windows. The deep notes of a heavy bass thudded through the ground and up into her feet. For a fleeting second, she wondered if she'd have been better off cuddled up at home, in her pyjamas with Polo beside her as they got to know each other better. Her shoulders tensed up as nerves coiled in her stomach. She'd been so busy she hadn't had a chance to feel anxious about going to a party on her own but now she was here nerves crept in. She knew Cesca and a few others but not many people. Who would she talk to? Would it be awkward? She tended to see the same faces each time she went to the gym, but this was for every member of the rowing club. Would those people be there? She could make small talk in a business setting but that was the professional her. Like a persona. Here, she'd have to be herself, let her guard down. Another chill ran through her and Beth gave herself a mental shake as the urge to run home gripped her again. She'd got all dressed up and styled her hair. She might as well go in for one drink. If she still felt the same way in half an hour, she could go home then. That's what she did when she didn't want to work out. She told herself ten minutes and if she wanted to stop, she could. She never did. At least she had the comfort of being fluent in Italian. Rolling her shoulders back, she walked inside.

People had spilled into the small hallway, and the music grew deafeningly loud as she entered the main function room. It was elegant with white-clothed tables and chairs and a dance floor down one end. The crowd of rowers and their partners were spread throughout, some talking in groups, some dancing on the crammed dance floor. A DJ played the typical party songs you'd imagine with a few home-grown Italian ones she'd heard on the radio. She spotted Cesca, dancing with a young man she hadn't seen before. Beth smiled that her friend was as uninhibited with her dancing as she was in life, moving her body in an unrestrained way that seemed so joyous and fun. When Cesca spotted her, she waved, encouraging Beth onto the floor, but Beth needed a good few drinks before she started throwing herself around. Holding her hands up in refusal, she signalled her need for a drink just as a deep voice from beside her made her stop.

'You're not a dancer then?'

She turned to see Marco and forced herself to keep her mouth closed and not let her jaw hit the floor. He looked stunning in a navy suit and crisp white shirt open at the collar. On someone else it might have looked too buttoned up, but he wore it with a confidence that was magnetising. She looked down to see a pair of worn trainers adding a casual edge and a touch of character to the outfit. She approved.

'I don't go near a dance floor unless I've had at least half a bottle of wine first.'

His eyes skimmed over her figure, sending a thrill through her, and she'd never been gladder that she'd kept this barely used dress. Like a gentleman, his gaze quickly went to her face, and he smiled. 'Then we better get you something before my sister drags you onto the dance floor whether you want to go or not. She likes to kidnap people if the "Macarena" comes on.'

'Is that a favourite in Italy? I thought that was just a cheesy UK thing.'

'No, it's everywhere. Unfortunately.'

'You're not a fan of dancing either then?'

'Not unless it's with the right person. So what will you have?'

'Red wine, please.'

She wasn't sure what to make of that right person comment and they headed towards the bar. She hadn't realised his hand was near her lower back until his fingers pressed there gently, as he guided her through the crowd.

A tingling seemed to ripple out from where he'd touched her. Once she'd picked up a large, delicious-smelling glass of red, the rich notes hitting her nose already, he signalled to a quieter corner, the opposite end to the DJ and disco lights, and they made their way over. So desperately unused to flirting, Beth felt suddenly self-conscious. Her lungs seemed to have filled with thorns and they were prickling her as she breathed in and out.

'So . . .' she began, then the sentence fizzled out. What should she talk about? What would a man like Marco be interested in? And should she speak in English or Italian? 'Thank you for the flowers. They really brightened the place up.'

'I'm glad you like them. I didn't get to ask what brought an Englishwoman here to Venice in the first place?'

Feeling back on sturdier ground, she told him about the galleria and the years of studying that had brought her to her secondment.

'You're not regretting the bookshop then?'

'Not yet.'

'That's good. Perhaps it's what was meant to happen.'

'Maybe. Did you know I've inherited a cat too?'

'A cat?' He laughed, throwing his head back, and she couldn't help but laugh along with him.

'It's mad, I know.' She told him about Polo and how he was now living with her at the apartment and being ferried to and from the book barge every day. Even to her ears it sounded an odd thing to have happened.

'I don't normally agree to impulsive things like that,' she added.

'Perhaps you should.' He chuckled again. 'I don't think I've ever heard of anyone doing what you have.'

'I'm not sure that's a good thing.'

'It probably is. Following your heart is . . . good . . . and fun.'

'I don't know if I've got time for fun. I've got a lot to do before the tourist season, and I've been thinking of ways to make money during the off-season too. I'd love to work with local artists more, given my background, maybe hosting events or even selling their works, but it's something I need to look into. I'm really only just getting started, but I can't wait too long. I need to earn money sooner rather than later.'

'What type of art interests you?'

She sipped her wine, and realised that the rich spicy notes matched that of his aftershave. A hint of sandalwood and dark berries had reached her nose, and it suited him. 'I don't know really. Anything and everything, I suppose. It could be paintings, ceramics, photography . . . all of it. My background is in art – Renaissance paintings and things like that – I've never particularly loved modern art, but I'm open to anything at the moment.'

'Hmm.' He sat back against the cushion, draping his arm across the back of it. She wondered what it would be like to shift over and snuggle in the gap, rest against his torso. She could imagine that being very nice indeed. The perfect way to binge-watch TV with Polo snuggled up beside her. 'Did Francesca tell you what I do for a living?'

'No, I – I assumed you worked in the family business. She's mentioned it a few times. Don't you?'

'I do, sort of.' That guardedness she'd seen at the gym when he and Cesca spoke was back. 'I also run my own PR firm for local artists. I try to get their work seen on the international stage. Mostly I work in Venice but also in Murano and the surrounding islands.'

'Oh, so you must know lots of local artists then?' This could be exactly the type of link she needed.

'I do. Many. It's a hard way to make a living with a lot of uncertainty. Creatives often struggle to market themselves; I hope to take some of that burden away so they can concentrate on the thing they love.'

'Do you think some might be interested in – I don't know – exhibiting work on the book barge or—'

'Would you want commission?' His demeanour and tone changed instantly, and it was as though a totally different side to him had come out, one that was professional and businesslike. The change threw her, but she quickly rallied.

'Umm . . .' She probably would want commission, wouldn't she? She needed to earn money after all, and that was the whole point of the idea. 'I think so, or perhaps a fee for use of the space to either display or run an event. The top of the deck needs clearing, but I'm hoping to have it as a mini events space. Do you think some of your clients might be interested?'

'Possibly, but I'd need more information on the price and terms.'

'Right, yes. Of course. I'll have a think and come back to you.'

'Here's my card.' He reached into his jacket pocket and pulled out his wallet, taking a card from inside and handing it over.

'Great, thanks.'

Her excitement was tinged with uncertainty at the change in him. Things had been going well until conversation turned to business, then it died completely and as they stopped speaking, the music filling the space between them, it seemed neither really knew how to get it back on track. Marco sipped his drink and smiled, but it didn't meet his eyes, and she couldn't think of anything to ask that wouldn't sound cheesy and like a desperate topic change. She'd had lots of awkward encounters with academics – they weren't generally known for their social skills – but this was definitely one of the worst. They glanced at each other, smiled awkwardly and both reached for their drinks, taking a sip and looking in different directions.

A few minutes later, just as Beth was about to make an excuse to leave or use the bathroom, they were saved by Cesca falling into the chair opposite her along with the handsome guy she'd been dancing with.

'I need a drink. I'm so hot!'

'Here.' Marco handed her his glass, and she took a grateful drink. 'Don't try and get me to dance,' he teased.

'She knows better than that,' the man said, glancing at a sweaty but wonderfully uninhibited Cesca. There was something in his eye and it didn't take a genius to know he had a bit of a thing for Marco's sister.

'Thanks for babysitting her,' Marco said. 'And keeping her out of trouble.'

'My pleasure,' he replied and even the low light level couldn't hide the way his cheeks turned even pinker.

'Beth,' Marco said. 'This is Emilio, my best friend.' He clapped a hand on Emilio's shoulder in that manly way guys do.

'Nice to meet you,' Beth replied.

Unlike Marco, Emilio was blond with long curly hair tied back into a ponytail, though a lot of it was falling out from the dancing. He had a short-cropped beard that was more like stubble and dark, hazel eyes. When they shook hands, his were heavily calloused, and his grip was incredibly strong.

'Sorry,' he replied, as she withdrew her hand, almost as if he knew what she'd been thinking.

'Em's a pro-athlete,' Cesca added, shooting a flirty look towards him. 'He rows for the Italian national team.'

That explained the vice-like grip and the rough skin.

'Really?' Beth asked, and Emilio nodded shyly.

'That's why I'm not here as much I'd like. I'm away a lot. There are a lot of rowing competitions all over the world that we compete in.'

From the corner of her eye, Beth noticed Cesca drop her

head almost sadly. Clearly, there was something going on between them, yet they weren't holding hands or acting like couples do.

Cesca leaned in and spoke quietly. 'Are you having fun with my brother?' She raised her eyebrows knowingly.

'We were talking business actually.'

'Right.' She stretched the word in such a teasing way Beth felt her cheeks flame. 'I know he stopped by the book barge. He kept asking me about it. I'm surprised really. He doesn't normally . . .'

'Normally what?' She knew she was playing into Cesca's hands by asking, but she couldn't stop herself.

'Like people. Open up. It's . . . weird. But good weird, I think.'

'Oh.'

'Are you going to go out with him?'

'No. We were really talking about business and anyway, what about you two? There's clearly—'

'We're just friends,' Cesca replied, frowning, the joy leaching from her face as she glanced at Marco. He was deep in conversation with Emilio and hadn't noticed his sister's reaction.

'Okay,' Beth replied. It was clear Cesca didn't want to talk about it. Beth would have to ask her when she was on her own. Emilio turned to them both and smiled, mostly at Cesca, who beamed back.

'I've never met an actual sportsman before. That sounds exciting,' Beth said.

'I'm very lucky to do what I love. Not everyone can do that.'

As if realising he'd said something wrong, his eyes shot to Marco and there was another strange and sudden shift in the mood, particularly between Cesca and her brother. Cesca glanced nervously at Marco from under her eyelashes while his gaze was fixed on the wine glass in front of him. Emilio, obviously aware of it too, cleared his throat.

'Right—' He held out his hand to Cesca. 'Ready for more?'

'Are you?' Cesca replied, ignoring his outstretched hand and standing up.

Beth was sure Emilio wasn't babysitting Marco's sister as a favour to him; he was spending time with her because he wanted to. They made their way to the dance floor, leaving her and Marco alone in the changed atmosphere. A Kylie party anthem was blaring, and it felt at odds with the silence they were in. Beth wondered what exactly was going on that kept causing these strange shifts. For a moment, Marco's gaze remained fixed on what was left of his wine, the small dribble in the bottom of the glass barely enough to see in the low lighting. His attention had turned inwards but rather than seeming angry or rude, he looked hurt, worried.

Though she knew it was none of her business, Beth felt compelled to ask, 'Is everything okay?'

'Fine. Why shouldn't it be?' As if realising how brusque his words had sounded and seeing the look on her face, he smiled, and his features softened. 'I'm sorry. I shouldn't have said that. It was rude of me and unnecessary. My problems are not your fault.'

She was grateful for such an eloquent apology. If it hadn't arrived she'd been debating walking away and even possibly telling him what a rude man he was. But what had Emilio said exactly that had upset him? Was it the comment about not being able to do what he loved?

'Italian families,' Marco said with a small laugh, then he sighed and took a drink of his wine. 'We are passionate about our family businesses, especially something like glass-blowing. It is important to Murano. Our heritage, our responsibility.'

'Cesca mentioned that there are sometimes . . . disagreements in your family.' He looked up and she quickly reassured him nothing bad had been said about anyone. 'We girls sometimes need people to talk to – that's all. Maybe with me being English she felt she could do that without judgement. My family made mostly bad decisions all their lives, so I'm not going to judge anyone.'

'Cesca doesn't have many friends, even though she is the life and soul of the party. I'm glad she has someone to talk to. She is our father's favourite. The only daughter. She gets caught between us even though I try to avoid it. It's hard for her. She finds it . . . *claustrofobico*.'

'Claustrophobic?'

He nodded.

'So your PR business, it's separate to your family business?'

'Sort of.' He was quiet for a second before speaking.

'With so many brothers working in the business, I wanted to do something else, so I started my PR firm.'

'You're not a fan of the glass-blowing?'

He shook his head. 'It's a skill and . . . not everyone has it.' That she could understand, but she couldn't shake the feeling there was more to this story than he was telling her. She couldn't blame him given they'd only just met. 'I hoped my father would let me use my skills for the family business too, exploring new ways of selling our products but he always refuses. It has caused some . . .' she watched him search for the right word '. . . difficulties.'

'How so?' He looked up, his eyes searching her face as if deciding if he should tell her or not.

'My father is a traditionalist and a technophobe. A difficult combination.' He stopped here, clearly feeling he'd said too much already, and Beth decided not to press. She didn't know him all that well and this wasn't the time or the place. It was a party after all.

'So—' He drank the last of his wine. 'Before we get another drink, or worse, get pulled onto the dance floor, shall I come and see the book barge again tomorrow?'

'Tomorrow?'

'Yes, if you want me to convince my clients to trust you with their work I need to see exactly where you're putting it and I wasn't sure from seeing it earlier.'

Remembering his first brief visit to the barge and then the flowers and the encounter that was over far too soon, Beth grew hot.

'Francesca's coming to measure up for some work I need doing. You could come with her.'

'Okay, I'll do that. Would you like another drink?'

She nodded. Marco moved past her in a waft of aftershave and her stomach somersaulted. The more she knew about him the more she *wanted* to know, and it wasn't just because she'd been in Venice for a whole year and this was the first time she'd met a man who made her tummy flutter like a schoolgirl with her first crush. Still waters ran deep, and Marco was interesting. The change in him as he spoke about business was a little confusing, but he was clearly passionate, and she'd always been the same way about her career. She was now about making the bookshop a success. She also liked his career choice and his wish to help creatives. She knew only too well how difficult it was to work in the arts.

He returned with another drink, and they began discussing art: her favourite paintings, his too, the museums and galleries they wanted to visit, the bookshops all around the world she wanted to see. He was a reader too, and though they had very different tastes in literature, for the first time in years, Beth didn't want the party to end.

Chapter 9

The February sun was slow to rise, and it was still dark as Beth wandered the Venice streets to the book barge, but Venice at dawn was as beautiful as any tropical sunset, in her opinion.

Lights from the streets and houses reflected on the canal waters and the sky was soon lightening to a dusky blue, splashes of light lifting the edges with colour. She wasn't sleeping well on the bed in the holiday rental and after waking at four she'd been unable to get back to sleep. She'd considered heading to the gym, but as her muscles still ached from her previous session, she decided instead to start the day early. Beth's plan to was to make a substantial amount of progress with the crazy amount of stock currently piled in the *Library of Words*.

Gosh, she loved that name. She looked down at the stupid cat carrier in her hand.

'How are you so heavy?' she asked Polo. He'd curled up and gone to sleep, ignoring her. But the thought of the book barge, even with carrying her new cat to and from, filled her with joy. The name was perfect for the place, but soon it would also be a library of art, if she were lucky. Her first job that morning was to create space for Marco's artists to display their work.

Marco. Her mind was stuck on an image of his face. After their tense interaction where he'd touched on the troubles with his family, they'd managed to pick up the conversation and had had a brilliant evening. He'd introduced her to lots of people and despite Francesca's attempts, both had managed to avoid stepping onto the dance floor. He'd relaxed in her company, and their love of art had proved a fertile area of common ground, giving them lots to talk about. He was passionate about new artists and moving Venetian art forward rather than it being stuck in the past, while she'd argued the past was more important than the present as people relied on social media apps and streaming services for their entertainment.

After a fun exchange, they'd agreed to disagree, and he'd cheekily said he might be able to convince her otherwise as she met the artists he represented. She was looking forward to the challenge. Realising she was smiling at the thought of him, she pulled her lips down. Cesca's comment that he didn't normally like people circled in her head. He seemed to like her and she certainly felt the same way.

Beth drew her mind back to the present because as well

as sorting out where Marco's artists would stage their work, she also needed to firm up her design ideas so she could describe them to Francesca. Normally, she'd have planned everything to the last detail for months before making a single move, but since she'd made the decision to buy the place, everything was moving fast. Too fast, it sometimes felt, and she was doing her best to go with the flow. She wasn't exactly enjoying it because it still made her feel unsettled and fearful of making the wrong decision, but she was getting used to it and kept telling herself she could always redo things further down the line if she needed to. That at least provided some comfort. After all, her academic life hadn't been all plain sailing either. She'd had to redo essays, retake exams, rewrite articles. Now she looked back on her previous career, it hadn't been as perfect as she'd thought.

Walking over a small bridge with iron railings, the water lapping against the houses, some of which looked like they were about to crumble into the canal at any minute, Beth took the time to inhale the tangy air. She hadn't done this before when marching to and from work with such speed, focusing on her to-do list and always trying her best to make a good impression, something that might lead to the next promotion. The only time she'd walked slowly was when she was searching for bookshops during her lunch breaks and even then she'd become frustrated because she had to get back to the office. She deliberately slowed her pace, moving the cat carrier from one hand to another. Was she really going to carry him there and back every day? She thought about letting him live on the barge but where would she put his litter tray? And there was no way customers would want to see that! He might get scared at night too and if he did, he wouldn't be able to curl up on her bed. She'd actually enjoyed coming back to him after the party, and hearing his gentle purring as she fell asleep while her fingers stroked his soft fur.

As she passed more houses, whose walls had seemed so pale five minutes before, she watched as they appeared to change colour. As the sun rose it was as though they'd taken on the stronger hues now slicing through the sky. The rich yellows made the red brick redder, and the pale cream walls brighter. The city was coming alive and soon it would be full of café owners like Giambattista, laying out tables, and shop owners readying tills for the day's trading. An overwhelming feeling of contentment spread through Beth and her shoulders dropped, even with the low temperature forcing them up to protect against the February wind. Still, the birds were singing, the sweet chirping growing louder as they too arose.

Beth arrived at the book barge and let herself in, placing Polo on the deck and opening the carrier. He immediately strolled out and stretched. The air hit her skin as she took off her coat, causing her to shiver, but she took a deep breath, inhaling the smell of paper and books, leather bindings and the safety of stories. Her first task was to light the fire and get some warmth in the place. That done, she flicked on the small travel kettle and made herself some tea. The milk was still fresh thanks to the freezing temperature and with a warm glow sweeping its way through the barge from the fire and the table lamps dotted around the shelves, Beth pulled on some fingerless gloves to keep her hands warm, and started work.

***

'Marco! It's even prettier than I remember!'

Francesca's voice broke Beth's focus and she placed yet another book down on the non-fiction pile. Whilst she loved a bit of non-fiction as much as the next person (maybe more being an academic) she had noticed a real lack of novels. She'd been clearing space and sorting the stock, stacking all the non-fiction books down one end of the barge and, as she stood, she worried the whole boat was about to tip over. Fiction, unless it was two hundred years old and a classic, clearly hadn't been Signor Balbo's thing. She'd have to change that. Tourists would most likely want holiday reads, so she needed a good supply and who didn't love disappearing into a book and forgetting about the real world for a while.

Marco's deep voice rumbled above, but she couldn't make out what he said. If he wasn't impressed, or at least saw the potential of the space, there was no way he was going to help her. A tingling in her lungs made her breath quiver and she told herself it had nothing to do with Marco and everything to do with her business.

Just as she turned, Cesca popped her head through the doorway. 'I can't tell you how much I love this place! Beth, it's amazing. I need to know all your plans right now.' She almost fell down the small set of steep stairs in her haste.

Marco followed more cautiously in a tailored peacoat and suit, and Beth wished she'd worn something more exciting than her usual pair of old trousers and jumper. She looked like a granny.

'And is this the cat you've inherited?' She crouched down and began stroking Polo, making cooing noises at him about what a good boy he was.

'He likes you,' Beth replied with a grin.

'What's his name again?'

'Polo. Like Marco Polo. Because he likes to go and explore all day then come back at night. Though he hasn't gone far today.'

'I'm not surprised,' Marco said. 'It's so cold.' He bent down too and began fussing the cat, edging his sister out of the way in a playful manner. She resisted, elbowing him back, then yielded and stood up.

'I really do love this place, Beth.'

'Me too,' Beth replied with a grin. 'So . . . welcome officially to the Library of Words.' She opened her arms wide. 'I was just sorting some more of the stock.'

'There's a lot isn't there,' Marco commented, leaving Polo who watched on, offended the fussing had stopped. He gazed around, his face unreadable.

'There is. Far too much. Signor Balbo just seems to have

bought more and more and more, without thinking about where he'd put it or how he'd shift it.'

'What will you do with it all?'

'Donate some to local libraries, I think. If they'd like them. Maybe set up a table on the bank next market day and just sell off as much as I can. I'm not quite sure, but I need to reduce the amount of stock to free up space and I'd like to avoid giving them all away for free if I can help it.'

'So what are you thinking in here?' Cesca asked.

'I think each area needs shelving that actually fits the space.'

Signor Balbo had used whatever furniture he could lay his hands on to display the books, but it meant the space wasn't as efficient as it could be and some areas were downright health hazards, with corners sticking out ready to be walked into. She already had bruises on her thighs from where they'd got her when she wasn't paying enough attention.

'But you want to keep the character, right?' Cesca asked. Beth could see her mind already working as she moved around the space.

'Definitely. You know I'm all about the heritage.'

Cesca moved to a dark mahogany cabinet and ran her hand over the wood. 'So we could reuse as much as possible, which'll keep your costs down and keep the character. But I think I could make you some lovely, unique shelving that fits the spaces perfectly and is a bit unusual.'

'That sounds great.' Another fizzle of excitement sprung up in her tummy.

'And what about the artwork?' Marco asked.

'So I was thinking,' Beth said, manoeuvring around the stack of books she'd made that morning and almost falling over in the process. She walked to the end of the barge where the armchairs sat. This area had the fewest books and the most free wall space. Small square windows were situated along the sides of the boat up to that point, but here they stopped, meaning she could hang items on the walls. She explained all this to Marco.

'So you'd only be looking for one or two pieces on each side, maybe three, depending on the size?'

'Yes, but I was also thinking about outside too.' He balked, the idea that expensive, beautiful artworks would be displayed in the open air, shocking him, but that wasn't what she meant.

Beth giggled at his wide-eyed expression. 'Come with me and I'll show you what I mean.' She led them outside and pointed to the cabinets on the exterior of the barge, the ones similar to those used by the booksellers on the banks of the Seine in Paris. 'I was thinking I could display ceramics or glasswork here. At least during the day. I'd lock them in the barge at night. And here on the deck—' She climbed up using a set of steps at the opposite end to the entrance to the lower deck. 'I'd like to hold events here. Mostly in the summer because of the weather, but we could have book readings, live bands, interesting talks. We could even open late. Once it's done up, I could do evening exhibitions here. I don't know what else but there must be a million options once the space is organised.' She righted a fallen flowerpot with the tip of her toe and turned to them both.

'We could put a roof on that,' Cesca said. 'Not a wooden one. But if I added some posts, we could add an awning, like the goods barges have for transporting things through the canals. That might help if you organise something and the weather suddenly gets bad.'

'That's a great idea!' Beth pressed her hands together. She should have thought of that.

Before, when she was working in the galleria, she might have blamed herself for not thinking of it. She'd have praised whoever did, but a small part of her, the driven part that wanted her and everything else to be perfect, would have told her she should have thought of that herself. Whether she had or not, it was a great idea, and she made a note on her phone so she didn't forget. Was she learning to be kinder to herself? She doubted it and instead, watched as Marco studied the place, his eyes flicking over every inch, his hands in his pockets. Beth held her breath, then reminded herself that regardless of his answer, she'd make it work somehow. She had to. His help was just a nice added extra if she could have it.

Finally, Marco turned to her and nodded. 'All right. We can start some discussions with my artists but no displaying anything until you've finished refurbishing. How long do you think it will take?'

Beth looked at Francesca. 'I can start work as soon as you've cleared everything.'

Ah. Now this might be a problem. 'The trouble is,' Beth began. 'I don't have anywhere to store anything except for here, so I'll clear as much as I can of the stock I don't want to keep, but what I do keep will have to be shuffled around to make room.'

'Can't you store anything at your apartment?' Marco asked and her cheeks grew warm.

'I'm kind of living in a holiday let at the moment. And they said I might have to move if they get a higher-paying, short-term booking. So no, not really.' She also had to definitely be out before the tourist season started. Oh, and she'd checked her lease agreement, and it quite clearly said she wasn't supposed to have pets either. She wasn't sure when she'd become such a rule breaker, but she was kind of enjoying it so far. As long as she didn't get caught.

'What?' Francesca said, almost shouting. 'Why didn't you say anything?'

Beth shrugged with embarrassment. The answer was simple: she hadn't thought they were that close. But maybe she'd underestimated her friend and their friendship. Cesca was kind and thoughtful and there was no reason to think that wouldn't have extended to her and her situation. Pride had kept her from saying anything. That and she didn't want people to think she was a failure. Guilt spread from her cold toes to the tip of her head.

'Life had gone a little crazy,' she replied, not meeting her eye.

Polo had followed them outside and was winding his

way around Marco's feet. He bent and fussed the cat again, grinning in a way that made Beth's heart melt.

'Well,' Marco said. 'I have a space you can use for storage if you need it. My office isn't too far from here, but as we can't use cars it'll be a lot of walking backwards and forwards.'

Venice was such a historic city, the streets so narrow with houses almost touching, that no cars were allowed. Beth loved it. London proved what pollution could do to beautiful buildings, turning their walls black. Venice had the right idea. But what Marco said was more than she'd been expecting. He looked again at the barge and smiled. She couldn't read his expression exactly, but she thought maybe he was . . . impressed? She hoped he was. She hoped they both were.

'Thanks, that's really kind, but give me another couple of weeks to get rid of as much of this as I can first. Then I can see what I'm keeping and get more of an idea of how much space I need. I need to plan it all out and decide where each section will go.'

'Section?' Marco asked.

'Yeah, like fiction split into different genres and non-fiction too.'

'Right, I see.'

'I want it to look like a proper bookshop.'

'Just a floating one?'

'Exactly.' There it was again: that friendly, open side to him she'd seen as they'd discussed art and history at the party.

'So,' Cesca interrupted, glancing between them. 'Two weeks to make some space then?' Beth nodded. 'That'll work. I've got a job to finish first, but it's nearly done.'

'Perfect! Shall we celebrate with tea?' Her Italian friends turned up their noses and curled their lips in disgust. Tea was not a favourite in Italy. Not when there was gorgeous Italian coffee to enjoy. Beth laughed. 'Okay, how about I take you to my favourite café instead then?'

'That sounds better,' Cesca said.

Marco agreed. 'I don't understand what you English see in tea. It's like drain water.'

Beth stepped down off the deck and led them back inside to grab her coat. She left a window open for Polo, who had already wandered off. As she stepped onto the pavement she said, 'Then you've clearly never had a decently made cup. Come on, I could do with the caffeine. I'm going to need it.'

Chapter 10

The following weekend, Beth placed yet another handful of books on a makeshift table she'd set up on the canal path. It was market day: a day the city came alive, even in the winter, and it had dawned bright and sunny, softening the breeze and blowing away the pale grey clouds she'd woken up to.

Further down the way, other sellers were beginning to organise their barges. One was stocked full of flowers and plants, another fruit and vegetables of every variety. They looked like works of art, as vibrant and colourful as the city during Carnevale. That amazing festival was coming up soon, and Beth hoped that both she and Cesca would have made some progress with selling books and sorting some shelving. She wasn't sure if it would be ready in time. She'd have to speak to Francesca about it. Perhaps even Marco too, to see if one of his clients made the gorgeous, decorated masks Carnevale was famous for.

Before she'd even moved to Venice, she'd loved the idea of Carnevale. She'd read about it in books and seen it on TV, but her first real experience of it had been not long after she'd moved here, and it had made the transition from England to Italy even more exciting. In the depths of winter, Carnevale cheered everyone up with its bright costumes, detailed, hand-painted masks and captivating performances. The timing of it changed each year as it came before Lent, but when it arrived, the parades and shows filled the centre of the city, concentrated in St Mark's Square, the most beautiful, historic backdrop to a festival that had its roots in the eleventh century. Everything about it appealed to Beth and she suddenly felt excited for it in a way she hadn't before.

Last year, she'd watched elements of it from the windows of the galleria. She'd dodged between crowds on her way to and from work, watching snippets here and there, but had otherwise kept her head down. This year, being her own boss and 'going with the flow', she'd make time to explore the city, watching the performances in the main square and in the side streets, enjoying every moment of it.

As Beth glanced to her right, she saw that a barge had set up selling coffees and pastries. The husband-and-wife team chatted as they readied their goods, their laughter louder than the crates being moved and organised further down the canal. The woman swiped the man with a tea towel as he nabbed a fresh pastry, just put on display, and took a giant bite. When he caught Beth watching, he winked, and she smiled back. The coffee barge had only moored up yesterday and she assumed it must move around the city. She was grateful for it though and decided to grab her wallet and head over just as soon as she'd arranged these last few books.

With a huge number donated to the local libraries, and even a few reference books given to the galleria, which Signor Sanna was particularly happy with, the book barge was looking much better. Stock was now organised, and she'd got rid of a quarter of it so far. She was hoping for at least a few sales today due to the knock-down prices. After all, some of the books were faded from the sun, the pages dog-eared, the covers pale and less than appealing. Others were better quality, but niche in nature. She wasn't holding out hope for fans of door frames and panelling, or cricket of the last one hundred years. Still, she'd try her luck. Nothing ventured, nothing gained, after all. She'd made a sign selling everything at under five euros and hoped people would overlook the state of some of them for such a bargain price.

'There,' she said to herself, adjusting a thick, hardback book that kept falling over, finally balancing it so it stood upright. She'd created quite a nice display, and in the summer, when she did this again, she'd add flowers and plants to the tables to make them pretty.

Polo sniffed around the table legs and as she turned to walk away, jumped up, knocking over the book she'd only just managed to balance.

'Polo! Shoo! Go away!' The cat sat in front of her,

knocking over even more books, and she stroked his fur and tickled behind his ears as she told him off again. 'You're going to get in the way today, aren't you?'

He lifted his head and without thinking she dipped hers so he could rub his face against hers. She'd never really been a pet person before but couldn't deny the bond between her and the silly grey cat. She could see how Signor Balbo had loved him and was afraid her heart was doing the same. She lifted him off the table and onto the floor and rearranged her books once more. Beth's stomach rumbled and so after nipping inside and grabbing her wallet, she went to the coffee barge.

The female owner smiled. Her dark hair was striped beautifully with grey and pulled back into a bun. Looking at the woman's full, rosy cheeks and warm eyes, Beth felt welcomed without saying a word.

'*Buongiorno*,' Beth chirped happily. '*Potrei avere un latte, per favore?*'

'*Sì, sì!*' The woman turned to her husband who began making the latte Beth had requested, and as the rich aroma filled Beth's nose, making her stomach rumble even louder, the woman said, 'You're the English lady, aren't you? The one who bought Signor Balbo's bookshop?'

'Yes, that's right. My name's Beth.'

'I'm Lolanda, and this is my husband, Galvano.'

Her English was heavily accented, and she seemed to struggle with some of the words, so Beth offered to speak in Italian.

'No, no!' Lolanda waved her hands. 'I like to practise. Before the tourists come.'

'You're doing very well already.'

'*Grazie.*' She smiled and nodded towards the tables laden with books. 'You're selling a lot today?'

'I'm trying to. I don't know where Signor Balbo got his stock from but there's a lot of it, so I'm trying to reduce it down a bit and make some room for new stuff.'

'He used to take whatever people gave him.' Lolanda was incredibly expressive and continued to wave her hands around as she spoke.

It was something Beth had come to love about Italy. Italian women took up space and made their opinions known. They weren't made to be small and fit into a man's world. They were vibrant and full of life, encouraged to share their opinions and take control. They took up all the room they needed, and Beth loved it.

'When anyone moved house,' Lolanda continued, 'they would hand him bags and bags of books, and he took them! Always! I didn't like going inside the barge; there was too much . . . stuff. Too much to see.'

'I can understand that,' Beth replied, not wanting to disparage Signor Balbo, who'd clearly loved the shop and had been incredibly kind to her. 'But then I used to work in a gallery, and they always have too much stuff too!'

Perhaps that was why she'd been drawn to the book barge in the first place. There were other bookshops in Venice, but she'd never thought about owning or running one of those. They'd always felt like shops rather than museums or galleries, spaces for history and heritage. But the book barge had felt the same as a museum – the slightly dusty air, the sense of time being frozen. She had to admit though, while that might be great for those type of places, it wasn't for a shop, as Lolanda had just demonstrated, so she needed to find a happy medium. She needed light and air and as much space as Francesca could make for her, but with the art on the walls, the cosy lighting, and the warming fire, she might manage the best of both worlds. Her nerves sizzled at the idea of her friend getting started and the way the book barge would soon be tidy and efficient and, most of all, customer friendly.

'What time do people normally begin arriving on market days?' Beth asked, slightly depressed to see she'd drunk most of her coffee already. Freshly made Italian coffee, made by artisans who knew exactly what they were doing, couldn't be beaten, but if she had too much caffeine she'd be jittery for hours.

'About eleven,' Galvano said, stopping beside his wife. He checked his watch. 'So it shouldn't be long. I think a few are beginning to come now.' He nodded up the bank where small groups were ambling along one behind the other. 'I hope you sell lots of books,' he said, his eyes flashing warmly before he winked at her again.

'And I hope you sell lots of coffee!'

Beth made her way back to the barge and decided to go inside and tidy the now more spacious lower deck. It would probably put people off if she was stood over their shoulder watching them, hoping they'd buy things. Nerves sprang up at the idea of talking to them, of not being able to disappear behind the scenes as she normally would have at the gallery. But it was talking about books, which she loved, and even if they didn't buy anything, she'd have a nice conversation with a fellow bookworm. She just needed to go with the flow.

After a while and few tentative conversations with people who enquired about the change of ownership, Beth felt more at ease and spotted her first real customer looking around for how to pay, a stack of books in their hand. She made her way outside with her portable card machine.

'*Hai una borsa?*' they said, and an icy chill ran down her spine.

A bag? Did she have any bags? She asked them to hold on and ran back inside, thankfully finding a bag stuffed full of other plastic bags. It wasn't exactly environmentally friendly, but it would have to do for now. As the customer left she made a note on her phone to get paper bags printed with the logo of the shop.

The day continued with a steady stream of customers Beth found incredibly pleasing. There were a couple of busier moments when she couldn't even see the table on the canal bank because so many people were crowded in front of it, but as the day drew to a close, seeing the number of books she'd sold filled her with joy. She'd spoken in both Italian and English to customers and, as she'd suspected, people who loved books were just nice.

As the afternoon sun lit the pale grey sky, and the customers ebbed away, the other barges began to pack up.

'You did well!' Lolanda said, calling over from the coffee barge as Beth began to take books inside.

'Yes, I'm very pleased! How did you do?'

'Very good. People were thirsty today.'

Galvano added, 'The cold makes them want to warm up. And Lolanda's pastries are irresistible.'

'I see.' Beth put down the books she'd just gathered and wandered closer. Galvano removed two pastries they hadn't sold from the glass display case. One was savoury with pesto and goat's cheese – like a mini pizza – and the other was a sweet called *sfogliatella*, shaped like a lobster tail and so delicate it looked as though it would break as soon as it was touched. 'Is this all that's left?'

'*Sì.*'

'Can I take them, please? I'm starving.' She hadn't had anything since that coffee this morning and a slice of toast before she left her grotty holiday let.

'Of course.' Galvano put them in two separate bags.

'I'll just grab my wallet—'

'No, no, no! Free. You have them for free.'

'I can't.' She shook her head. 'I couldn't possibly.'

'Of course you can,' Lolanda added. 'We will only throw them away. Take them!'

'Thank you. That's really kind of you.'

'We will see you next week!'

They waved and Beth took the bag, tucking into the

savoury pastry as she cleared up. The goat's cheese and pesto were perfectly balanced, the pastry fluffy and chewable, and the *sfogliatella* was crumbly and sweet. She was just putting down the trestle table she'd bought and trying to manoeuvre it through the barge doorway without falling down the steps when Marco appeared.

'Oh! Hello. I hadn't expected to see you today.'

In fact, she hadn't known when she would see him again as they hadn't made any plans.. Seeing him now, her ribs tightened around her heart, and she almost lost her balance on the steep stairs.

'Do you need some help?' Marco asked.

She thought about continuing on her own to show she didn't need anyone's assistance, but then, why struggle when a strapping, handsome Italian man was offering to help? 'Can you take that end for me?'

He did as he was asked, and she safely got down the steps before taking the weight of it and moving it inside.

'Thank you. What are you doing here?'

He looked as handsome as ever, a smattering of weekend stubble on his jaw. He was wearing dark denim jeans, almost as navy as his peacoat and black boots. A striped scarf added a splash of colour at the opening of his coat. Italian men really knew how to dress. He looked like a model.

'I thought I'd come and see how your first day selling books has gone.'

'Very well actually.'

She told him all about the day and about meeting Lolanda

and Galvano next door. Through one of the windows she saw them beginning to move away, the boat steadily gliding through the water. She hoped she'd see them again the following weekend.

'And what are you doing now?'

'Bringing the rest of that inside.' She pointed out of the window. 'Then sinking into a hot bath and drinking a huge glass of wine.'

His gaze whipped to her as she mentioned the bath and it made her nerves tingle.

'Why?' she asked, ignoring the feeling.

'Because I want to talk to you about some of my artists. I've already spoken to a few and they're interested.'

'Really? That's brilliant!'

'Shall we go for a drink? Do you think you can manage that before you sink into a bath?'

Her cheeks grew hot, a warm fuzziness filling her lungs, and she attempted to ignore the beautiful ice-blue eyes watching her. 'Sure. Do you want to sit down while I finish off? Polo should be back soon too and I better leave him here while we go. I don't think anywhere nice will let me bring a cat carrier inside.'

'Maybe not,' he replied with a chuckle. 'But I don't mind helping. Then you'll be done more quickly.'

A sizzling feeling began to spread through her limbs, and she put it down to her body finally warming up after being in the cold all day, though deep down she knew it wasn't to do with that at all. As six o'clock neared, Polo returned from his day's expeditions, and she left him with some water inside the book barge while she headed out with Marco.

He took her to a canal-side bar a few streets away and the tinkling sounds of a piano were just noticeable under the chatter as Marco led them to a table. The green marble that Venice was famous for covered the walls, the polished surface and pale, almost white veins in the stone reflecting the light. Gilt-edged mirrors spread the soft orange glow of the numerous table lamps all around the room and the place screamed class as though it was coming through a loudspeaker.

Beth felt grubby and dull in her boring trousers and jumper, her hair tied in a plain ponytail and the dust from the book barge, that always seemed to be there, covering her skin. She brushed a hand down her trouser leg as she waited for Marco to return from the bar.

He handed her a glass of wine and placed one in front of himself as he slid into the chair opposite.

'This place is beautiful,' she said, wondering how he knew it and who he might have brought here. Elegant, gorgeous women with glossy hair and long legs, no doubt.

'You've never been?'

'No, I . . . I was so focused on my job I didn't get out much.'

'I know that feeling,' he replied casting a gentle look at her. The softness reminded her of the Marco she'd seen before at the gym, bringing her flowers, but then he swallowed and something shifted. 'I sometimes bring clients here. This place—' He signalled to the room. 'It encompasses

Venice and they like looking out over the lagoon. It always impresses them.'

She followed his gaze to the view out of a floor-to-ceiling window. The Venetian Lagoon, the enclosed bay in which the city sat, was a wonder of the world. The city itself was a UNESCO World Heritage site. The waters were growing choppy as the wind picked up, but it was busy nonetheless, water taxis moving to and from the small islands and barges of goods being transported. She drew her gaze back to Marco to catch him watching her.

'Are these clients for your family business or your PR firm?'

A slight stoniness entered his expression but then was gone as quickly as it came. 'Mostly for my business. My father, he doesn't like me trying to "sell" what we do. He thinks it is . . . tacky, you English might say.'

That sounded a little short-sighted to her, but she didn't say so. Instead, she said, 'Every business needs publicity, even the most successful ones.'

'Exactly.'

'You said a few of your clients were interested in the book barge. Do I get to know who?'

'You do.' He sipped his wine, and his Adam's apple bobbed as he swallowed. She drew her eyes down to the ruby liquid in her glass. 'That's why I wanted to meet. They want to meet you. I was hoping to set up some appointments. Is that okay?'

'Yes, of course. Please do. I'll be there whenever they can

see me. Francesca said she can start work on the barge this week, so I'll need to keep out of her way anyway.'

He smiled fondly at the mention of his sister. 'She's very excited. She loves projects where she can have some freedom.'

'I'm happy to take her advice. I know she's going to do a great job.'

'She is very talented.'

'It's rather an unusual career for a woman, though, isn't it? A carpenter. That may sound sexist, but – well, I think she should be very proud.'

'Our family are all practical, hands-on people, but she has always hated the heat from the furnace. As do I,' he added. For a second he didn't speak as his eyes glazed, and his gaze seemed to turn inwards. He rubbed a small area of his wrist and Beth noticed some scarring there. Had there been an accident? 'She was terrified of the molten glass as a child. Instead she'd make things from wood and my father was happy to encourage her career.'

But not yours, Beth thought, wondering why.

'I'm very proud of her,' Marco finished.

Again, a piece of her melted even though Marco was being nothing but professional. 'So who are we going to see this week?' she asked with assumed brightness.

'A lacemaker who makes incredible pieces of art using traditional Venetian techniques, and a portrait artist. Don't worry, he isn't like the ones who con the tourists in St Mark's Square. He is a very talented man and a friend. There may be more, but I'm waiting for some people to get back to me.'

'That sounds amazing. I'm very, very grateful.' She could just see the far corner of the book barge with items like this on the walls. Or maybe she could do takeover days where the whole barge was used by a single artist as working and exhibition space.

'What?' Marco asked. 'Your face has—' he ran his finger in a large circle around his own face '—contorted.'

Beth laughed through her embarrassment, wishing she hadn't let her emotions show on her face. 'I was just thinking of an idea, that's all.' She told him what had just occurred to her and he nodded.

'I like that idea very much. I think my clients might too.'

'We could do it once a month and even open into the evening with wine and nibbles.'

'Nibbles?' He was the one making a face now and Beth laughed again.

'Gorgeous Venetian *cicchetti*.'

Cicchetti was the Venice equivalent of Spanish tapas. Though you could get it almost anywhere now, it was traditionally sold in bars called *bacari*. Again, she'd only been to a couple with her friends from the museum on staff nights out to celebrate the opening or closing of an exhibition and had always been home early. Academics liked an early night.

'Ah, I see. Good. I was worried it would be sad English food that has no flavour and is made from bread or flour.'

'You know, not all of our food is bad. And we only like stodgy food because it's always so cold and rainy. If we had weather like you do here, we'd eat more salads and fresh fish. We only don't because it's always freezing, and no one wants to eat salad when it's drizzling.'

'Drizzling?'

'Raining constantly but not heavily.'

He seemed surprised at her outburst and laughed. It was free and easy, a deep throaty noise that changed his face, the serious, businesslike layers dropping away. 'I do understand; it isn't your fault.'

She cocked her head, scowling at him in mock annoyance. 'I'll convince you one day, I'm sure.'

He laughed again, and as it died, something shifted and the softness of moments before was gone, concern now visible in the shallow lines around his eyes. He took another sip of his wine, only a little remaining at the bottom of his glass. Beth did the same, hoping that he might suggest they have another. When he didn't she was just about to ask him herself, but he abruptly stood.

'Well, I will call you when I know more.' He took his coat from the back of the chair and slipped it on.

'Oh, right. Of course. I better go and get Polo anyway.' Beth almost knocked her glass over as she quickly placed it back on the table, shocked at the sudden end to their discussion.

'Have a nice evening, Beth. Do you need me to walk you home?'

He'd said it like it was a chore and not something he wanted to do at all, so she shook her head.

'No, thank you. I don't live far and like I said, I need to head back and collect Polo.'

'If you're sure.'

'I am.'

'Okay. Then have a nice evening.'

With a brisk nod of his head, he was gone, weaving through the tables, leaving her watching after him and wondering what had happened to make him run away. Had she done or said something? Had she offended him? She flopped down, questioning what had brought about such a sudden change. Their conversation had only just started. When the barman caught her attention, he signalled to see if she'd like another and without hesitation she nodded. As much as she wanted to fetch Polo and fall into her bath and bed, she wanted to figure out what had just happened.

With a new glass of wine, Beth pulled out her book, ready to read, but she couldn't help replaying the conversation from start to finish. No matter how many times she ran it through, nothing stood out and the only conclusion she could come to was that it had been a business meeting and nothing more and that Marco wasn't interested in getting to know her in any other way. She had to admit, given he was the only man she'd been remotely attracted to in the year she'd been here, the disappointment hit hard. As she tried to fall into the pages of her latest crime novel, this one featuring a doctor in modern-day Venice, she sighed. The hero in her hands had no hope of measuring up to the man who'd just left.

Chapter 11

When Monday morning rolled around, Beth found herself jumping out of bed before her alarm had even gone off. Before, even though she loved her job, there'd still been days when she hadn't really fancied getting out of bed and spending the day in a freezing cold gallery. She didn't know how long this feeling would last, but she did know that owning her own business and living by her own timetable was definitely something she was enjoying. Plus, Cesca was starting at the boat today and she wanted to be there early to ensure everything was ready and to grab pastries on the way to show her thanks.

Dressing in her usual outfit of trousers and a jumper, and tying her hair in a ponytail, Beth caught a glimpse of herself in the mirror. Her hazel eyes were bright and her skin was glowing, freckles dancing across her nose, but when had she started dressing so conservatively? So . . . boringly? Even in the height of summer last year Beth had stuck to her uniform of (if she were honest) unflattering trousers, swapping out her jumpers for a vest top or T-shirt, but still wearing a blazer over the top so people took her seriously. She wore low-heeled boots every day and everything was black or grey – dull, muted colours that showed no personality. Everything was corporate.

It was time for a change. As soon as she had enough money, she'd treat herself to some new clothes – just a few bits that were bright and cheerful and didn't make her look like someone's great-nan. She picked up a bright red scarf she'd bought on a whim last year and swung it around her neck, adding an extra layer of warmth and a pop of colour against the boring black coat. It instantly made her skin look brighter, her lips pinker. It wasn't much, but it was a start, and she nodded at her reflection before grabbing her keys and Polo's cat carrier.

He'd been fast asleep on the armchair when she returned to collect him after seeing Marco and hadn't been bothered at all. Beth was beginning to like his independent personality, which was very much like her own.

Cesca was already waiting at the barge as Beth arrived with two takeaway coffees and a bag of pastries in one hand, the cat in the other. A pile of tools were laid out at her feet.

'You haven't been here long, have you?' Beth asked. 'It's freezing! I feel bad now.'

'No, only a minute or so. I had to come as soon as I

woke up. I couldn't wait to get started. Did you row this morning?'

'Not this morning. I might go later though.'

'You really should try the water and not the machines in the gym.'

'I will. I'm just . . . working up to it. Coffee first, yes?'

Cesca grinned. 'Of course!'

Beth placed the cat carrier on the ground, found the keys and opened up, letting Cesca in first and then handing over the treats. Beth lit the fire saying she could put it out once Cesca got to work, but for now they both needed to warm up. As they sat in the two small armchairs, Polo having a roam around, Cesca said: 'Did you enjoy the rowing club party the other night?' Her left eyebrow rose slightly and Beth ignored her friend's unsubtle enquiry into the time Beth had spent with Marco.

'I did. It was fun.'

'You and Marco were talking for a very long time. He barely spoke to anyone else all evening.'

'I think he felt sorry for me. Not wanting to leave me on my own.'

'Yes, yes, that was it. Nothing more.' Cesca's tone was teasing, and hope rose that maybe Cesca was right. But then, why had he acted so strangely when they were having a drink the other night?

'What about you?' Beth asked, raising her eyebrows in return. 'You seemed to be enjoying yourself.' When Cesca didn't reply, and instead watched Polo sniff then leap up the steps and head outside, Beth added, 'Emilio's a very handsome man.'

Cesca's cheeks coloured, turning her gorgeous olive skin ruddy. 'Is he? I hadn't noticed.'

'Oh come on!' Beth laughed. 'I might have forgotten what it's like to flirt with someone, but you two were flirting like crazy.'

'No, we weren't!' Cesca wasn't smiling and Beth felt a heavy weight in her stomach. 'We're just friends. Nothing more.' Cesca suddenly swallowed the last of her coffee and stood up. 'I better get started.'

Beth frowned in surprise. What was it with this family? First Marco shifting from friendly to super-professional and now Cesca?

What had she said? What had she done to upset her friend? She followed Cesca as she made her way out onto the canal path and began organising herself.

'Oh, okay. Sure. I—' The cool air bit at her skin since she'd left her coat inside. 'Cesca, I'm sorry if I spoke out of turn. I didn't mean to upset you. It's none of my business.'

With her back still to Beth, Cesca stopped and took a deep breath. Beth watched her shoulders rise and fall, then her head drop.

'I really am sorry, Cesca. I didn't mean to make you uncomfortable. Is – is everything okay?' she asked tentatively.

Finally Cesca turned, looking defeated, and Beth's heart shot up into her throat. 'There's something I need – I want –

to tell you. Emilio and I – we're not just friends. We're . . . together.'

'Oh!' Beth felt the wrinkles forming on her forehead as she frowned in confusion. 'Have you had an argument or something?'

'No. We're very happy.'

'You don't look it.' In fact, Cesca, who was always cheerful and the life and soul of the party, looked like she was about to cry.

'No, I am. We are.' She wiped at her nose.

'Then what is it?' Cesca lifted her head, but didn't speak, her eyes glassy with unshed tears. 'Shall we go back inside?'

Cesca nodded and they both marched back to the armchairs and the warmth of the fire and flopped down.

'Emilio and I are very happy. We've been together for a few months now and it's going well, but . . .'

Beth waited, hoping whatever Cesca had to say wasn't that serious or was something easily sorted, but from her reaction so far, that didn't seem to be the case.

'It's Marco,' Cesca continued. 'He doesn't know. No one knows.'

'Why not?' Beth clasped her hands together between her knees.

'Because Marco would hate the idea. All my family would. Emilio – he's had a few girlfriends in the past, sometimes more than one at once. He's not like that anymore and what we have, it's been growing between us for a long time. But Marco, he knows what a . . . a . . . playboy he's been and will be angry. He'll think that his best friend is taking advantage of his little sister. Italian brothers they . . . they can be very overprotective of sisters. Especially younger sisters.'

'I'm sure that's true of brothers everywhere. And I get Emilio might not have had the best past, but why would he think that? And anyway, you're a grown woman able to see who you want. It's not really any of his business is it?'

'We're Italian, Beth,' Cesca replied, deadpan. 'Everything is everyone else's business.'

A small smile pulled at Cesca's lips and Beth's too. 'Oh yes, I forget that.'

'Marco's very protective. He's had some knockbacks, you would say. He finds it difficult to trust people and he'll see it as a betrayal. I know he doesn't want me to get hurt but he won't believe Emilio's changed, even though I know he has. He's shown me he has, and I trust him implicitly. He's told me he loves me.'

Beth's eyes widened. That was a big thing to say. 'And do you love him?'

Cesca nodded. 'But you cannot say anything to anyone, especially Marco. I just . . . I just had to tell someone. You're the only real friend I have. My brothers scare off friends as well as boyfriends.' She smiled at Beth and Beth cocked her head, reaching out and taking her hand. 'The girls I grew up with on the island, they're nice enough but they wouldn't understand. They've known us both for too long. They still only see the Emilio he was before, but people change.'

Beth knew that herself. Look at how much she'd grown

over the past month, but the thought of keeping Cesca's secret from Marco didn't sit well. She hated lying to people. But Cesca was her friend and had been before she'd even seen Marco. She had no choice but to keep her friend's secret.

'I promise I won't say anything, but you should think about telling your family, especially Marco. I'm sure they'll understand.'

Cesca scoffed. 'I wish that were the case. With Marco trying to get Papa to move into the twenty-first century there's enough tension at home without adding anything else. Telling them this will be like setting off a bomb.'

'But you can't keep it secret forever, and if you think this is the real deal then at some point you'll have to tell them.'

'I'll find the right time. When they've seen for themselves how Emilio has changed. It just might take a while as he's always travelling to competitions.'

'You know your family better than I do,' Beth conceded. 'But I'm here if you ever need me, okay?'

'Thank you,' Cesca said. 'So, shall we get started?'

Suddenly brighter after unloading her secret, Cesca began work in a flurry of activity, but Beth found it harder to move on from their conversation. She felt torn and reminded herself that Marco was a business partner and his and Cesca's family life was none of her business. All she could do was encourage Cesca to speak to them sooner rather than later.

They decided to start where the armchairs were, where Beth intended to display different artists' work. She'd chosen a neutral colour for the walls, as Beth knew it often worked well in exhibitions, allowing the customer to focus on the art without interruption. She'd also selected some bolder colours in royal blue and deep, Regency red for smaller alcoves in the boat to give the place some colour and keep the cosy feel. They'd look so good around the fire, and she didn't want it to feel sterile like a chain bookstore.

Together they cleared books and took furniture out onto the street, which Cesca then broke up, Cesca measuring the pieces and cutting them to size to make new, sleek shelves. Polo stayed out of the way, deciding at one point to go on a little adventure, and he disappeared from sight down the side streets and alleyways away from the barge. Beth still worried a little about him but was growing used to him returning when he felt like it, and always by six o'clock, ready for his dinner.

The morning went quickly, and both were surprised to see Marco arrive at lunchtime carrying bags of food and another tray of takeaway coffees.

After their strange meeting a couple of nights before, Beth wasn't sure how to act around him and now, with Cesca's secret on top, she felt even more uncomfortable. He smiled warmly at them both.

Cesca shot Beth a concerned glance, so she smiled back, reassuring her friend that, as she'd promised, she wouldn't say anything.

'How is it going?' Marco asked, perching on the small brick wall that lined the other side of the canal path.

'Good!' Cesca replied, checking the length of a piece of wood. 'We're making excellent progress. I don't think this will take more than a week. Well, to do the inside anyway.'

'Really?' Beth replied, jiggling in her excitement. 'That means I can be open for Carnevale!'

'The outside will need more work,' Cesca said, leaving the wood and taking her coffee from Marco. 'But we can tackle that after, if you like.'

'Yes, that'd be great.'

'Here,' Marco said, handing Beth a coffee. 'This is for you.'

'Oh, thank you.' She took a tentative sip, surprised that he'd remembered her order from before.

'I risked being thrown out of Italy, ordering your latte.'

Beth laughed. 'You're very brave.' He gave her a flirty smile in return.

What was with this guy? Sometimes he could be relaxed and charming, and at other times he reverted to such a stony, businesslike approach she felt spun around. The hit of strong coffee gave her the energy boost she needed, though she hadn't realised it.

'What's in the bag?' Cesca asked sneaking a look.

'Get your nose out and I'll show you,' he teased. 'I thought you might be hungry. Both of you.'

Marco glanced again at Beth, and the fizzing she'd experienced every time they met returned. This time though, she couldn't help but wish Cesca had never unloaded her secret on her, even though she'd clearly needed to.

Marco pulled out three tuna and olive stuffed *tramezzino*: soft white bread sandwiches cut into triangles. They were a simple food, but always delicious because of the quality of the ingredients. Beth took hers greedily, her stomach rumbling.

Just as she was taking a bite, Marco said, 'Are you free this afternoon, Beth? One of my artists would like to meet you.'

She hastily covered her mouth while she chewed, then wiped her lips with the napkin. Meeting a client with tuna breath? It wasn't ideal. She'd have to grab some mints on the way. 'Yes of course. Is that okay with you, Cesca?'

'Of course!' she replied brightly.

'I can give you the spare key in case I'm not back by the time you want to finish. You did start stupidly early this morning.'

'That would make life easier.'

'Let me get it now before I forget.'

'No!' Cesca and Marco both cried in unison, their hands shooting out to stop her moving.

'What? What is it?'

'Eat first,' Cesca said, pointing at her sandwich. 'We Italians always prioritise our food.'

'Always,' Marco added with a glint in his eye that made Beth slightly hot even though she didn't have her coat on.

They ate in comfortable silence, Marco and Cesca making odd snippets of conversation about their family business and the general excitement for Carnevale. When he mentioned Emilio's next race, Beth had to stop her eyes flying to Cesca, who was acting as if this news was the most uninteresting thing she'd ever heard.

'You always talk about him,' she said dismissively. 'It's boring.'

She seemed to realise she sounded like a teenager as she winced a little, though Marco didn't see.

He laughed. 'He's my best friend, and I'm proud of what he's achieved. You remember how he was at school. Always in trouble. Never doing the work. I'm glad he's found something he wants to work hard at.'

'Is he away often?' Beth asked, trying to show as much interest as she normally would but not go overboard or act rudely uninterested. Again, an uncomfortable gnawing started in her tummy.

'Quite a lot. He lives his life on the road, really. It's not for me, but he seems to love it. He works hard and plays hard.'

'No he doesn't,' Cesca replied without thinking and then turned back to the book barge, pulling out her tape and pretending to remeasure something. Beth could see the redness clawing up her neck and onto her cheeks.

'He does,' Marco replied. 'Or at least he used to. He has grown up a lot lately; I will give him that. He takes his training a lot more seriously now he's getting older and can't rely on youth to get him through.'

Beth reminded herself that she and Marco were only business associates, and it wasn't her place to tell him anything. Though she did wish Cesca would just be honest with her brother. She kept her mouth shut and finished her sandwich.

Cesca returned to work without another word, only wishing Marco goodbye. He didn't seem to notice the change in his sister as he cheerfully said to Beth, 'Shall we go? We'll have time to walk to Signor Zambelli's studio.'

'Is he the portrait painter you mentioned or the lacemaker?'

'The portrait painter.'

'Fabulous. I'll just get my coat.'

She gave Cesca the spare key and snapped a few pictures of the space to show him when they met. 'If Polo comes back before you leave, just shut the windows and leave him in there. He has water.'

'And if he's not back?'

'Just leave a window open, he'll climb inside and be asleep by the time I return, knowing him.'

'Seems like you've got used to him already,' Marco said.

'I have,' she replied with a huge grin. She was beginning to love the silly creature and was glad going with the flow had brought him into her life.

The crisp wind she hadn't noticed as she and Cesca had worked on the boat nipped at her face, and though the sun was shining a little more than it had on previous days, it didn't quite kill the chill in the air. They walked towards the sixth *sestieri*, the artists' quarter, and after a short silence, Marco spoke first.

'I should warn you about Signor Zambelli. He is . . . urgh . . . I think you say, eccentric.'

'Eccentric how?' Beth chuckled. She'd met more than her fair share of eccentrics. Creatives and academics were known for being unconventional. One particular male curator at the National Gallery in London had been known for always wearing odd socks and mismatched cufflinks. He'd always claimed it was an accident, but she suspected he did it on purpose just to play the part. He was one of the curators of the more boring areas.

'You'll see,' Marco replied, grinning. 'I wouldn't want to spoil the surprise. But he is very nice and very talented. I think people will like his work and it could sell well on your boat.'

'Great.' She took a deep breath, enjoying the walk through the city.

They navigated the streets and Beth took a moment to appreciate the different names Venice had for them. In the rest of Italy, streets were mostly called *stradas* but in Venice, because it had always been a floating city, accessed via waterways, there were different names like *calle*, which meant alleyway, or *campiello*, which meant a square. They walked along a paved *fondamenta* – the pavement next to the canal, brushing shoulders as the road tightened.

Beth's excitement over Cesca saying they might be able to open before Carnevale couldn't be contained. 'I can't wait to open properly,' she said, slightly embarrassed by her joy.

'Carnevale is always here before you know it, and it's a good time of year for artists. A real opportunity to showcase their work. Were you here for it last year?'

'I was but I saw most of it from my office window.'

They were so close together on the *fondamenta*, her hand brushed his and his aftershave carried towards her. 'You didn't explore the city? Enjoy the parades?'

'No. I should have. I should have come out and soaked up the atmosphere, but I was too busy working on some items in the gallery storerooms. I'm hoping they'll put it on display one day.'

'Your taste runs to the classic?' he said, though it was more a statement than a question. 'I remember from our conversation the other night.'

Beth's nerves fizzed that he remembered, but then, his job was to tempt and schmooze, and part of that was making people feel seen. 'I suppose I've always been drawn more to traditional art. It's why I love Venice. I don't think anything can beat works by Titian or Canaletto. But that's not to say I don't appreciate other art too. I'm very open-minded.'

'Good, because some of my clients are not old-fashioned.' He flashed a smile, his eyes glinting in the sunlight.

'Does that include Signor Zambelli?'

'No, he is just . . . odd. Nice, but odd.'

Beth giggled and Marco looked down at her. His face softened again as though the mask of professionalism had fallen away for a moment. They continued on, discussing artists old and new, the architecture of the city and the places Beth had and hadn't been.

They'd already been walking for ten minutes, when they turned down a cobbled street and over a bridge till they came to the artists' quarter. The buildings surrounded them on all sides, so close together it looked like you could lean from the window of one house and shake hands with someone on the opposite side of the street. They walked down winding *calle* until Marco stopped in front of a dark red house. The door and windows were flung wide open despite the chill of the day, and the tinny sounds of a radio blasted out. Beth glanced at him, and he signalled for her to go first. She knocked on the open door that was splattered in paint and stepped over the threshold.

'Signor Zambelli? Signor Zambelli?' She glanced behind her and with Marco's nod of encouragement, made her way further inside. The hallway was dark, and she passed a small living room heading towards the back of the house. Through an open doorway she could see a light airy kitchen and as she stepped further forwards, she called his name one more time.

'*Sì?*' He appeared in the doorway in a giant paint-smattered smock like a painter from the Middle Ages would have worn. He carried a loaded palette in one hand and a long-handled paintbrush in the other. One was also stuck in his mouth and another tucked behind his ear. '*Buongiorno!*' He smiled as he saw Marco behind her. 'Marco, my friend! Come in, come in!' He spoke in Italian as he ushered them forwards, waving the paintbrush enthusiastically. Beth hoped she wasn't about to get covered in paint. 'And who is this?'

'This,' Marco said in English, 'is the lady I told you about who is opening the book barge.'

That he hadn't referred to her as a friend or even a colleague or business partner caught her attention, but she didn't say anything. If anything, it simply reiterated she was right to be keeping her friend's secret as she was nothing to Marco and he was nothing to her.

'Ah, yes,' Signor Zambelli said. 'Shall I show you my work? Marco has told me all about the book barge. It sounds like an interesting place.'

'It is. It has a lot of potential. We should be opening in time for Carnevale too. At least inside. I should be clear that the top deck will need some work still.'

'I am grateful for all the opportunities to sell I can find,' he replied with a grin. 'But not everyone will be. We Venetians, we love our traditions.'

'But everything must move forward,' Marco added.

'Exactly!' Signor Zambelli burst out loudly, the paintbrush once more being waved about. Beth felt a smattering of dampness on her cheek and wiped, hoping there weren't now smears of acrylic paint on her face. She tried to check her fingers for spots of colour as he ushered them inside. She glanced at Marco to see who should go in first and found his hand gently reaching up.

'There is a little—' His fingertips almost touched her face, then he pulled back. 'Just there.' He pointed and Beth wiped, heat radiating through her veins.

'Come and see my work,' Signor Zambelli said, stepping aside so they could walk into the light and airy space.

The back of his house had been turned into a kitchen-cum-workshop. At one end was a small kitchenette with a breakfast bar separating it from what would, under normal circumstances, have been a dining room, but was in fact his studio. Paintings were lined up against the wall and hung on every available surface. An easel was set up with his current work in progress.

For all Signor Zambelli's eccentricities, he was indeed a talented portrait artist. Beth noticed some sketches on the breakfast bar and found herself wandering towards them. They were like something Leonardo da Vinci would have done: gentle, soft line drawings on what looked like parchment. She had to resist tracing her fingers over the delicate pencil strokes, her appreciation for talent moving her.

'These are beautiful,' she said, turning to see Marco watching her, a strange look on his face. How long had he been doing that? Did he think she was silly for reacting to them in that way? As a fellow lover of art, she hoped not, but it was always difficult to tell with him.

'You're very talented, Signor Zambelli,' she said, leaving the sketches and taking a step back towards him.

'You like those?' he said with a shrug, as if they were doodles he'd done in his spare time.

'I do, very much. I don't have much space at the moment, but if you had anything like this you wanted to sell, I could definitely see book lovers also being attracted to these.'

There weren't just portraits of people but of animals too. He'd drawn some still life with charcoal shading.

'You do not want my real art?' he asked sadly, motioning to the easel where a huge portrait of a woman and her parrot sat half painted.

'Umm . . .' She looked at Marco for help, not wanting to upset him, but she couldn't see fellow bookworms like her nipping into the floating bookshop for a new thriller and picking an enormous canvas of someone they've never met (and their parrot).

'It's a space issue,' Marco replied.

'But perhaps once I've got the upper deck sorted we could hold an exhibition of all your work,' Beth added, feeling guilty at his downcast expression.

'Yes!' Marco added. 'During the height of the tourist season. They may seek you out for commissions.'

Signor Zambelli's eyes flicked between Marco and Beth for so long she was beginning to feel uncomfortable, then all of a sudden, a huge smile grew on his face. '*Sì, sì!* I like that idea! I will paint you, Signorina Beth. You are very beautiful. Isn't she beautiful Marco?'

Marco's face froze and Beth's lungs seemed to spasm. A deep redness was just visible above the collar of his shirt, as he adjusted his scarf but didn't actually answer.

Beth waited, both wanting his answer and wishing she was somewhere else. Was it a particularly hard question? She didn't think of herself as either pretty or un-pretty, really. She'd always been content with her looks and though she knew her face could seem harsh when she was thinking or concentrating (she had the original resting bitch face) she felt like she'd been smiling a lot more recently, and she was certainly smiling now, or at least had been until Signor Zambelli threw a verbal hand grenade into the room.

The silence grew uncomfortable, and Beth felt a similar redness creeping into her own face. Her skin was prickling, and she could feel sweat forming under her arms.

Eventually, after what felt like a millennium, Marco muttered something in Italian. Though fluent, it was harder to make out with his inarticulate murmuring and the ruffling of his coat as he reached up and scrunched the hair on the back of his head, but she thought it was something like: '*Yes, she is very beautiful.*'

He wouldn't meet her eye so was obviously just being polite, and Beth felt like she'd been punched.

'So,' Marco said in English, overly loudly. 'Do you want to pick say six small pieces for Beth? Is that enough, Beth?'

She nodded dumbly. She wasn't even sure if she had room for six, but right now it was hard to focus on anything except his begrudgingly calling her beautiful and the way he'd clearly now rather be anywhere else than with her. She'd find room for them all somehow. To be honest, she just wanted to get away too.

'And commission will be ten per cent, yes? Standard gallery rate.' Marco was looking between her and Signor Zambelli. The businesslike, professional side of him back to the fore. Again Beth nodded dumbly. She hadn't had time to even think about commission rates, and supposed a standard gallery rate was fair.

'*Sì, sì.*' Signor Zambelli threw his hand out as he walked back to his easel and began painting. His patience for boring business things had run out and he began wielding his paintbrush, filling in the parrot's feathers with expert skill.

Marco turned and smiled at Beth, the deal done, and she did her best to respond in a way that showed her genuine gratitude, though she worried her grin was strained. It felt strained, like her mouth just didn't want to move into any kind of smile right now.

Together, they made their way out of the house and back into the chill February air.

'That was a good result, yes?' Marco asked, catching up with her as she marched along.

'Yes, great. Thank you.' Her voice sounded professional and clipped, and she began to overcompensate, feeling guilty. The fact was, this *was* a great result, and it would help her earnings once the boat was open properly. 'I couldn't have done it without your help. I really am grateful for the introductions.'

'And the negotiations,' he added.

'There wasn't much negotiation,' she replied, unable to stop herself.

'Standard rate. We can negotiate next time when we know how sales have been.'

'I suppose so.'

She began to slow her pace as her cheeks cooled in the air, the humiliation fading the further they got from Signor

Zambelli's workshop. She turned to Marco, putting the mumbled compliment that he clearly didn't mean behind her. 'I better get back to the boat and see if Cesca needs me. And of course I need to find the bloody cat and take him home too.'

'I think you secretly enjoy having him around.'

'Maybe.' She gave a teasing smile.

'You don't want a celebratory drink first?'

The request shocked her. She just couldn't figure out how the two different sides of Marco existed or what made each one come out. In that instant, she decided that if he was going to be so businesslike one minute and friendly the next, blowing hot and cold, the easiest thing to do was to remain super professional. Especially as she was also hiding Cesca's secret from him, which given the way her heart burst into life whenever he was near was only going to complicate matters further.

'Maybe another time,' she said and headed away. He didn't move and as guilt threatened to prick at her, she called back, 'Thanks again though. Let me know when the next appointment is and I'll be there.'

It took every drop of self-control she had, but she didn't look back again, and for some reason, an image of his handsome, shocked face remained burned into her eyeballs.

Chapter 12

That night, after checking in on the book barge and seeing the amazing progress Cesca had made, and collecting Polo (though Beth still got strange looks as she walked through the streets of Venice with him), Beth returned to her rented apartment with a spring in her step.

The furthest end of the barge now looked like a bright and airy space. The book storage Cesca had created gave her lots of room, and there was space to move and browse without knocking into things. All Beth needed to do was start painting, which she would, first thing tomorrow, while Cesca worked on the next section of the barge. She'd have to pick up some pastries on her way in the next morning as a thank you. She couldn't believe how much Cesca had achieved already.

As Beth approached her flat, she noticed a man leaning up against the wall, one leg scuffing the paintwork. He looked incredibly young, as if he'd only just left school, and as she drew closer she recognised him as the junior estate agent who'd come with the more senior one when she'd looked at, and decided to rent, this apartment.

Oh no.

She wasn't supposed to have pets and here she was carrying a basket with a cat in it. And there was nowhere to put it. Thinking quickly, she dived into an alcove, took off her coat, picked up the cat carrier again and laid the coat over the top, hiding as much of it as possible. Polo meowed loudly.

'Shhh! Just be quiet for a few minutes. They must just be checking in with me or something.'

Knots formed in Beth's stomach. Spiky, uncomfortable knots that prodded at her. She wasn't a natural rule breaker. How much trouble could she get into for keeping a pet when she shouldn't?

'Hello?' she said, drawing the young man's attention up from his phone.

'Ah, Miss Thorpe.' He began speaking quickly in Italian and it took her tired, panicked mind a moment to translate what he was saying.

'Wait, wait, wait,' she said in English, holding up her free hand. Moving had caused the cat carrier to rock and Polo meowed again.

The young man frowned, looking down at her coat. 'Was that—'

'I didn't hear anything. But that's not important. Are you saying that you have another booking?'

'*Sì.*'

'For this flat?'

'*Sì.*'

'For when?'

'Two days,' he said in English, stating the words slowly and carefully.

'Two days!' Her words echoed around the quiet space and Polo gave an angry mew as his carrier shook again. She echoed the sound to make out it was her, and the poor estate agent's eyes widened in terror.

'What am I supposed to do? Do you have anywhere else I can stay?'

He shook his head, taking a step back from her in case she made the strange sound again. Beth felt quite sorry for the poor boy. 'I'm sorry, Signora, but the bookings have started coming in and you did know—'

'I know, I know, I just—' She sighed. She'd been so busy hiding Polo and his stupid noises, the reality of what he was saying was only just sinking in. 'I thought I'd get more notice than this.'

He gave another shrug. 'I'm very sorry. We will need to get in tomorrow and clean the apartment.' He eyed her coat. 'Especially if you have kept a pet we didn't know about.'

'Pet?' She laughed hysterically and it echoed around the empty hall. 'I don't have a pet. Don't be silly.'

Polo made a strange noise like he was about to bring up a furball and she coughed loudly to cover it. 'And you don't have anywhere else I can go?'

He shook his head. 'I am very sorry.' He ostentatiously checked his watch and sighed. 'I have another appointment I must get to. Please drop in the keys tomorrow.'

Beth watched as he virtually ran down the stairs and away from her. Beth's shoulders slumped as Polo gurgled again.

'Oh hush. You think you've got problems? Where am I going to sleep from now on?'

Instead of a nice evening with a gorgeous pasta dinner and her feet up, it looked like she'd be filling her suitcases and lugging them to the book barge. She couldn't afford to waste money on hotels. Not when she needed to restock the bookshop, and with such a tight deadline, she'd have to sleep there until she could find a cheap hotel or something nearby. Frustration and irritation tensed her muscles, and her hand tightened around the keys. Closing her eyes to stop the tears from falling, she opened the door and set Polo down. Her feet ached as she made her way to her suitcase and began packing her things. She'd have to make several trips to move all her books. Going with the flow was proving a lot more difficult this time. She'd dealt with everything thrown at her as best she could for the last month, but this was proving more difficult to accept.

A sudden longing for her old flat, for the safety of her job and the dusty air of the galleria gripped her. She flopped onto the bed and Polo jumped up, leaning against her so she could stroke his fur. The rhythmic movement of her hand calmed her for a moment, and she gathered herself.

'Right, Polo. We better get started. If we don't, it's going to be a long night.'

***

After dragging two heavy suitcases inside the barge for the final time, Beth fell into one of the armchairs and wrapped a blanket around her, too tired to even light the fire. Thanks to her exertions she wasn't cold, and her appetite had all but disappeared with the stress. Polo looked at her in confusion at being back at the book barge, and after stretching and eating his dinner, he jumped onto her lap, affectionately padding the blanket as she stroked his fur. The comfort of having him hit her again and she sent a thank you to Signor Balbo for this unexpected gift.

Beth's eyes felt too tired and heavy to read. Tomorrow, she'd have to put her decorating plans on hold and go and find a new place to live. She wasn't even sure if she was allowed to sleep on the book barge. There were always strange, ancient by-laws in Venice pulled out by officials when the occasion called for it. She just hoped no one would report her.

After grabbing another blanket from a suitcase wedged open, filling the narrow walkway, her eyes were just closing when her phone rang. Seeing who it was, she cursed. As much as she loved her friends she wasn't in the mood to speak to them right now, knowing how much they'd worry if she told them the truth. She didn't like lying to them either, much as she didn't like lying to Marco, but if she told them the truth tonight of what had happened, they wouldn't sleep, and she'd only feel guilty for worrying them. No, it was better to stay quiet about it all, at least until she'd moved into somewhere new. She thought about not answering at all rather than lying, but missing their call would be even worse. She'd receive multiple text messages from both of them checking on her and asking for updates. It was simply better to get it out of the way and make sure the conversation focused on them and not her.

Beth sat up, plastered on a smile and turned on her camera. 'Hey, you two, what's up?'

'Oh my God, are you still at the book barge?' Daisy asked.

'I am,' she replied, adjusting the blankets so they were out of sight. 'Working late to get it ready.'

'Good for you!' Elsa said, and then an eerie silence took over while her friends glanced at each other, smiling like loons.

'What's going on?' Beth asked tentatively.

They were clearly up to something, and their inexpert whispering came through the microphone, Elsa saying, 'You say it.'

'No you say it.'

'Say what?' Beth asked, a grin pulling at her mouth for the first time in hours.

Her best friends looked at each other, then the camera and shouted in unison, 'We're pregnant!'

Beth's mouth fell into a wide O, her jaw slackening, her eyes widening. Happiness flooded her body like a wave. 'Oh my God, you guys, that's amazing! I'm so happy for you!'

Knowing her friends had been blessed with something they'd wanted for so long, her own troubles faded, and joy filled her, easing away all the negative thoughts of the day. She watched them smiling at each other, Elsa kissing Daisy's cheek, Daisy kissing her temple in return.

'It's quick,' Daisy said with a shy smile as they looked back at the screen and Beth. 'But the IVF took really quickly. We're so lucky.'

'We really are,' Elsa echoed.

'Wow! I mean . . . wow! I'm – I'm so happy for you.' She said it genuinely as tears sprung to her eyes. A dark niggle in her mind reminded her this would likely never happen for her and before she could stop it, her thoughts were racing with the questions she'd always fought with about having her own children. The guilt at thinking about herself at a time like this ripped at her throat and she swallowed the hard lump down, tears springing to her eyes.

'Don't cry!' Daisy wailed. 'You'll send me off too!'

Beth wiped her eyes, pushing those miserable thoughts down. She'd deal with them later. For now she wanted to know all about how her friends were doing and share in their excitement and happiness. It had been hard won, and they deserved every second of this joy. 'It's the best news. I honestly am so, so happy for you. So what happens now?'

Daisy caught a tear on her finger and sniffed. 'I'll be having regular check-ups and additional care but so far, everything looks really positive. We have the first scan pictures. Look!'

They held some fuzzy black and white images Beth couldn't make head nor tail of, but she took their word for it that they were of a baby.

'We can't chat long,' Daisy said. 'We need to tell the rest of the families. You're the first person we've told.'

She'd never felt more honoured or more loved and almost started crying again.

'Don't!' Elsa commanded.

'I'm honoured,' Beth replied smiling, and a swell of love overrode her own mixed emotions. 'You better go then and we can catch up properly another night, okay? But I'm so, so happy for you. You're going to be great mums!'

'We love you!' they chorused as they rang off and Beth sank back into the chair.

As the screen went black, tears formed in Beth's eyes. It wasn't that she wasn't happy for her friends, she was – ecstatically – it was just that, up until that moment, the thought that she'd never go through this herself had been on the periphery of her mind. A decision for future Beth to make.

There'd been times the idea of children had surfaced, of course there had, but she'd ignored it because it hadn't been a priority as she focused on her career and building her own life. But now she was getting to an age, as her friends were, that children and families became the next logical step. Her PCOS meant the chances of her conceiving were slim and she wasn't even sure she wanted children. That in itself made her feel strange because it wasn't the done thing. Women had children. They became mothers. To want children was natural, to not want them was unnatural. It wasn't fair, but that was how so many people saw it. Yet, she'd never really seen children in her future, and couldn't imagine them as part of her life. As much as she loved a quick cuddle with a friend's baby, a game with a toddler visiting the gallery, and was looking forward to building a children's section in the Library of Words for the kids to visit, being around them simply didn't inspire any kind of maternal feeling inside her.

Beth wiped her eyes knowing that the tears were for her finally coming to terms with a decision she'd struggled with for so long. A fact about herself she'd previously ignored and refused to face.

Life could be so utterly confusing at times. Not to mention bloody hard work. She looked around the book barge where she'd be sleeping that night and for the foreseeable future as if that were proof enough of her point.

A heavy sigh helped the tension and emotion ease from her body and mind, and she made herself a cup of tea, the cold sneaking back into her bones as she moved around the barge. After changing into her pyjamas and an extra jumper for warmth, she snuggled back on the armchair, under her blanket, with Polo by her side, reaching for her latest read: a comforting, feel-good romance. She needed to disappear into a world where everything turned out all right in the end. Right now, she had to believe that was what happened in life and that things would work out for her too.

Chapter 13

As the morning dawned, Beth knew she had to do something to get a handle on her emotions. Sleep had been fitful, and though her body felt tired and sluggish, there was only one thing to do. She dressed quickly into her gym gear and made her way to the rowing club.

The streets were deserted, the city quiet and only the lapping of the canal water against the buildings could be heard. It calmed her. A few birds were singing and Beth concentrated on them, rather than the messy noise in her head. As she drew closer to the larger expanse of water and the rowing club, she could feel the electricity pulsing through her muscles, eager for release. She'd feel better after this; she knew she would. She just had to make herself get started but the thought of hitting the gym with its energetic, loud music simply wasn't as appealing this morning. Instead, she looked at the boathouse.

Cesca had said she was good enough to go on the water now and though she should really go out with someone else for her first time, she didn't see the harm in trying it alone. After all, she wouldn't go far and she was a strong swimmer if she did get into any trouble. She didn't know why she'd put it off for so long. She went inside the boathouse and was about to take down a single-person boat when she was interrupted by someone coughing. She turned to see Marco.

'Sorry, I didn't want to startle you.'

'You're here early,' she said, still reaching out for the single-person boat.

'I like this time of day. It's calmer. Peaceful. If this will be your first time on the water,' Marco said, 'you should take it easy and maybe wear a life vest. Are you a good swimmer?'

'I am,' she replied and as she turned to him, his eyes widened as he studied hers. Could he see the red, the puffiness from her lack of sleep and the tears she'd shed? She quickly turned back. 'Actually, I think I'll stick to the gym.'

'I can take you out on the water if you'd like?'

'No, it's fine. I'm not sure today's the day to start anyway.' She stepped away and was about to make her way back outside when he stepped closer to her.

'Why not? It's a beautiful morning and there's nothing like rowing in the lagoon.'

He pointed to the sky that was lightening as the sun came up. The water too was calm and serene. There wasn't much of a wind today and she could imagine the crisp air on her cheeks as the boat moved through the water, the feeling of peace as she listened to the movement of the oars.

'Don't you need to get going?' she asked tentatively, a part of her hoping he would say no.

Marco chuckled. 'Not yet. I only just arrived and—' he looked at his watch '—it is only seven-thirty. Why are you here so early?'

'I couldn't sleep.' She would have said more but a lump formed in her throat.

It wasn't that her friends were having a baby. She was honestly happier for them than it was possible to imagine. It was simply that her own non-baby choices were causing chaos in her brain and had been all night. What if she met a man who did want children? How would their relationship continue? Was she now destined to be on her own forever?

She looked up, realising her brain had taken over again and she'd gone quiet.

Marco stepped towards her, his voice kind. 'Is everything all right?'

'Fine.' Beth plastered on a smile – the type you'd see in a horror movie. 'Absolutely fine.'

'Hmm.' He walked past her and into the storage area, taking out a two-person boat. 'Can you get the oars, please? *Grazie*.'

'But—'

'Come on. You'll enjoy it, I promise. And it's a calm day. The best type of day to be on the water. It's much nicer than being in the gym breathing other people's sweat.'

'Well, when you put it like that . . .'

As he carried the boat as if it weighed nothing and placed it on the water, she had no choice but to follow. Automatically, she grabbed the oars and he gently placed the boat down. Marco climbed in and Beth handed him the oars, and he placed them in the oarlocks so they were ready to go. He held out his hand for her and she took it, stepping down into the boat. It took a moment for her body to adjust to the swaying, and she flopped down ungracefully, but with her mind still full of Daisy, Elsa, their baby and the difficulty of her own feelings, she didn't care.

'Ready?' Marco asked and she nodded. He cast off and began calling the rows. 'One, two, one, two, one, two.'

Before long they were gliding through the water, and the beautiful city passed before her. White foam splashed as the oars slid in and out of the sea, and the incredible architecture of the Renaissance buildings with their arched windows, shutters still closed as those inside only just began to wake, passed her by. She inhaled the fresh, salty air, taking it deep into her lungs and tasting it on her tongue. She spotted the rooftops of the most iconic Venetian buildings huddled in the middle of the city, the towers and spires watching over them. Boats and gondolas lined the shore, some quiet and still, others being prepared for the day. The water taxi men were coming to life, coffees in hand, cigarettes hanging from the corners of their mouths.

As the boat moved forward, cutting through the tide, Beth enjoyed the feeling of pressure in her arms, the resistance of the water forcing her muscles to work. Her heart rate increased with every stroke and as she pulled and released, it was as though her emotions were being freed every time, just a little bit more. It was the same in her legs and core as she braced her body in the rocking boat. She could feel her abs burning and enjoyed the sensation, knowing she was making her body – herself – stronger every second she endured it. She breathed heavily through her mouth, sweat forming on her temples, dampening her hair. Right now, she didn't care how she looked. All she cared about was the thoughts fading from her mind as she pushed her body.

Marco, whether sensing her mood or simply enjoying his own row, didn't speak to her for a good twenty minutes. Not until they'd gone some distance and their pace was naturally slowing down, leaving the main island behind them. As the pace decelerated, her body calmed and all the emotion that had been kept inside seemed to flow out of her in one giant sob. All the energy and tension had been released from her muscles and with it the emotions she'd locked inside. She couldn't stop the tears no matter how hard she tried and her breath, already ragged from her workout, grew even more frantic.

'What the—Beth? Beth? What's wrong?'

Before she knew what was happening, the boat rocked, and Marco was crouched in front of her. His ice-blue eyes met hers, crinkling at the corners with concern. As she looked at him, his expression kind, she thought that she'd quite enjoy seeing that face every morning, but then the maelstrom of emotions swept her up once more.

'Breathe. Take a deep breath. What is it? Are you all right? Do you need water? Air?' His expression changed to panic, all his usual standoffishness washing away, and stupidly, it made her laugh.

'I'm fine,' she said, taking a breath. 'Well, not really fine, but I'm not having a heart attack or anything. I just – just got some bad news last night that's all.'

'What is it? Are you ill? Is it the book barge? Can I help?'

She shook her head, the tears returning and spilling down her cheeks. 'It's my friends. They're pregnant.' She buried her head in her hands knowing how ridiculous she sounded, but how could she explain her own existential crisis to this man? A man she barely knew, and anytime she did get to see the relaxed version of him, he pulled back.

'Oh.' Marco's brow creased. 'Is that – is that not good news?'

She lifted her head, partly because she was so hot and sweaty she thought she might die, her tears mixing with the perspiration still pouring down her face. This was not a great look for a heart-to-heart with a gorgeous Italian man.

'It is! It's amazing news! I'm so happy for them.' She collapsed into sobs again and his warm, strong hand gripped her knee. She liked the feel of its reassuring pressure.

'I'm sorry, I – I don't understand.'

Realising how crazy she sounded she took a deep breath.

'I'm happy for my friends. I really am. It's just . . . do you really want to know?'

'Of course.' His genuine concern made the hairs on her arms stand on end.

She wasn't really sure why she began to tell him everything, but she'd unlocked her emotions through her physical workout and now, they couldn't be locked back up. 'I don't know if I can have children. I have PCOS, which means it'll be really hard for me to conceive and to be honest, I don't even know if I want children at all, but I feel like I should, you know? That that's what's next, isn't it? But I don't – I just don't think it's for me.'

'Why does it have to be what's next?' he asked gently. 'You get to decide what your life looks like. No one else. If you don't want children, that's fine. People should respect your choices.'

She knew it made sense, but it felt somehow more difficult to own that part of her personality. To accept this decision. 'But what if I meet someone and they want children? What do I do then?'

'What if you meet someone and they don't want children? What will you do then? I'm not being flippant,' he reassured her. 'But you cannot worry about a future that isn't here or think about all the different possibilities that are out there. You'll drive yourself mad. You could meet someone who feels exactly the same way you do, and it won't even be an issue.'

For a moment, their eyes met, and something seemed to pass between them, an invisible signal that she couldn't clearly identify. The connection that kept appearing between them as it had at the party, during their drink in the bar and even at times the day before grew stronger. Suddenly more aware than ever of his hand on her leg, she wanted to reach out and take it, wrapping her fingers in his. He'd been so kind. Marco dropped his eyes away and Beth cleared her throat. The morning air stung her damp skin but quickly dried her tears.

The boat was floating peacefully in the water, drifting on the tide, and the sky had lightened considerably just as the weight on her shoulders had.

'I'm sorry. You probably didn't expect that this morning did you?' Beth asked with a small smile.

Marco laughed and scrunched the back of his hair as he had when he'd called her beautiful. 'I hadn't, but I'm glad you told me. I'm glad I could listen. Sometimes that's all we need from people is just to listen.'

She nodded her agreement. 'It's not always easy though is it?'

'No, it's definitely not. I'm sure my father would say I'm not a good listener and I'd say the exact same thing about him.' He stood and the boat rocked as he made his way back to his seat. 'If you're ready, shall we turn around and head back?'

'Yes, Francesca will be arriving soon, and I need to clear up my—' She stopped herself just in time.

'Clear up your what?' he asked with a laugh. 'Or shouldn't I ask?'

'I umm—' She'd been so totally honest with him up to

this point and he hadn't balked, so she decided to continue. 'I need to clear up my makeshift bed.'

'You slept at the boat last night?' His voice was higher than she'd ever heard it and though she couldn't see his face, the shock had stopped him rowing.

She felt the weight of the boat's movement fall to her and her tired limbs protested. 'Can you maybe . . .' He picked up his oars and the boat moved a little easier. 'I had to sleep on the boat because I've been kicked out of my holiday let. Today I need to find somewhere else to live. There must be another rental I can take.'

'Holiday lets are not the answer. And with Carnevale near, it might be harder than you think.'

'I know, but I have to try and I'll just have to take what I can get.'

'I suppose so,' he mumbled.

They rowed back to the pontoon outside the club and washed down the boat. It was important to remove the dirt and grime, but especially the salt that could damage the hull and oars. Once everything was back in its place, Beth turned to Marco.

'Thank you for taking me out on the water. Despite my mini-meltdown, I actually really enjoyed it.'

'So did I. I – we – should do it again.'

'I'd like that,' she replied, and as they smiled at each other, neither moved. Beth had no idea what she looked like – probably not good – but Marco's cheeks were flushed with exertion, and it only added to his appeal.

The sun was up fully now and even though the air was still a tiny bit wintry, the sun's golden rays, when they broke through the cloud, gave a burst of heat. The blue of the sky was reflected in the lagoon, and it seemed like it was going to be a beautiful day.

As they walked towards the gym and the showers, Beth felt calmer for speaking about her feelings. Marco was right: she couldn't worry about a future that hadn't yet appeared. She'd do what she always did and plan. When she decided she wanted to date, she'd make sure she met the right person, with the same values and ideas as her own. She'd make well-thought-out decisions and ensure she had no regrets. But something inside told her this wasn't the end of these feelings. That this issue would come up again and again and no amount of preparation would prevent it from throwing her life into disarray. She ignored the dread in her stomach and focused instead on what she could control: her floating bookshop and finding a new place to live.

It was time to get to work.

Chapter 14

'What's this?' Cesca asked with a grin as she reached out for the smoothie. 'But tell me, why is all your stuff inside the boat? I couldn't move to get started.'

'I know. Sorry.' Beth winced and explained all that had happened with the estate agent, including her futile attempts to hide a cat carrier under her coat.

Cesca giggled as Polo, hearing his name strode over to them for some attention. 'Poor Polo and poor you. That is a horrible thing to do. Couldn't they just move you somewhere else?'

'They didn't have anywhere and even if they did, I'm not sure he wanted to. He thought I was mad.'

Cesca laughed again but then changed to concern. 'What will you do?'

'Tidy up!' Beth replied breezily. 'We need to get to work.'

She edged past Cesca and stuffed her things back into the suitcases. 'I'll put them up on the deck for now. At least it's not supposed to rain today. Then we can get started.'

She would paint the area Cesca had completed while her friend worked on the next section. Once the case was up on the deck, Beth returned and together they manoeuvred the cabinet Signor Balbo had installed, which was more like an old-fashioned bureau with a pull-down writing desk, out onto the canal path. Cesca immediately started taking it apart, holding up the desk inlaid with green leather.

'I think we can use this somewhere else, don't you?'

'Definitely. What will you do with the sides?'

'Do you like the colour of the wood?'

Beth scrunched up her nose. It was dark walnut and made the interior of the barge feel small and gloomy.

Cesca laughed. 'That's a no then?'

'It's just so . . . dark.' There was no other word to describe it.

'The wood's good quality though. I might sand it and get some of this horrible varnish off. The wood underneath could look beautiful stripped back.'

'Let's do that then.'

They got to work, and the morning passed quickly. Beth almost forgot about her need to find somewhere to sleep and had just decided on a cheap hotel for the night when Marco called.

Seeing his name on her phone she felt a flush of embarrassment after her outburst this morning, not that he'd made her feel stupid. He'd been incredibly kind and understanding, giving good advice. She just hoped he wasn't calling to check in on her. That would be mortifying.

'Hi,' she said, her eyes going to Cesca who was out on the canal path sawing wood. Beth felt suddenly guilty as she was reminded of the secret she was keeping and swallowed.

'Are you busy?' Marco asked cheerfully. 'Sorry, that's a stupid question. Of course you're busy, but can you spare an hour? I have another artist who can see you but as Carnevale is starting she doesn't have much time.'

'Yes of course. Send me the address and I'll be there.'

He rang off and Beth was grateful he hadn't mentioned anything about the morning. She worked until the appointment time neared, then quickly pulled some smarter clothes from her suitcase and nipped back inside to change. Cesca kindly waited outside while she did so.

'Make my brother buy you some lunch,' Cesca said just as she was leaving. 'You haven't eaten all day.'

'Neither have you. Make sure you stop soon, okay?'

'I'm Italian,' she replied with a grin. 'Of course I will stop for lunch!'

Beth giggled as she walked away, searching on her phone for a cheap hotel she could stay in that night. She somehow managed not to fall into a canal while looking at the screen and soon ended up at the location Marco had given her. As she walked through the beautiful Venetian streets to the most expensive shopping area of the city, she felt more and more confused. Had she entered the address wrong? No, she couldn't have as she'd used Marco's pin. Had he got it wrong? She was just about to call and double-check she was headed in the right direction when she spotted him outside a shop.

'Hello,' she said, spying his three-piece suit with his usual navy peacoat over the top and a deep blue scarf. She'd never been gladder she'd changed into her uniform of smart trousers, jumper and tailored coat.

'Hello,' he replied with a smile. 'What do you think?'

He motioned to the window and Beth's eyes widened as she saw the type of shop they were visiting. On the other side of the spotless glass, a mannequin wore a dress with an enormous train, both made entirely of intricately woven lace.

She gasped. 'Is this . . . is the owner . . .'

'One of my clients?' He grinned. 'Yes, she is. And she's incredible. Very talented. Gifted, even.'

'She made this?' He nodded. 'It's exquisite, but it won't fit on my boat and I'm not sure bookworms like me are in the mood to buy massive dresses for extremely special occasions when they're looking for a new historical crime or romance to read. Not that I'm not grateful but—'

'Do you trust me?' Marco asked and the question shocked her.

After their row that morning though, she knew the answer without a second thought, which made her feel even worse about holding Cesca's secret for her. 'Yes, I do.'

'Then come on, let's meet Marcella and I'll tell you both about the idea I've had.'

Marco opened the door and held it open for Beth. A young woman met them, stepping forward from behind a desk. The place had that high-end feel you get in designer shops. It was brightly lit with glossy surfaces and was entirely spotless. The young woman walking towards them looked elegant and sleek in a fitted, conservative black dress.

'*Buongiorno, come posso aiutarla?*'

Marco responded in Italian, greeting her and adding, 'We've an appointment with Marcella.'

The assistant smiled and said, 'This way,' motioning them towards the back of the shop. They went through to a back room where Marcella, curly blonde-grey hair piled high on her head, glasses on an expensive-looking gold chain falling to the bridge of her nose, was working on another delicate piece of lace.

Marco waited patiently for her to finish before he spoke. 'That looks beautiful, Marcella.'

'*Grazie*, Marco.' She stood and kissed him on both cheeks. Marco introduced Beth and she did the same thing, Beth noticing the expensive perfume she was wearing. The floral scents were subtle but not overpowering and filled the air as she moved.

There was no way she could afford, or even safely display any of Marcella's work and she wondered what Marco was up to. But, as she was learning to go with the flow, and she trusted him, she sat back while he led the conversation.

Marco turned to Beth. 'I had a conversation with Marcella this morning after our row.' She fought the blush that was threatening to rise up her cheeks. 'And we came up with a genius plan.'

Marcella tutted, then spoke in English just as Marco had. '*You* came up with a genius plan. I can take no credit.' She placed a hand on Beth's arm as she moved from her workstation to a corner of the room and took a drink from a water bottle. 'But I think it's a good idea.'

'I'm intrigued,' Beth replied.

Marco grinned. She'd been waiting for his usual businesslike armour to appear, but it hadn't as yet. 'I had an idea that Marcella, as the foremost lacemaker in the whole of Venice—' she tutted again, and Marco smiled fondly at her '—might have some use for the smaller pieces she makes.'

'Use for them?' Beth echoed, still not catching on.

'What do all bookworms need when they purchase a new book?' he asked.

A slow smile spread over her face as she realised where he was headed. 'A bookmark!'

'Exactly. Marcella has lots of small pieces of lace that are cast-offs—'

'Or not good enough,' Marcella added.

'And those pieces, she throws them away.' Marco tossed his hand to illustrate his point. 'Into the bin. It is a waste! I've been telling her for years it's a waste. And now, I know how we can use them to both your advantage.'

'I can make bookmarks with them?' Beth asked, a little unconvinced. She wasn't exactly a crafty person. There was a very good reason she'd hired Cesca.

'You can if you like but look—' He led Beth to a workstation and Marcella joined them, taking over the explanation.

'These are all no good for my dresses or artwork,' she explained, pointing at the slim, narrow pieces. They were beautiful and Beth couldn't see what was wrong with them. She said as much, and Marcella laughed.

'Here.' She took a small handheld magnifying glass, the same sort of thing jewellers used to check diamonds, and held it over a corner of one of the pieces. 'There is a stitch missing. My dresses cost thousands and thousands of euros and are worn by movie stars, celebrities, world leaders. They must be perfect. This—' She gestured to it again. 'This is not perfect.'

'So you'd put it in the bin?'

'I would, unless you want them.'

Beth studied the beautiful pieces. Some were already the perfect shape for a bookmark, others were more unusual, but the beauty couldn't be denied. She could definitely see them taking up space in the bookshop. Maybe on a special counter made with the green leather writing desk she and Cesca had moved out of there that morning. But just as excitement filled her at the idea, she needed to know how much it would cost. Yes, Marcella said she would normally throw them away, but with her dresses costing thousands and thousands of pounds, would she charge a fortune for these too?

'I love the idea,' she said, glancing at Marco who seemed to pick up on where she was headed.

'So this is what I'm proposing,' he began, outlining the cost Marcella would charge, the commission Beth would receive from each sale and how it could all work in practice. Beth was impressed and though the pieces would be expensive, they would absolutely be worth it for their beauty and craftsmanship, and she was sure booklovers would want them. Especially tourists so they had an amazing souvenir to bring home.

The deal was done, and she thanked Marcella, shaking her hand. As she did, Marcella studied her and then didn't let go, her eyes narrowing.

'I recognise you from somewhere.'

'Oh, really?'

Marcella nodded still holding her hand. She finally let go and pushed her glasses up the bridge of her nose, standing back to take her in once more. Marcella began to wave a finger up and down the length of her body.

'You looked different though.' She suddenly clicked her fingers in the silence, making Beth jump. 'It was at a ball last year.'

'The galleria's masquerade ball,' Beth said, suddenly remembering seeing this woman in a long velvet dress with a gorgeous lace mask over her face. She must have made it herself, Beth realised now.

'Yes, that's it,' Marcella agreed. 'Signor Sanna always invites me. Are you going again this year?'

'I am. Even though I no longer work at the galleria. It'll always be a highlight of my time here in Venice.'

'And now you are here to stay.'

'I am,' Beth confirmed with a grin.

'Then I will see you there.'

'I'll look forward to it.'

They made their way back outside, Beth fully aware of the flirtatious goodbye and fluttering eyelashes Marco received from the assistant who showed them out, and jealousy flittered through her chest. She reminded herself she had no right to be jealous of anything, but she was still relieved when Marco didn't reciprocate and, in fact, barely even noticed.

As the afternoon wore on, the sun dipping in the sky casting a strong golden yellow glow over the city, Beth tightened the belt of her smart coat and pulled the lapels tighter. A colder wind now wound its way through the narrow streets and Beth couldn't wait to get back to the book barge and light the fire, though she'd still enjoy the walk, the smells of the city and the simple feel of the place.

'Well thank you for—'

'Before you go,' Marco said, a nervousness she hadn't seen before clouding his expression. 'There is one other thing I wanted to show you. If you have time.'

'Oh umm . . .' She checked her watch. 'Sure, okay. Is it far?'

'No, and it's back towards the book barge so it's on the way.'

'Oh, great. Is it another amazing studio?'

'Not exactly.'

She wondered what type of artist she was going to meet this time and where they worked if it wasn't a studio. They walked for about ten minutes, chatting through how well the meeting with Marcella had gone.

'You're very good at your job, you know.'

Marco smiled shyly. 'I am now. It's not been the easiest road.'

'Because of your father?'

'That and other things. Businesses take a lot of hard work to make them successful and sometimes they fail for reasons that aren't your own fault.'

She frowned, trying to understand what he'd said and place it in the context of what she knew about him. As she only knew bits and pieces, it was impossible, and as they walked the narrow, cobbled streets and tiny bridges over the canals, his gaze seemed to have turned inward.

They stopped outside another historic Venetian house, and Marco fumbled in his coat pockets for something. The waters of a canal could be heard just behind the building, lapping against the pale pink stone. With a huff of frustration, Marco pulled a set of keys from his pocket and opened one side of the large medieval-looking door. Frowning in confusion, she followed him in and he found another key and opened a door on the ground floor.

Beth's mouth fell open.

It was a flat.

An empty flat.

A beautiful, empty flat.

'What are we doing here?' she asked.

He glanced down at the ground, shyly, scuffing the toe of his polished black shoe on the tiled floor. 'When you said this morning about sleeping on the boat, I called a friend who has some properties. This one is looking for a tenant. I thought you might like to look at it before he puts it on the market.'

Beth's mouth fell open again. She really needed to learn to act shocked more elegantly. She didn't know what to say.

He'd done that for her.

'Do you like it? I'm sorry if I've overstepped.'

Realising she hadn't yet spoken, just gazed around in awe, she was quick to reassure him. 'No! Not at all! Thank you! I – I love it. It's perfect!'

She began exploring the apartment properly. The living room they'd entered had wooden beams across the ceiling and was painted a gentle cream. There was room for a bookcase, maybe even two. At one end of the room, a doorway was cut into the wall leading to a kitchen filled with cupboards that matched the wood of the beams. At the other end was a bedroom large enough for a double bed, a wardrobe and a chest of drawers. From the window she could reach down and almost touch the water of the canal, but its gentle lapping reminded her of being on the barge and a sudden feeling of home engulfed her.

The bathroom was plain white, but well sized and as she returned to the living room where Marco had remained, she couldn't stop the smile reaching across her face. 'It's perfect! Absolutely perfect! How much is the rent?' When Marco told her, she shook her head. 'It can't be; it's too low. Not for somewhere as nice as this and in such a good neighbourhood.'

'He is happy to charge a lower rate. And he's happy for you to have Polo here. He just wants someone in here and as you might be here for a while, he's happy to charge less.'

'I'm going to be here forever,' she said, realising she was saying it to herself as much as him. 'Marco, I . . . thank you! Thank you so much!'

There was already a sofa and kitchen appliances, so she could move in as soon as everything was arranged. Marco handed over the keys.

'What are you doing?'

'My friend will come by tomorrow to the book barge with the paperwork. He's happy for you to move in now. Shall we get your stuff and bring it here?'

'I – I can't believe it.' Marco smiled and Beth's heart melted, 'are you sure you don't mind?'

He shook his head. 'I don't mind at all. I'm just happy you won't be sleeping on the floor of your barge amongst the wood shavings tonight.'

'Hey! Cesca always cleans up after herself at the end of the day. You wouldn't even know she's been there.'

'Good. My mother will be pleased.'

At the mention of his sister, Beth felt swamped with the weight of the secret she was keeping from him. There was no denying that despite not knowing exactly how he felt about her, she was beginning to develop real feelings for him. She wanted to open her mouth and tell him everything, but she could picture Cesca's face, the betrayal she'd feel and the damage it might do if not handled properly. She'd speak to Cesca again and tell her she had to tell Marco and her family about her relationship before people got really hurt. It wasn't much, but it was all she could do.

They shared a glance and as he fidgeted shyly she expected the professional side of him to take over and the shutters to come down, but they didn't.

'Well,' Marco said, clapping his hands together. 'Shall we get you moved in?'

Without a moment's hesitation, Beth nodded.

Chapter 15

Marco dropped her heavy suitcase on the living room floor and rotated his shoulder.

'If there was one thing I'd change about Venice it would be that cars could be used in exceptional circumstances.'

Beth lowered a suitcase. She knew his one was even heavier as it contained mostly books, but she hadn't wanted to say so. 'Ah, but then the buildings would get covered in black pollution *and* it would sink even lower.'

'That is true, but it can make life awkward. Do you mind if I sit?' He motioned to the small sofa.

'No, please do. Would you like a glass of wine?'

Earlier, while Marco was taking a bag to her new home, she'd gone to the local shop and bought some crostini, good wine, ready-made panzanella and garlic and rosemary focaccia. She'd already invited Marco to stay. It was the least she could do. Now, her stomach was rumbling, and she couldn't wait to dive in. Neither could Polo who'd been retrieved from the book barge and was currently circling her feet waiting to be fed.

'Will it be a large one?' Marco asked, cheekily.

She laughed. 'It definitely will. And here, Polo. You greedy cat.' She placed his food down on the floor in the corner of the kitchen she'd decided was his space.

The small kitchen was already beginning to feel like home and thanks to being fully furnished it had everything she needed. Finding two glasses and arranging the food on several plates, she brought them over and placed them on the small coffee table in front of the two sofas arranged in an L-shape. With the gorgeous beams overhead that ran through the entire apartment, it really did feel special. It was small, but perfect for her.

They'd opened the windows to air it but as they sat, they didn't feel the chill wind after their exertions. Beth could hear the water lapping against the building and enjoyed its soothing sound. Sometimes she forgot how water was everywhere in this city – its lifeblood – and reminded herself never to take being here for granted. She could never have planned to have achieved the things she had, or if she had been imaginative enough to plan this course, it would have taken her months to bring it to fruition. Her tendency to consider all options and think through every possibility would have delayed her progress. It went to show that sometimes, taking chances and acting on instinct (or should that be impulse?) wasn't the worst thing to do.

'I'm excited for Marcella's lace,' she said as they both settled back into their seats. Her body ached from the busy day, but her soul felt at peace as some of her worries lifted. 'She's incredibly talented.'

'She is. We've been able to raise her profile, so designers are contacting her, asking her to make lace for their designs. Sometimes she has to turn them down she is so busy.'

'And that's thanks to you?' she asked, trying to eat the delicious focaccia at a reasonable rate and not stuff it all into her mouth in one go, as it was too delicious to resist.

'It's thanks to her talent,' Marco replied, helping himself to some of the food.

'But I'm sure you helped a little,' she teased.

'Maybe a little.'

Suddenly, Beth realised how much the deal he'd just brokered had helped her rather than Marcella. She'd be the one truly benefiting from the sales; Marcella didn't need the money if she was turning down work from big-name designers. Hope sprung in her chest. Did that mean something? That he'd done it only for her? Her fingers tingled and she watched him as he continued speaking, her heart beating louder in her chest.

'She should think about expanding, but she won't let anyone else make the lace. Not if it has her name on it. I just wish my father would let me do the same for our business. He likes the old ways and no matter how much I prove myself he won't let me help.' Polo jumped up and snuggled next to him. Marco smiled.

'Is it struggling?' Beth asked, surprised at his honesty. Was it tiredness forcing his guard down?

'No, but it could do better. My father doesn't want to see it that way though. He thinks as long as we are doing fine, that's enough.'

'But it isn't for you?'

She sat back, sipping her wine, and again, waited for a brisk change of subject but instead he said: 'You have to understand, it's not about the money. Yes, I would like my parents' retirement to be secured, for the business never to have to worry about cash flow and my brothers to pass it on to their own children, but it's also about telling others about this amazing gift – this amazing history – my family has.'

'I understand,' she said quietly as he reached for his glass. Again, he pushed his hair back, scrunching it in his fist at the back of his head. She was beginning to realise it was almost a nervous gesture. Did that mean he'd been nervous when he said she looked beautiful and wasn't just forced to say it? Heat rose in her chest, and she sipped her wine to calm herself.

'What made you turn to PR in the first place?'

'I—' He stopped, and she looked up, food halfway to her mouth. She lowered her hand as his eyes clouded, and he rubbed the small spot of scar tissue on his wrist. Beth prepared herself to be brushed off.

'There was an accident when I was younger,' he said, and Beth softened.

'I'm sorry. Please, if you don't want to talk about it, that's fine. I'll respect your privacy; you don't have to say anything.'

He looked at her, his ice-blue eyes piercing hers. Her breath hitched a little.

'It's okay. Everyone tells me it wasn't that bad really. That no one died. But I – I slipped when I was blowing glass as a teenager and Cesca got hurt. I got hurt too but . . . She pretends like it was nothing, but she won't blow glass now and neither will I.'

That explained a lot, not just about him, but about Cesca, and the tensions between father and son.

'If it was an accident you can't blame yourself, and it sounds like you were young too.'

'I was a teenager. I probably shouldn't have been doing it anyway, but you start young when it's in your family.' He took a deep breath. 'But thank you for saying so.'

'You don't believe me,' she replied, tilting her head.

'I don't believe anyone who says that, and they've been saying it for years. Now—' He took a crostini and chewed, following it with a drink of wine. Beth drew her eyes away from him, worried she might stare. Was there anything more attractive than a man being vulnerable? And a truly handsome man at that? 'How do you feel about opening properly?'

'I'm excited. And—' An idea had just occurred to

her and this was the perfect opportunity to ask. 'Umm, Marco . . .'

He looked up, panzanella stacked on top of a piece of focaccia almost falling to the tabletop as he paused with it halfway to his mouth.

'I was wondering, umm . . . you remember Marcella talking about the masquerade ball?'

'Mmm hmm.' He pressed a hand to his mouth as he chewed.

'Well, I was thinking, you've done so much to help me already and this might be a way I could pay you back a little.'

'What could? You're already paying me back by paying my clients commission.'

'I know, but, let's be honest, while I hope it'll make them some decent money, it probably won't for a while. Not until people really know where I am and I start to build the business up, but in the meantime, I was thinking . . .' It was now or never and if he turned back to business and refused, she'd have to face that embarrassment. 'Why don't you come with me to the ball? There'll be a lot of artists attending, maybe some you can convert into clients, and there'll be people from all the galleries and museums coming too. You could form some useful links, I think. I mean, I know you have lots already, but I just thought—'

'I'd love to,' he replied, before she'd even finished speaking. Their eyes met and they smiled at one another.

Happiness flashed in his eyes and he seemed truly excited.

'There is someone who goes to the ball every year who I've never been able to sign to my agency despite my best efforts.'

'Oh, who's that?'

'A woman called Signora Cadora. She's a famous mosaicist. She doesn't really need PR but if I could represent her it would be a big coup for my business.'

'Great!' Beth said, her nerves vanishing.

'But Beth,' Marco said kindly. 'I normally try to keep my personal and professional lives separate, but you didn't have to convince me; I'd have been delighted to go whether it helps my business or not.'

Beth's breath hitched as their eyes met and the words seemed to carry far more weight than anything else he'd said. 'You would?'

Marco's eyes stayed on her a moment too long and in that moment, all the air seemed to be sucked from the room and replaced with a heavy, electric atmosphere. Something stirred deep inside her body, sending her nerves tingling with anticipation.

'Yes. We're . . . friends, yes?'

'Yes!' she replied a little too loudly. 'Friends. Umm . . . great. That's . . . great. I'll—' Why couldn't she form sentences? Was it happiness that he'd said yes or disappointment that he saw them as just friends. 'I'll umm, send you all the details.'

Still watching her in a way that made her chest fizz, his gaze finally fell away, and he drank the last of his wine. 'I should probably go. You must be exhausted from today and

I understand from Cesca that you have a lot of work to do tomorrow.'

'I do,' Beth replied with a laugh, feeling back on firmer ground. 'I've been slacking with the painting and I'll have some catching up to do.'

'Then I'll say goodnight. I'm still talking to my clients so if another wants to meet, I'll let you know.'

'Thank you, I appreciate it.' She stood too and, unexpectedly, Marco took a step towards her, placing a gentle kiss on her cheek. His lips touched her skin so lightly she was surprised at the burning sensation it left as her mind imprinted the sensation in her memory. 'Goodnight.'

'Goodnight,' she managed, her words barely more than a whispered mumble, her senses thrown into a tailspin.

He began to walk towards the door and with the heat of his lips still on her skin, she found herself glued to the spot. She heard the door close softly and the sound of his footsteps fading through the open window.

Coming to, her cheek was still tingling as she tidied up their plates. Why had she ever agreed to keep Cesca's secret? She felt like the worst person imaginable. Marco was being so kind and helpful, and now he'd agreed to go to the ball with her, which sent tingles down her spine. She was attracted to him, and not just physically. She liked him. Really liked him. She felt wretched. But despite her guilt, knowing they'd soon be spending an evening together made her happier than ever that she'd stayed in Venice, and as she spent the first night in her new home, the worry and doubt of the morning couldn't have been further from her mind. Still, as she readied for bed, the creeping guilt that she knew something Marco didn't, something that Cesca thought would upset him, something that might ruin her chances with him, if those chances even existed, tinged the night with worry and frustration. Cesca had to tell him. And soon.

Chapter 16

Beth awoke the next morning after the best night's sleep she'd had in ages. The gentle splash of the water against the side of her building (the same she heard on her barge every day) was becoming a calming soundtrack to her life. The sun began to stream in through the windows, and the sky was blue and cloudless. Spring was on the way, the morning slightly warmer, buds emerging on the flowers and trees. She took a deep breath, spinning in a circle, her arms out in her gorgeous bedroom, and promptly fell back onto the bed. Okay, so it wasn't quite big enough to pretend she was in her own musical, but it didn't wipe the smile from her face. After a quick breakfast, she headed for the gym.

She paused at the boathouse and considered going out on the water, but the idea of doing it alone was still a little too much. She decided to head into the gym instead and though she looked out for both Cesca and Marco, neither were to be found.

After a quick pit stop at her flat to change and pick up Polo, Beth went to the book barge, ready to paint every inch Cesca would allow her to.

As she'd expected, Cesca was already set up on the canal side working on cutting shelving from some wood she'd purchased. They'd reused as much as they could, but the tatty cabinets Signor Balbo had kept for years would only go so far. As Beth walked towards her, Cesca was sawing fiercely at a piece of wood, her face stern, and Beth had a feeling it wasn't just because of the effort she was putting in. She let Polo out of his carry case and after a stretch he began to wander.

'Everything okay?' she asked nervously.

Cesca finally finished and the wood clattered to the ground. 'No. It's not.'

'Oh.' Cesca was normally so cheerful that to see her respond like this was worrying. Was she concerned Beth growing closer with Marco put her secret at risk? Or had she told him? Hope that she had rushed through Beth. 'Is it me? Something I've done? The barge?'

'What?' Cesca looked up, her eyes wide. 'No! Why would you think that?'

'Because I know I've been nipping off and you've been doing so much work. I haven't exactly kept up with my fair share, have I?' As if to prove that she was there to work and not go anywhere, Beth took a can of the paint they'd chosen and opened it, giving it a stir before pouring it into a pot to take inside. She grabbed a couple of brushes and newspaper too.

'You've been having business meetings, not just doing nothing. Unless—' She looked up. 'Unless you've been going on secret dates with my brother, then I'd be annoyed that you didn't tell me. Not that I'd want the details but . . .'

Beth felt her skin flush, especially remembering his friend comment of the night before. 'All business, I assure you.'

'I'm not annoyed at you or Marco or *La Libreria delle Parole*.' She sighed heavily. 'I'm annoyed because Emilio is going away. Again. I get that it's his job, but I miss him so much. I wish . . . Oh, never mind.' She went back to massacring the piece of wood.

'What do you wish?' Beth asked gently.

'I wish I could go with him and that we could tell people about us.'

Beth dropped her painting gear and went to her friend, gently rubbing her arm. 'It must be hard. Is it perhaps time to tell everyone?' She had her own reasons for asking, but she did genuinely think it would be good for them if they could get it out in the open. Sneaking around was never any good for any of them. 'No matter what they might think?'

Cesca shook her head. 'I wish it was, but I really don't think so. Not yet, anyway.'

After her evening with Marco the night before, Beth wanted more than ever to tell him so there was nothing weighing on her conscience. He was being kind in helping her and had even opened up a little more. Not telling him was becoming more and more problematic, but if she told him, she risked losing Francesca's friendship, which she'd had for far longer than Marco's.

'I'm sure they'd understand,' she tried again. 'Marco would, I think.'

Cesca glanced at Beth from the corner of her eye, and Beth turned her attention back to the paint pot and brushes, sweeping them up from the floor.

'Marco is a good man – a good brother – but he's protective of the family. Too protective, maybe.'

'I can see that. He told me about the accident.'

'He did?' Cesca's eyes widened.

'Is that strange?'

'Very. He never talks about it. Ever.'

A thrill that he was opening up to her in a way he didn't with other people rocketed through Beth's body. It made her want to smile, but now wasn't the time.

'He must trust you a lot. Like you a lot.'

Beth didn't say anything and dropped her eyes. Cesca continued.

'It's what's caused all the problems with our father. They both want to preserve the family business but in different ways and knowing how much he values reputation, Emilio's will work against him. Even though he's changed.'

'But maybe you should give him a chance. If you tell him on his own, maybe he'll react better than just blurting it out.

He's so proud of you Cesca; I'm sure he'll only want what's best for you.'

'Maybe.' She clapped her hands together. 'Anyway, speaking of my family, my mother wants you to come for dinner.'

Beth, who had made it down the first step to the lower deck, almost lost her footing and scrambled back out onto the bank. 'I'm sorry. What did you say?'

Cesca giggled, her face easing for the first time that morning and her normal grin returning. 'She wants you to come and have dinner with us and when I say us, I mean *all* of us. So be prepared. She knows all about the book barge from me and from Marco and she wants to meet you.'

'Why?'

'Why?' Cesca began sanding the wood she'd cut, smoothing its edges. 'Because they want to meet you, and because it is the start of Carnevale and we always have a big family dinner at the beginning of the Carnevale season. It's tradition. To do with Lent,' she added.

'But—'

'And,' Cesca continued, stopping her protesting, 'you're invited because you have no one else to celebrate with. Italian mammas don't allow people to be on their own when it's a big celebration or normally a family occasion. You'll be one of us for an evening.'

One of us. Beth felt tears sting the back of her nose. She had Daisy and Elsa, and they were her found family, but she hadn't ever experienced this sort of thing. This was why she'd fallen so in love with Italy. It wasn't just the place; it was the people too. They were just so nice. But she couldn't possibly accept. She couldn't sit and have a family dinner with Marco and his sister, and all his brothers, not while she was holding on to Cesca's secret.

'I'm sure Marco won't want me there. Not when he finds out. Like you say, he's professional and he won't want to mix business and . . .' The idea of saying pleasure in relation to Marco when she could still feel his kiss on her cheek made her body heat like someone had put her in a pot of boiling water, so she settled for: 'not business.'

Cesca smirked. 'Marco already knows and he's fine with it. We discussed it last night on the family WhatsApp. My other brothers are dying to meet you too. And Mamma will be upset if you don't come. So you will come, or she will never forgive you. You're not busy tomorrow are you?'

'I—'

'I know you're not. So don't say you are.'

Caught out, Beth found a smile creeping onto her lips and tugging at her cheeks. 'Okay, then. I'd be honoured to come. Thank you.'

'Good. I'll send you the address. Have you ever been to Murano?'

She shook her head, unable to speak.

'It's beautiful. You'll love it. Marco can give you a tour before dinner.'

Knowing argument was futile, Beth shuffled back into the boat and began painting. After a few minutes, she grabbed her phone and began playing some music, singing along quietly as she worked.

With only a quick stop for lunch and a few cups of tea, Beth ended the day shocked at how much they'd achieved. She wasn't quite caught up with Cesca, but her friend's work (which was excellent) was nearly finished. The inside of the book barge was almost done. As soon as she finished painting and it had dried, she'd be able to restock. She'd spend the evening placing some orders so that at the end of the week, she could fill the shelves. Not only would the book barge be open for the tourist season, it'd be open for Carnevale too! This was much better than anything she'd thought possible. But then, once they'd cleared most of the stock, there still wasn't that much room in the galley of the small barge anyway. Soon she'd talk about plans for the upper deck but for now, she'd kick back and relax at her new apartment.

After clearing up, Cesca left, and Beth made her way back home, Polo under her arm. She was actually considering getting him a little harness as he was quite heavy, but wasn't sure if he'd like that.

Once home, Beth decided it was time to call Daisy and Elsa. It had only been a couple of days since they'd broken the news, and she had texted them every day as usual, but she still worried that her own feelings on parenthood had shown in her reaction, and she wanted them to know how happy for them she was.

Marco's words floated around her head as she kicked

off her shoes and jumped in the shower. *You cannot worry about a future that isn't here, or all the different possibilities that are out there. You'll drive yourself mad. You could meet someone who feels exactly the same way you do, and it won't even be an issue.*

Would she get that lucky? With all the luck she'd had so far, she didn't know if that was possible. But what she did know was that she was loving her life and the future she was building for herself. When she pictured the book barge, her as old as Signor Balbo, she just didn't see children or grandchildren with her and was slowly coming to terms with the fact that, though it was still kind of frowned upon by some people, a family just wasn't what she wanted for herself, and there was nothing wrong with that.

Wrapped in her fluffy bathrobe, with her hair tied in a towel, she grabbed a glass of wine and settled on the sofa as her phone rang.

'Hey, you!' Daisy called as her face appeared on the screen. 'Ooo! You look cosy!'

'I am.'

'Where are you?' Elsa asked peering around, her face coming into view.

'My new apartment!'

'What?! When did this happen? Tell us everything.'

Beth gave them a tour and enjoyed their oohs and ahs as they saw the beams and the view from her bedroom window.

'Won't you get guys on gondolas looking in?' Daisy asked and Beth giggled.

'No, this isn't one of the main gondola routes.'

'Good. They might see you wandering around naked.'

'I do not wander around naked!'

'You did in your first ever flat. That one back in Fulham.'

'That was once, and I never did it again after you let yourself in with the spare key to borrow milk not realising I was home.'

'I learned my lesson the hard way.'

'Now,' Beth said. 'Tell me what's happening with you two. I want to hear all the pregnancy news.'

Daisy and Elsa launched into lots of technical details about the process and all the additional scans and checks Daisy was due to have. She moaned about morning sickness and then admonished herself for not being grateful for it, given how lucky they were.

Beth laughed as she said, 'Daisy, you don't have to enjoy vomming every morning—'

'And evening. It's pretty much all day, actually.'

'Then you have every right to be grumpy about it. And don't let Elsa tell you otherwise.'

'Hey!' Elsa giggled, knowing her friend was teasing. 'I'm buying her ginger biscuits and making her ginger tea and everything.'

'Good, I'm glad to hear it.'

'So—' Daisy sipped her mug of tea and grimaced. Beth presumed it was the ginger tea they'd just been talking about. 'Tell us all about the book barge.'

Beth began excitedly telling them about the progress

she'd made with Cesca and the artists she'd spoken to with Marco.

'Marco, hey?' Elsa teased. 'Is he handsome?'

'Very. But all Italian men are handsome.'

'Umm, no they're not.'

'They are. I promise,' Beth replied trying to deflect.

'Why are you blushing?' Elsa asked and then gasped. 'Oh my God, do you fancy him?'

'What?' Beth pulled the collar of her dressing gown tighter. 'No. Of course not. This is a business relationship.'

'You do!' Daisy declared, shoving Elsa out of the way. 'I can see it in your face. You do, don't you?'

'I – no!'

'You do so!'

'Maybe a little bit. But only because he's a handsome Italian man. And anyway, he said we're just friends.'

'When did he say that?'

Beth took them through the other evening.

'I think he wants you to be more than friends,' Daisy said.

'Daisy, he literally said he didn't. You're such a romantic, you'd think that anyway.'

'I mean, I do think you're gorgeous enough that all men should be trying to grab hold of you and snog your face off every two minutes. You're a fox. But that's not why I'm saying it. You just look different when you talk about him. There's something in your eye.'

'Glaucoma.'

'Shut up!' She giggled.

Beth hadn't felt much of a fox in a long time. Maybe she'd make an effort with the masquerade ball and stop living in boring trousers and jumpers. She thanked her friend for the confidence boost and explained about the times Marco had blown hot and cold, but also how he'd helped secure her this amazing apartment and kissed her cheek last night after helping her move in.

'It sounds like he likes you.'

'I'm also having dinner with his family!'

'What?' they both screamed.

'Calm down, before you do yourself a mischief. He hasn't invited me; his sister has. Their mum heard about me from her and invited me along. It's an Italian thing.'

'Umm,' Elsa began. 'I know Italians are known for being friendly and welcoming and you've certainly found that in Venice, but they wouldn't invite you if they didn't want to.'

'I don't know whether to go or not.'

'Why not?'

'It'll be weird. Marco likes to keep his personal and professional lives separate. He told me so. So I need to keep everything business.' Elsa snorted. 'And Cesca's my friend and was before I even met Marco so there's, like, all these weird different relationships: some business, some not. It's going to be . . . difficult to navigate.' She hadn't mentioned the secret she was keeping or how it was driving her crazy.

'It's simple really, Beth,' Elsa said. 'Marco has the hots for you at least a bit, even if he doesn't want to admit it to himself, but he's not sure what to do because you're working together.'

'Do you think?' Beth asked, unable to tear her eyes away from the screen, eager for her friends' reaction. They both nodded emphatically.

'Why else would he have helped find you a place to live, helped you move in and then stayed for dinner! I love you, Bethy,' Elsa said. 'But you can be so blinkered sometimes.'

Daisy shot Elsa a warning look and softened her friend's words. 'You've always been focused on the next plan, but I think Elsa's right. And maybe his aloofness is him trying to navigate his own feelings and not knowing what to do.'

'Maybe,' she replied, still unconvinced, but unable to shake their words. If only she could tell them what he'd also said on their morning row, but that would mean admitting her own difficulties and she wanted them to know how happy for them she was. She turned the topic back to the baby and when she should plan coming to visit.

'There's actually something we wanted to ask you,' Daisy said nervously. Beth took a breath, unsure what was coming. 'Will you be godmother, please?'

'What? Me?' Tears immediately sprang to her eyes and started falling down her cheeks. 'Are you guys serious?'

'Absolutely!'

Even Elsa was wiping her eyes and sniffing.

'I'd love to! Thank you! Thank you so much!'

A swell of love and gratitude filled her chest, warming her from the inside. And another part of her feelings seemed to slot into place, the messy emotions becoming clearer. While she didn't want children of her own, she would relish the opportunity to be there for her best friends' children, to help them when they needed her and guide them when she could. This felt more natural to her than the idea of being a mum. It felt right.

'I can't believe you've asked me!'

'Of course we've asked you! You're our best friend and we can't think of anyone better to help guide our little one.'

'Thank you. I'm truly, truly honoured. When he or she's sixteen, they can come and stay with me here in Venice.' The line went quiet, and Beth scowled. 'What is it?'

'You really see yourself being there forever?'

Beth considered for a moment. Though the words had simply slipped out, she'd meant them with all her heart. 'Yes. Yes I do.'

Her friends grinned back at her. 'Then you better fix up a spare room,' Daisy said.

'Or at least buy a sofa bed!' Elsa added.

Once the book barge was fully up and running and hopefully turning a profit, she'd do exactly that.

Chapter 17

Carnevale began in an explosion of colour, music and pageantry Beth hadn't appreciated before. Last year, she'd seen snippets of it from her office window and on her walk home, but she'd always been up too early to see it on her way into work. The city was bustling with activity as though it had suddenly awoken from a long sleep. There were noticeably more tourists than there had been a week ago and the city was alive with music, song, shouting, cheering and performances that would take your breath away. She'd already made a promise to herself to explore this evening after the barge had closed for the day and make the most of this most brilliant occasion in the Venetian calendar.

As the busy vibe of the city seemed to leak through the canals, reaching out into all the different *sestieri*, and she unpacked a couple of boxes of new books she'd ordered from a wholesaler, she was ready to fling open the doors and reopen *La Libreria delle Parole*. The Library of Words was looking far less crowded and much more elegant while still keeping the cosy vibe Signor Balbo had created with his table lamps dotted here, there and everywhere and the wood-burning fire. She was waiting on the artwork from the portrait painter and until then, had created some small prints of famous literary quotes and had put them in frames on the wall. She could easily swap them over when his work arrived and until then, it wouldn't look bare or like something was missing. She missed Marco's flowers and thought about buying another bouquet to give a gorgeous splash of warmth and colour too.

Beth filled the last of the books into the 'New in!' section and stepped back. The rugs that had come with the barge had been hauled outside and swept and brushed, and whilst they weren't exactly as good as new, they were at least less grubby. She still wanted to purchase some cushions for the armchairs and give them a good polish to make the leather shine, but they were all things she could do as the season progressed. Some were even jobs for when there were no customers around, though she hoped there would be more than enough to keep her busy. She still felt slightly nervous at the prospect of talking to them, conscious that she might not have what they were looking for or be up to date with all the news from the book world, but she'd been reading trade papers and would just have to make do with what knowledge she did have. She had her love of books and, for most bookworms, that was enough. It had been before when she'd been selling Signor Balbo's old stock on the canal side and she'd had one of her happiest days ever. Today would be even better than that.

The coffee barge was back next to her, and she planned to nip next door for a treat to start the day, something to give her lots of energy and see her through to the family dinner tonight. Nerves swirled in her stomach as she thought of seeing Marco and meeting his enormous family. Was it possible Elsa and Daisy were right, and Marco did like her more than she thought? No, she couldn't go there today and shook her head to ward off the thoughts. She'd already bought a bunch of flowers to give to Mamma di Rienzo, knowing it would be rude to turn up empty-handed. She'd deal with the evening when it got here; there were other things to think about right now. Like breakfast, though she wasn't actually sure she'd be able to eat anything but she didn't want to feel sick. She'd have to force herself which, given Lolanda's amazing skills, wasn't that much of a hardship.

'*Ciao*, Lolanda; *ciao*, Galvano,' she said, unzipping her purse. She continued in Italian, asking them if they were ready for a busy day. Polo, who had hopped onto their barge for a sniff and a fuss, hopped off again and went off for a wander.

'*Sì, sì!*' Lolanda replied, then switched to English. 'Carnevale is always busy! Every street in Venice is full. I love this time of year. And it is a good time to trade.'

'Yes, I'm glad I've managed to get the inside refurbished in time. I wasn't expecting to when I first took the place over.'

Beth looked along the canal path where two performers were strolling along. They were in huge Renaissance dresses, gorgeously made in rich colours of red and gold and detailed with lace, buttons and ribbons. In their hands hung *colombina* – half-length masks that Venice was famous for. In fact, the city was well known for its many different styles of masks. The *bauta* were the plain white half-masks while the *colombina* were decorated on the cheeks in bright, even glittering paint. Sometimes people added feathers, veils or lace so they became huge works of art in their own right. The only ones she didn't like were the *medico della peste* – the plague doctor masks. She knew their history, and why they'd been made in the shape and style they had, but she'd never been able to shake the horror-movie look of them and they still sent chills down her spine. The couple stopped next to her at the coffee barge and Galvano began to serve them, while Lolanda took her order.

Beth listened as the conversation took place in Italian between Galvano and the couple. They were going to be performing on the canal side just down from them, dancing traditional dances and acting out set pieces. Beth couldn't wait to see it and told them so.

'*Grazie, grazie,*' they replied as they took their coffees, the takeaway cups looking entirely out of place compared to their costumes and the famous waterways of Venice.

Beth wished Lolanda and Galvano a good day and went back to the book barge. The owner on the other side of her smiled a greeting and congratulated her on the changes she'd made. She thanked them and headed inside to await her first real customers.

Though it was a slow start, it wasn't long until the canal-side street grew crowded with early season tourists and locals enjoying Carnevale. She sold books old and new and noticed she'd been right about the tourists wanting bestsellers and the latest, hot reads to relax with. Her mind began to race to the upper deck and the outside of the boat. With Cesca's help, the Parisian-bookseller-style cabinets could hold the eye-grabbing covers and exciting titles of the romance, thriller and crime genres she loved. Maybe she could even have a children's section?

'Well,' came a deep voice, speaking in Italian. 'I can't believe the difference already. You young people have so much energy.'

Beth turned to see Signor Balbo stepping down into the book barge. She greeted him enthusiastically. 'It's so lovely to see you.'

He shuffled to the armchair and sat down, Polo having spotted him and appearing at his heels. 'It is very different though.'

'I know. But good different I hope?'

He peered around. 'I think so.'

It wasn't the resounding yes she'd hoped for but she'd take it. 'What have you been up to?' she asked.

His smile grew wide. 'I've been seeing my family and enjoying not getting up early or moving heavy books around.'

'Well that's good.' She laughed.

'And I'm going to Padua soon to see my children.'

'I'm so pleased.'

'Perhaps I'll take my daughter a book. What would she like? She loves love stories.'

Knowing his daughter was older than her, Beth went to her new releases and pulled a romance from one of her favourite authors off the shelf. The cover was of a gorgeous café on a canal, similar to Venice, and with a swoony hero and feisty heroine, it was sure to be perfect. 'Here. Take this one.' He reached into his pocket and Beth held her hands out to stop him. 'I won't accept any payment.'

'You can't run a business like that!'

'I can if it's the man who sold the business to me.'

'Fine,' he grumbled, making his way back out of the barge. 'I never got to enjoy Carnevale before, but I will this time.' He kissed Beth on both cheeks and squeezed her hand. 'Till next time.'

She watched him go and wished she'd thanked him for changing her life. She'd make sure to say it next time.

At around lunchtime, the crowd died down as people found restaurants and cafés to settle into for a delicious lunch. Her stomach was rumbling, and she was just about to head to Lolanda and Galvano's when Marco's tall frame appeared on the street outside her window.

'Hi,' Beth said, as she took in his pale ice-blue eyes. The colour looked softer today, almost grey, and her nerves twitched as she thought about what Elsa and Daisy had said. Could he be interested in her? There was no denying her feelings for him were growing the more time they spent together, the more he opened up to her and she to him. She had to admit she certainly wouldn't say no if he asked her out. When he smiled warmly at her, she felt herself melting. 'What are you doing here?' she asked, tidying up some books that had been perused and then left on the side.

'It's Carnevale!' He grinned. 'The city is at its best and I thought you should see it. I didn't want you to miss it like you said you did last year.'

'I should really stay open,' she said, motioning at the empty book barge and then eyeing the empty street.

Marco shook his head. 'No, you shouldn't. No one will be out for the next hour at least. Everyone is eating. Come and explore with me. There is so much to see.'

For a moment, she hesitated. It was time to work, not play. But no one had ever anticipated her needs like this before, or knew she needed a little bit of prodding sometimes. It reminded her of Daisy and Elsa's relationship. One she thought was perfect. Did it mean that if things were different they would be perfect for each other? She immediately chastised herself for being fanciful and letting her imagination run wild. But her new life in Venice was about balance, going with the flow and enjoying being her own boss. If she couldn't close up for an hour to go and have lunch herself, what was the point? Besides, if she was staying forever in Italy, she had to act like an Italian and they always prioritised food. It was time she embraced their more laid-back culture.

'All right then,' Beth said, grabbing her coat and keys, a smile pulling at her face. She left a small window open for Polo to get in should he deign to return while she was out, and Marco helped her secure the outside bookcases. After she'd locked up, she asked, 'So where's the best place to watch the Carnevale fun?'

'St Mark's Square of course. Come on.' For a second it was almost as if he was thinking of offering her his hand, but then he stuffed it into his pocket and instead, made an awkward gesture with his elbow, which made him look like he was pretending to be a teapot. Beth repressed a giggle, but despite seeing the funny side, she wished he had taken her hand. She could imagine his strong fingers wrapping around her own. She placed her own hands in her pockets, flexing her fingers as though she could rid herself of her imagined feelings.

They followed the sound of the music, loud voices and general noise as they made their way to St Mark's Square. The square was always breathtakingly beautiful with the Doge's Palace, the Basilica and the tower dominating the view. But today, these historic gems were all but hidden behind troupes of performers, covering every inch of the piazza. Some were dancing, some performing, their actor voices projecting over the din. There were mime artists, and one troupe must have been acrobats from the way they were tumbling and throwing each other around.

Everywhere she looked there was colour: the elaborate medieval-style costumes, lace, ribbon and masks. Performers were on the water too, in gondolas in the lagoon and in the canals winding through the city. She loved the way the water was such a part of Venice, central to its existence for thousands of years and would continue to be well into its future.

Then there was the music: old-fashioned, medieval tunes mixed with drums, loots and lyres. She felt like she'd stepped back in time, but that all time periods were happening at once. Her senses felt overloaded, but she could still pick out the rich scents of freshly cooked tomatoes and garlic drifting on the air from the nearby restaurants. Her mouth watered as she realised how hungry she was.

As they wound their way through the crowd, Marco turned and held out his hand. Beth released hers from her pocket, allowing his long, strong fingers to intertwine. It felt unaccountably intimate, even amongst all these people, and the warmth of his skin travelled through her own, up into her heart, quickening its beats.

'This way,' he said, guiding them towards a side street and down to a small restaurant away from the hustle and bustle of the tourists.

Beth had to admit she was grateful for the peace and quiet. As they moved away from the crowd, she'd expected him to let go of her hand, but he hadn't yet and a smile formed on her face. She glanced at him from the corner of her eye and found he was already watching her. He smiled and focused on the building ahead, motioning with his other hand at their destination.

'I didn't know this place existed,' Beth said, then added, 'But to be fair I didn't know any places existed outside of my walk to and from the galleria.'

'You were married to your work,' Marco replied as his hand finally left her own to open the door for them. She noticed its loss immediately, needing the weight of it back.

Though the weather was bright, it wasn't quite warm enough to sit outside, and Marco pulled a chair out for her at a table by the window so they could still hear the music from the piazza.

Beth undid her coat and shrugged it from her shoulders, placing it on the back of her chair. 'It's a cliché, but I was. I tend to get sort of laser-focused on things. I like goals I can head towards and ultimately achieve.'

'Like with the book barge?'

She laughed as Marco slid into the seat opposite her. 'No, the book barge was the opposite of something I'd normally do. If I'd ever thought of doing such a thing it would have taken me years of planning. No, that was very much a go with the flow, take a chance kind of thing.'

'And how do you feel it's working out?'

The waitress came over, making eyes at Marco, and a stab of jealousy forced Beth to sit back and relax. He was here with her, she reminded herself. Albeit as friends. The word seemed to form differently in her brain as though she hated thinking it. Her feelings for Marco were certainly growing, perhaps more than she'd allowed herself to realise. They ordered a coffee each and a light lunch, Beth opting for *cicchetti* with different toppings and Marco a salad.

'Are you looking forward to dinner tonight?' Beth asked as she sipped her coffee. The Italians really knew how to make a good cup. The bitter liquid softened by the sweet, frothy milk.

'Yes, I am. I always like to see my family.' She couldn't quite read Marco's tone and when he shuffled a little, Beth worried it was her presence at the family meal that was making him uncomfortable. But then he spoke again and she realised with a wave of relief, it wasn't. 'You know things can be difficult sometimes, but I do like seeing my brothers and their wives and children. And Mamma. I think you'll like her. I should warn you my father might be a little . . .' He struggled to finish the sentence.

'Are things still difficult between you?' Beth asked gently.

Marco sighed. 'Always. I tried to convince him to let me contact a new shop opening in Milan. They'd love to sell our Murano glass, but he's determined not to see this as a good thing. He thinks if people want glass *from* Murano, they should be willing to travel to Murano to get it.'

'What?' Beth couldn't keep the incredulity from her voice.

'I know.' He rolled his eyes dramatically and both smiled. 'But what can I do? I cannot start another argument. It isn't worth it. He thinks I would appreciate the craft more if I got back into the workshop, but I've told him, I cannot. It isn't for me.'

Her eyes drifted to the small scar on his wrist, almost covered by his shirt cuff.

'Anyway,' he continued, his tone brighter. 'All my brothers will be there with their families tonight too and they're looking forward to meeting you. Has Francesca warned you it will be very noisy?'

At the mention of his sister's name, Beth grew tense, the guilt of the secret she was keeping from him growing heavier in her stomach. Her bond with Cesca had been formed first, but there was undoubtedly a bond between her and Marco now. Something sizzled between them and whilst they remained *friends* at times it seemed so much more than that. She'd speak to Cesca again She had to convince her to tell *him* the truth, if no one else. 'She hasn't actually, but that's okay. I thought it might be. And I like being around kids.'

'But you don't want any yourself?'

The question was so direct and so surprising, she didn't know what to say.

Marco's eyes crinkled at the corners as he winced. 'I'm sorry, that was insensitive of me. Stupid. I should not have overstepped.'

'No, it's fine.' Seeing his face flame with embarrassment that made him so deliciously vulnerable she wanted to kiss him instantly, she took pity on him. 'It's actually nice to have someone to talk about it with. No one ever seems comfortable broaching the subject because it's the opposite of what's expected. And you're right. I like being around kids, especially when they get old enough I can talk to them about art and history, but . . . no.' She shook her head. 'I don't want any myself. Does that shock you?'

He shrugged so casually she wondered if he was faking. 'No. You'd be surprised how many people feel the same way.'

What did that mean exactly? Did he feel the same way?

Their food arrived and the topic seemed to have come to a natural conclusion, though she couldn't deny she was curious to know more. They ate discussing Marco's artists, ideas he had of other people who might be interested in displaying on the book barge and his plans for an early morning row the next day.

'Won't you be too full of wine and good food from dinner?' she joked.

'My mother's wine and good food is exactly the reason I'll need to go. If I was still living at home, I'd have to row full time to stay in shape. But I was wondering—' He wiped his mouth with the napkin and Beth felt her eyes follow the movement of his lips. She turned away as soon as he looked up, not wanting to be caught staring. 'Would you like to join me?'

'Oh—' She hadn't expected him to ask that, and the question floated in her mind as her body reacted to the invitation with instant longing. 'I'd love to.'

'Great and shall I pick you up to go to Murano tonight?

I'm in Venice all afternoon with meetings; we could catch a water taxi together?'

'Yeah, that'd be great.' Beth congratulated herself on the casualness of her tone, though inside it was like fireworks going off.

'I'll meet you at say six-thirty?'

'Can't wait.'

Marco's eyes met hers and from the enthusiasm in her reply, she'd clearly lost the coolness of moments before. Neither of them moved, the moment too loaded with expectation and feeling, words unsaid dancing between them. Their hands were on the table, almost touching and Beth felt, rather than saw, Marco's fingers inch towards hers. They brushed hers gently and she looked up, his eyes pinned on her. A second later, he cleared his throat and wiped his mouth with the napkin.

Suddenly, she couldn't wait for dinner.

Chapter 18

The sun was setting as Marco and Beth sat in the *vaporetto* – the water bus – on the way to Murano. She'd taken Polo back to the apartment and changed into a tidier pair of trousers and a cuter jumper, but now more than ever realised her wardrobe needed a shake-up. It still needed to be practical, but she could definitely branch out into something more stylish and, dare she say it, more colourful. She hoped Marco's mamma wouldn't hold it against her. She smiled nervously at him. Their hands were nearly touching as the boat lifted over the gentle waves.

'Don't be nervous,' he said, leaning into her so his breath tickled her ear. 'My family are nicer than I am.'

'You don't think you're nice?'

'Do you?' The air was suddenly charged as Marco caught her eye, his expression different to anything she'd seen before. He was teasing her, his mouth lifting at the corner and his eyes shining mischievously. He continued without waiting for her to answer. 'I know I can be . . .' He looked around at the Venice skyline in the distance. 'Too focused on my work.'

'You have drive and ambition; there's nothing wrong with that. If there is, my whole life has been wrong.'

'Then maybe we are similar.'

He turned away and, feeling heat rising underneath her clothes, she focused on the rippling waves that surrounded the boat as it made its way through the water. As the water bus pulled up and they disembarked, Beth chastised herself for never coming here before. Murano was like a smaller version of Venice, just as beautiful, but with far fewer tourists. Many of the shops sold the colourful hand-blown glass the area was famous for, and Beth couldn't wait to get to Marco's home and hopefully see the workshop his family operated.

They walked away from the main streets towards the furthest part of the island, coming to a stop outside a large cream house. It was gated and at first appearance looked elegant and expensive, but as she looked closer, she could see marks on the walls from the leaky guttering and paint flaking from the iron fence.

At the gate, Marco entered a code, and it swung open. As they walked in, the front door flew open before they'd taken more than a few steps and a woman Beth knew instantly was Marco's mother came out. She was short and round, with rosy cheeks lifting into a smile. She had Marco's ice-blue eyes, and her hair was still dark and luscious though a few grey hairs scattered the crown of her head and at her temples.

'*Benvenuto*! *Benvenuto*, Signora Thorpe! *Benvenuto a casa nostra*!'

It was the most effusive welcome Beth had ever received. Before she could reply, a dozen small children of various sizes ran around Mamma di Rienzo's legs, swarming Marco who chuckled as he almost tripped over them. His face instantly relaxed, losing the closedness it carried when they spoke about business. When he relaxed, there was a light in his eyes, the same teasing gleam she'd seen earlier on the way over.

Beth felt a rush of attraction for Marco as once more she saw the man underneath the business exterior. His mamma rushed forwards, shooing the children away with a tea towel that had been slung over her shoulder. She embraced Marco, speaking quickly in Italian, saying how well he looked (if a little thin!) and that she was looking forward to feeding him and hearing all about his week. As soon as he could speak, he cleared his throat and spoke in English.

'Mamma, this is Beth.'

'It's lovely to meet you,' Beth said, handing over the bouquet of flowers she'd brought with her.

'Oh! *Grazie, grazie*! Thank you! You're so kind. And pretty! Isn't she pretty Marco? I can see why you like her. Come in, come in!'

He liked her? Beth's cheeks grew hot. She knew he and Cesca had been talking about her, but she hadn't thought he'd say anything more than they were working together. Then again, she could see how his mum might misread his interest and their relationship. They were hustled inside, the children all speaking quickly at Marco, talking over one another as they vied for his attention.

'You can call me Paola,' she began gently, then stopped to chastise her grandchildren in Italian, telling them to leave their uncle alone so he could get in the house.

Beth giggled as they moved into a large open-plan living room. Cesca immediately stood and walked over to her. They hugged, and kissed each other's cheeks and Cesca hooked her arm.

'Let me introduce to you to everyone.' She began pointing at her brothers and introducing them and their wives and children. There were so many names, Beth worried she wouldn't remember them all, but they all smiled or waved happily, seemingly glad she was there.

'And this is Papa,' Cesca said, as a man came in from the garden wearing grubby overalls. 'Papa, this is Beth.'

'Call me Elio,' he said with a smile. 'I won't shake hands until I've cleaned up. Look!' He held up his blackened hands, the fingernails dark with muck.

Marco had inherited Elio's height and strong jawline. Age and hard work hadn't dampened the brightness of his gaze or the strong set of his shoulders. When his eyes fell on Marco, he stiffened slightly, then smiled at her again and went off to change. She glanced over her shoulder at Marco, but he was busy watching after his father.

'Don't worry about them,' Cesca said. 'Things are always a little weird at first. They'll be all right in a while. Papa has just come in from the workshop. Marco was going to show it to you—'

'After dinner!' Paola announced, wagging a finger at them all.

Beth felt about twelve years old, but in a comforting way, as if she were part of something again. Something bigger than herself. Marco, Cesca and Beth all shared a cheeky look as the two siblings responded, 'Yes, Mamma,' in unison.

As Paola left for the kitchen, several conversations erupted at once with questions fired at her while others were talking amongst themselves. Her senses were overwhelmed with noise and colour, and she was almost growing concerned she wouldn't be able to cope when she felt the weight of Marco's arm around her, his hand settling perfectly into the dip of her waist. The warmth of his skin through her thin jumper was comforting. Like being given a hot water bottle to hold when you walk in from the cold. He dipped his head to speak to her, his voice, husky and deep, cutting through the racket.

'I told you it would be noisy, didn't I?'

'You did, but I admit, I didn't expect it to be this . . .'

'Crazy?'

She giggled and he looked at her in a way she'd always

hoped a man would. Once more, the words just said stayed in the air between them as if they understood each other perfectly. Marco cleared his throat and she said, 'It's wonderful but also . . . a lot.'

'I know exactly what you mean. Shall we step outside for a few minutes? Get some fresh air before dinner?'

She nodded and he led them outside, his hand moving to the small of her back, through the door Elio had just come. The cool air hit her cheeks, and she studied the darkening sky. A pale pink glow was just visible above some of the rooftops as the dense navy and soft black of the night crept in. No stars were visible yet, but it wouldn't be long. She'd never seen sunsets as beautiful as those in Venice and it thrilled her to think that the centuries-old artists she loved had looked up at the same sky.

'I understand my family can be overwhelming,' Marco said. 'They take friendliness to a whole new level.'

'I think most Italian families can be overwhelming. They're all so big and loving. It's wonderful, just . . . not what I'm used to.'

'Are your family not like that?'

'No. I'm an only child and my parents weren't the most responsible of people. They used to make random, last-minute decisions – going places, buying things – that threw everything into chaos.'

'And that's why you like to think slowly? To plan?'

She nodded again, thinking how no man had ever 'got' her the same way Marco did. 'I don't like regrets. I've seen too many from them and I try to avoid them. But—' She brightened. 'Now they're enjoying their retirement and I'm here living my own life. I have Elsa and Daisy; they're my family really and have been for years.'

'How is the pregnancy?'

She smiled at his concern. 'Good. Everything's fine. They've asked me to be godmother to their baby.' Her grin widened, Marco's matching it.

'And how do you feel about that?'

'Happy. Blessed, actually. I feel more comfortable with that than being a mother.'

'Parenthood isn't for everyone,' he said gently. 'And that's okay.'

She couldn't help but notice he'd said parenthood, not motherhood. Were his thoughts similar to her own? Unless he volunteered the information she didn't feel she could ask. A knock at the window drew their attention and they turned to see one of Marco's nephews, aged around eleven, blowing a raspberry on the glass so his entire mouth was visible. Beth dissolved into laughter, Marco too, even more so when Marco's sister-in-law noticed and told him off in whispered Italian for creating a bad impression with Beth. Catching each other's eyes, Beth and Marco laughed again. Beth knew this was exactly the type of situation where trouble lurked for her in the future. Men like Marco, who enjoyed their big families, would they want children and what would they do when they found out Beth didn't? Worry threatened to knot her stomach like a vice.

'She doesn't need to worry,' Beth said, hoping to move her own thoughts on by speaking of something else. 'It would take more than that to create a bad impression with me.'

'I feel I did,' Marco said, again being so direct it caught her off guard.

'You? When?'

'At the rowing club party. I know I change when talking of business. I know I often seem . . . difficult.'

'I wouldn't say difficult. Perhaps a little . . . corporate. But then, I suppose we all change when talking about our work. I used to turn into a different person when giving tours. I found it easier than trying to be myself. I've always preferred being behind the scenes.'

'I know what you mean. Can I admit that I'm nervous about the masquerade ball?'

'You? Why?'

'I want Signora Cadora to work with me, and I worry I'll get tongue-tied.'

'You'll be fine. And I'm sure she'll be interested in meeting you even if she doesn't agree to anything right now. The night won't be wasted.'

'No, it won't.' He glanced at her again, his words loaded with meaning she was almost too scared to think about.

She wasn't sure if it was intentional, but Marco's body pressed a little more against her own, and she found herself relaxing into the noise and mayhem behind her, her shoulders dropping.

'We should go in,' Marco said. 'Ready?'
She nodded. 'Let's go.'

***

Sat around the enormous wooden table with Paola and Elio at each end, the family gathered around the middle. Conversation flowed easily. The table was laden with dishes of baked pasta, a delicious-smelling leg of lamb, and several types of vegetables cooked in multitudes of ways. Beth couldn't imagine how long it had taken Paola to prepare it all, but her mouth was watering at the smell of artichokes, herbs, cooked meats and cheese-infused pasta. Everyone included her in their discussions and were curious about the book barge and her change of career.

'I'm grateful to Cesca and Marco,' she said, glancing around the table as dishes were passed to her and she loaded her plate. 'Cesca's skills have been invaluable, and Marco's contacts will really help me to offer something different. I hope I can make some money for his clients too, of course.'

Elio made a grumbling noise, and Paola shot him a warning glance. The temperature in the room dropped as though someone had poured a bucket of ice on the table.

'It's not always about money,' Elio said in Italian, ignoring his wife's pursed mouth and hard stare. 'It is about the work and tradition.'

Beside her, Marco's hand clenched around his fork, then dropped below the table and did the same in his lap. As discreetly as she could, Beth moved her hand on top of his and gently held it. He didn't move, but she felt him relax slightly under her touch.

'I understand,' Beth began, answering Elio in his own language. Elio's eyes widened in surprise, a ruddy redness bringing two spots of colour to his cheeks. For a second, Beth worried she should have kept her mouth shut. But the grin Cesca was giving her and Paola's delight in seeing her husband contradicted made her continue. Marco's eyes shot to her in utter surprise, the blue bright as he watched her. She continued speaking in Italian.

'But PR isn't a bad thing. All the great artists of the Renaissance had patrons, people to advocate for them and promote their work. Titian had Emperor Charles V, Tintoretto had the physician Tommaso Rangone, and many artists acted as a sort of patron for the pupils they themselves taught. It's not uncommon in the arts at all and – well, actually – it's been going on in Venice for hundreds of years. The way I see it, what Marco does is just another, more up-to-date form of a time-honoured Venetian tradition.'

Elio's mouth was hanging open, as was everyone else's around the table. Even the children, who'd been annoying each other with shoves and kicks, or picking the bits of vegetables they didn't like out of the pasta, had stopped and were watching her. Beth's neck prickled and it crept slowly up her spine. Oh no. She should have kept her mouth shut. She'd been invited into the di Rienzo home and had embarrassed Marco's father. She'd never be invited back here – that was for certain – and now, everyone would hate her. Her only solace was that she was unlikely to see them all again. 'That's just my opinion of course,' she added lamely.

After a silence that seemed to last for hours, Paola let out a huge, mirthful laugh.

'You see!' she said, slapping Elio on the arm. 'This is what I've been saying for years. Marco does a good job. A necessary job.'

'Hmm,' Elio grumbled, his cheeks still pink. 'Maybe. Maybe we should visit this book barge of yours.' He scooped some pasta and chewed.

The table then erupted once more into life and the meal ended without Beth embarrassing herself any further. She had no idea how Marco had felt about it because his expression had remained unreadable, even now as they were readying to leave and he'd handed her coat to her.

'I'll see you tomorrow?' she asked Cesca.

'Oh yes. I'm staying here tonight, but we have a lot to talk about tomorrow.'

Not least of which was her secret and that she had to say something for everyone's sakes.

Marco slipped on his coat too.

'When will you move back to Murano?' his mum asked.

Marco rolled his eyes. 'I don't know, Mamma. I like Venice.'

'Murano is nicer than Venice.' She tutted, but smiled as she kissed his cheeks, then Beth's.

'Thank you for inviting me for dinner.'

'It was our pleasure. And—' she leaned in and spoke

quietly '—thank you for standing up to my husband. He is too old-fashioned sometimes. You've never brought a girlfriend home before, Marco. You should do this more often. I like her. A lot.'

'She's not my—'

Paola made shooing noises, and Marco gave up trying to argue, bundling them outside, but it was clear he thought she'd overstepped the mark.

The night was dark, and the stars were now visible in the sky, glittering like drops of fairy dust. A half-moon shone brightly, and as they approached the water bus, the silver light reflected on the deep black of the water. The skyline of Venice could be seen in the distance and Beth felt a longing for her apartment. She was tired after a busy day, and the evening had been more eventful than she'd expected.

Still not speaking, they climbed into the water bus, and it glided over the lagoon on the return journey. The chill evening wind sent goose bumps over her skin as it wound its way inside her coat and up her sleeves. She shivered and Marco pushed back the fluttering strands of his hair before grabbing the back of his head – the nervous gesture she'd come to know. He unwound his scarf, gently draping it around her neck.

'Here, have this.'

'Aren't you cold?'

'Not really.'

'I'm sorry if I embarrassed your father,' Beth said, staring at her fingers.

To her surprise, Marco laughed. 'You didn't. It's about time someone told him that what I'm trying to do isn't sacrilege.'

'Then why were you so quiet? You've barely spoken to me since dinner. I thought I'd humiliated you or something.'

'I'm sorry. I – I was in my own head, that's all. Thinking of something.'

'What?'

His gaze pierced hers as he studied her face. 'It doesn't matter.' After a second, he added, 'My mother likes you.'

'Really? I was worried I was going to get kicked out of dinner. Is your dad always so . . . sombre?'

'Only when I'm around. Did you see him with his grandkids?'

Now she thought of it, she had seen him laughing and joking with them, being silly and tossing the littlest ones into the air and catching them again, making them giggle. 'Is it all because of your career choice?'

'That and no longer blowing glass and moving away from Murano. He likes to have his family close.'

'But you aren't far! Only a—' she motioned to the water '—a *vaporetto* away.'

'We've grown apart since I started working with other artists. Perhaps he sees it as a betrayal of the family. I don't know.' The hurt on his face made her reach out again and cover his hand with her own. He didn't move away, and Beth's stomach somersaulted. 'Your point was well made.' His voice was gravelly as though he were struggling to speak. 'And in Italian too. Thank you.'

'I thought—' Her voice was as husky as his, almost inaudible. 'I thought he might take it better that way.'

As she turned to him, his head moved slightly towards her and she wondered if he were about to kiss her, but she couldn't be sure if it was just the swaying of the boat. As they moved over a choppier wave it forced them apart and both of them looked towards the Venetian skyline. The moment gone, the spell broken.

The rest of the journey was taken in silence and when they climbed onto dry land he offered to walk her home.

'Oh, you don't need to do that.'

'I'd like to.'

Delight surged through her and their hands gently brushed as they hung by her side, a tingling electricity shooting up her arm. He made no attempt to hold her hand but the longing for him too pounded in her heart.

'Even though I'm nervous, I am looking forward to the ball,' he said as they strolled through the quiet, deserted streets towards her apartment.

The moon shimmered off the quiet canal water, lapping against the houses, and the silence of the night surrounded them. The day's Carnevale activities were over and the city was once more asleep.

'Me too. I was working last year so was so busy making sure no one was leaning against any of the paintings or drunkenly falling into them. I didn't really get to enjoy it.'

'I hope you will this time. I can't believe it's only a week away.'

Beth paused, almost falling over her own feet. 'What did you say?'

'Have I got the date wrong?' Marco began swiping at his phone. 'Next Saturday, yes?'

'Is it?' Beth pushed a hand through her hair. 'I thought it was further away than that. I don't even have a dress!'

Marco laughed. 'Please don't panic. There are so many shops in Venice, you'll find something to wear. Can't you wear what you wore last time?'

She crossed her arms over her chest in frustration. 'Of course I can't! Everyone will know and this isn't just any old do, this is the galleria's masquerade ball. Okay,' she said to herself. 'Don't panic. I'll sort something out.'

'I'm not panicking. Beth—' He put his hands on her shoulders and stared into her eyes. She suddenly realised how close he was. 'You will look lovely in anything. You always do.'

He stared at her for a second too long then began walking towards her apartment, saying he'd meet her at seven for a morning row. Beth followed and at the door, he kissed her gently on the cheek as he said goodbye. Like the night she'd moved in, she could feel his lips long after he'd left, and she resisted drawing her fingers to the spot to see if she could feel the tingling in her fingertips. But then, something happened. From somewhere inside her, the voice telling her to go with the flow took over and she called Marco's name.

He turned, only a few steps away and led by some invisible force, pulled by some invisible string that seemed to have thrown them into each other's paths, she took a step forward. Her heart beat frantically in her chest, pounding against her ribcage, her lungs, and echoing in her brain. Now barely an inch apart, she lifted her head to meet his gaze. Excitement rather than fear filled her body as he tilted his head towards hers, drawing closer to her. The perfect Cupid's bow met her lips, sending a shockwave through her body, and what started as a gentle, tentative kiss grew fiercer as his hand slipped around her waist, drawing her close while another threaded into her hair.

Beth had no idea how long they were lost in each other, but then they separated, Marco's cheeks pink and Beth knew her own were too. They smiled.

'You are a very surprising woman, Beth.'

'That's probably a good thing, isn't it?'

He laughed and kissed again, gently. 'This has been a good day.'

'It has.'

'But I should say goodnight.' With another final kiss, plus one on her hand, which made her want to melt, he left, wishing her goodnight.

As if controlled by a robot, or some kind of magic, Beth went inside, turning on the television just to hear some noise. She needed a few minutes to clear her head. Trying to sleep was going to be hard enough after the dinner and that amazing, incredible, gorgeous kiss, not to mention his compliments about her looking lovely in anything. And how had she forgotten the masquerade ball was coming up in a matter of days? She'd be spending an entire evening with him and there'd be champagne and dancing. Just the thought of his hands on her waist sent her heart thudding against her chest again.

She tried to focus on the television as she changed into her pyjamas, trying to control all thoughts of Marco, but no matter what, there he and his kiss lingered, and she knew he wasn't going anywhere.

Chapter 19

Beth met Marco at the boathouse, and she watched as he carried the boat onto the water. He'd kissed her gently in greeting and the effect of it was still buzzing around her body as they got ready to row. She walked behind with the oars, admiring the tension in the muscles of his broad shoulders. The cool air seeped under the layers of her workout clothes, but it was pointless adding more as she'd only be hotter once she started moving.

Soon they were on the water, finding a natural rhythm so quickly that Marco didn't need to call the strokes and instead they enjoyed a comfortable silence. The blades of the oars cut through the water, and the sound of birdsong filled the air. As they moved away, the city was a sea of terracotta, the bright tiles of the roofs, stark against the pale stone of the buildings, seeming brighter in the white light of the morning.

'I don't think I'll ever get bored of this,' Beth said, happy to be putting her memories of that last emotional row behind her.

'I haven't yet,' Marco replied, a little out of breath. 'And I think this is my favourite time of day to see the city.'

'Me too.'

It wouldn't be long, and Venice would once more be alive with Carnevale, all the calm lost. Spring would soon be here, the mornings warmer, the sun brighter, and she was looking forward to watching the city bloom.

Beth wondered if this was her chance to ask about Emilio and Cesca. To try and warm Marco up to the idea of them being together and therefore soften the impact of Cesca's secrets. After the kiss last night, they were moving into new, uncharted territory. Her feelings for him were deepening with every day, every kiss.

'Doesn't Emilio train on the water?'

'Emilio?' Marco seemed startled by the question. He gave a sardonic laugh and then sighed.

A silence grew, but Beth quickly interrupted it. 'How long have you been friends?'

'Since we were children. He's a great rower. I'm proud of him.'

'Cesca mentioned he's been more focused lately.'

'He has, but it won't last. It never does. I love my friend, but he has faults. He is led by passion and has little self-control.'

'Surely he must have some as a sportsman?'

'He does what his coaches tell him, but he relaxes too much when he can.'

'Cesca said—'

'Cesca doesn't know him like I do, and she should remember what he's like. She's always had a crush on him.'

'But she is a grown woman,' Beth said over her shoulder.

'She'll always be my baby sister and I've warned her enough times to stay away from him. I love him, but his reputation with women isn't great. I know my friend and that means knowing his faults, and they're not faults I want anywhere near the women I know.' His tone changed, suddenly loaded with suspicion. 'Has Cesca said something . . . to you . . . about him?'

'No, no!' Beth replied quickly, her heart rate increasing. Guilt tightened her throat so she could barely speak. 'No I was just asking about him, wondering what a sportsman like him does day to day; that's all.'

The sky was lightening all around them, the water brightening as the sun began to shine down, turning the navy blue to a glistening aquamarine.

'Do you mind if we head back now?' Marco asked, his voice breathy from the effort, and she worried she'd annoyed him. She could see why Cesca was so worried about saying anything, even though Marco was acting with the best of intentions. 'I have a meeting at nine.'

'Of course not. I'll see you Saturday for the masquerade ball, yes?'

'Yes, but I will come by before then. If you don't mind . . . ?'

'No. No, of course not.'

'Shall I pick you up for the ball or meet you there?'

'Meet me there. It'll be easier.'

As Marco made conversation, they made their way back to the shore, enjoying the sounds of the city coming alive. Boats moved through the lagoon and chatter exuded from the gathering people. Marco smiled and kissed her before leaving, his lips gentle and firm against her own. She knew this thing between them was serious from the way her body reacted to his every touch, and reluctantly, they said goodbye and she headed home to shower and collect Polo. She'd have to speak to Cesca again about coming clean. Marco's reaction made her feel even worse and when he found out she'd been keeping the secret from him, what would he do or say? She had to see Cesca as soon as possible.

When Cesca arrived at the book barge, Beth pounced on her before she'd even put her toolbox on the ground.

'What's the matter?' Cesca asked, looking panicked. 'What's happened? Is it sinking?'

'Sinking? What, the boat? No! Why would you say that?'

Cesca shrugged. 'What else could it be?'

'The book barge isn't sinking. It isn't Polo either – he's asleep on the armchair. We're going shopping. I need your advice.'

'Shopping?' Cesca slowly lowered her toolbox and crossed her arms over her chest while frowning in confusion. 'For what?'

'A dress. I have this masquerade ball coming up and I have

nothing to wear. Literally nothing. All I have are trousers and jumpers—' To demonstrate her point even more, she tugged at her clothes. 'In boring, muted colours. I don't even own jeans. Why don't I own jeans, Cesca? I'm not ninety!'

Cesca laughed and placed her hands on her friend's arms. 'It's okay, calm down. We'll go shopping for a dress. I know just where to go. It's a very elegant event so you need something beautiful. We can start with the dress, and fix the rest of your boring wardrobe later. When is it?'

'Saturday!'

'That's okay, we'll find something. This is Venice! But first, we need coffee.'

Cesca stowed her toolbox inside and linked her arm into Beth's as they walked to Giambattista's. Her friend's presence calmed her a little and she actually started to believe she'd find something to wear that didn't make her feel like one of the Carnevale performers. She wanted to feel sexy and elegant, something she didn't feel very often. Maybe her narrow vision had seeped into more areas of her life than she'd realised.

After two strong coffees each, they were suitably caffeinated to face the Carnevale crowds and navigate the busy streets as they marched to the most upmarket shopping area of Venice.

'Are you ready for how much this is going to cost?'

Beth nodded. She had thought about hiring a dress, or even borrowing one, but this was a masquerade ball during Venice Carnevale at one of the city's most historic galleries.

She had to look her best and she wanted to impress Marco. She wanted him to be proud she was on his arm and for him to goggle comically when he saw her dressed so differently. For his eyes to light with longing and maybe even lust.

'And I have to ask,' Cesca began, 'is some of this for my brother's benefit?'

Beth felt her face freeze into a mask of horror. The moments they'd shared the evening before – the kisses – floated through her mind.

'It is, isn't it? It's okay. I'd be happy if Marco dated you. Very happy. Our mother would be happy too. She likes you very much. She didn't stop talking about you after you left. Does Marco know you like him?' Cesca squeezed her arm as she said it, slightly teasingly.

'I think so,' Beth replied, knowing she sounded like an embarrassed teenager but not wanting to go into details of what they'd been up to with his sister.

Cesca chuckled. 'It's all right; I know how handsome women find my brother. It makes me feel a little sick but I'm not an idiot. I know the world thinks he's gorgeous.'

Beth thought about continuing to deny it, but Daisy and Elsa's thoughts lurked in her mind and last night had changed everything.

'I really like him,' Beth said tentatively.

'I'm glad. He likes you very much; I can tell. He's more open with you than he is with most people. I like seeing him happy. I just wish I could tell him about Emilio so he could be happy for me in return.'

'I tried to talk to him about Emilio today.'

'You did what?' Cesca paused. 'What did you say?'

'I didn't give anything away. I just hoped I could smooth the way for you. Warm him up to the idea.'

'And?'

Beth shook her head sorrowfully. 'It didn't work. I don't think he sees how much Emilio has changed.'

'I knew that already.'

The Carnevale streets were still busy and a dancing duo bowed to them both, letting them pass before continuing with their act. The number of shops they went in and out of was exhausting. As was the number of dresses Beth tried on, but nothing seemed quite what she wanted. She either felt uncomfortable at the level of detail, or overexposed as her pale white skin was there for everyone to see. As usual she was drawn towards darker colours while Cesca seemed to be grabbing bright jewel colours that washed her out.

Time was marching on as they walked to the next shop with nothing to show for their efforts. Beth worried about closing the book barge for this, but she knew she had to get it sorted.

'You need to try something different,' Cesca said as they opened the door and walked into the air-conditioned store.

'I know,' Beth replied. 'I know you like colour, and that's fine, but I just don't suit bright tones. They make me look ill. I'm too pale for them.'

'You're not comfortable in them; that's not the same as not suiting them. You actually suit a lot of brighter colours, but you insist on staying in greys and blacks. Why?' Cesca raced to a rack and began studying the clothes.

Beth grew uncomfortable. 'I don't know really. I've always had a uniform. It helps me stay focused on my work and I guess it's just comfortable. It means I don't have to spend headspace thinking about what to wear and I can use that energy on something else.'

'Well Venice Carnevale is the time to embrace colour and something a little daring. Try on some of these.'

She bundled Beth towards the changing rooms. Every dress was made of thin, satiny material that clung to her less-than-sexy underwear. The colours were far too bright and only highlighted how she had bags under her eyes and needed a new moisturiser. She was about to give up when a hand shot around the curtain waving a long black velvet dress.

'This is the only black dress I'll allow you to wear.'

Beth took it, already feeling a connection with the garment. She held it up to view its full length and was relieved to see it would fall to the floor. It had a Bardot neckline and a thigh-high split that was sexy without putting everything on display. She slipped into it. Even without heels her legs looked good from all the rowing. She stood on tiptoe and ran her hands down her hips. She pulled her hair into a high ponytail and turned in the mirror, deciding if having it up made it look nicer. It did. Her neck looked long, her shoulders toned, and she felt comfortable – like herself but . . . fancier.

'Can I see?' asked Cesca, and Beth pulled back the curtain. Cesca gasped, her hands shooting up to her face.

'It's perfect. Now all we need are heels and a mask. And a red lip.'

Beth shook her head, letting her hair tumble from her hands. 'I've never worn a red lip.'

'Then it's time you started. You have lovely plump lips and with a black or gold mask, you'll look incredible. Trust me,' Cesca added, seeing her waver.

Go with the flow, Beth told herself. *Go with the flow*. She looked again at herself in the mirror and wondered what Marco would make of her. He'd seen her sweaty from workouts and rows; he'd seen her covered in paint from working on the boat. Would he recognise her? A smile crept over her face. Cesca wouldn't steer her wrong and she always managed to look stylish, even in her work clothes.

Beth grinned. 'All right. Let's go.'

Chapter 20

Beth stood at the entrance to the *Gallerie dell'Accademia*, her mask in her hand. She'd opted for a black half-mask with gold detailing and gold lace at the top, and she and Cesca had spent ages choosing a red lipstick that would complement her pale colouring. Her hair was pinned up in a beautiful clip they'd found, and she wore a gold necklace that sat at the base of her throat, a small solitaire diamond nestling just above the hint of cleavage.

A dark, velvety sky overhead was covered in clouds, and she hoped it wasn't going to rain. Guests were already arriving, and Signor Sanna welcomed them. When he spotted Beth, his face lit up.

'Beth! I am so happy to see you.' He smiled warmly, embracing her.

'It's lovely to see you, Signor Sanna. How are you?'

'I am well, of course. And you?'

'I'm good.'

'Really?' He ducked his head, catching her gaze to make sure she wasn't lying.

She grinned widely. 'I really am. I'm enjoying running my own bookshop.'

'You always loved books as much as paintings.'

'I suppose I did.' Though she hadn't let herself realise it, working so hard on her career and focusing only on the next step.

'So you are happy?'

As the feeling flooded her body, she didn't hesitate in replying. 'Yes, I am. Very.'

'Good, good! Now, I must go and greet the other guests. Have fun tonight, Beth. You deserve it.'

She kissed him goodbye and hugged him tightly to let him know how happy she was with the change of direction her life had taken.

'Beth?'

She turned as she heard Marco call her name and was pleased to see him pause, his eyes scanning her with obvious surprise and, she was pleased to see that hint of longing and lust she'd hoped for. The smile that spread over his face sent a thrill through her. He didn't look bad himself wearing a black suit with a crisp white shirt and black bow tie. His mask was in his hand, and he'd opted for a plain black velvet one with ribbon detailing. As he smiled, her body tingled.

'I – you . . .' He cleared his throat, a blush rising up his cheeks. 'You look stunning, Beth. Beautiful.'

'Better than my normal black trousers and jumpers, I think.'

'You *always* look beautiful.'

He stressed the word *always* as he met her eye and, despite the cold, a warmth grew in her chest. He stepped closer, taking her hand and she moved into him, lifting her head so he could kiss her. His lips were gentle, not disturbing her bold red lipstick, but the slight touch was enough to set a fire inside her heart and for her to want him to know just how much she was falling for him.

He crooked his elbow for her to take his arm, and she slid her hand through. Below his jacket she could feel the movement of his muscles, the tension of biceps worked hard by rowing. Inside the entranceway, the one she'd walked in every day, she took a glass of champagne from the tray offered to her by a server. Marco took one too and sipped. She watched the movement of his throat, a smattering of stubble on his jaw.

'How does it feel being back here?' he asked, adjusting his collar.

She was surprised by his question, and Beth looked around taking in the paintings, inhaling the familiar smell. 'It does feel strange. And a little sad.' They moved through to one of the galleries. The central seating had been moved away to create a large, clear space. They paused in front of a Tiepolo and her skin prickled as she took in the delicate brushwork. 'I miss seeing paintings like this every day. Being in a museum or gallery it just feels like a – a gift. But I've always loved books and reading too, and being surrounded by them all day – and the people who love them as much as I do – is incredible. I can't deny as well—' she lowered her voice and moved nearer to him so Signor Sanna wouldn't hear '—I'm also loving the freedom of being my own boss. I've never had that before and it's scary but also . . . wonderful.'

'I know what you mean. I've always loved it too and I wouldn't have had that if I'd gone into the family business like my brothers.'

Someone tried to edge past and knocked into Beth, giving their apologies. Marco's hand circled her waist, and she turned to him, suddenly realising how close they were together. His eyes were drawn once more to her mouth, and she'd never felt more naked but also, as she'd hoped, confident. She flicked her eyes up to meet his face, and before his grip loosened so she could move back to where she'd been standing, as if he couldn't help himself, he placed another gentle kiss on her lips. Her body grew hot. 'So shall we find Signora Cadora and see if we can convince her to sign with you?'

He took a gulp of his drink. 'Do we have to do it right now? Can't we see some paintings first?'

'I suppose we can, yes.' She giggled. 'But you can't put it off forever.'

'A few minutes will be enough.'

He was nervous and if he had a free hand he would have scrunched the hair at the back of his head. They moved through the crowd, smiling and chatting with people they both knew. Beth was able to introduce Marco to some experts he hadn't met before, and though they were mostly curators or conservators, she hoped they might still prove useful to him one day. Networking, she knew from experience, could never be underestimated.

As they moved into another gallery, Marco paused. 'There she is.'

Signora Cadora was surrounded by a group of people, who all rapturously listened to whatever it was she was saying. As she reached the punchline of her joke, they all laughed.

'Are you ready?' Beth asked seeing the nervousness in his jaw.

'No.'

She laughed. 'It's going to be fine.'

'What will I say? She always makes me so nervous. I can't just go in and say, "Do you need PR? I'd love to help".'

Beth laughed again. 'No, don't do that. Just introduce yourself and say how much you enjoy her work. Is there anyone else there you know?'

He studied the group. 'The lady with the long dangly earrings is a ceramicist I've worked with before, but she prefers to hire me for occasional shows.'

'Then leave it to her to mention your PR.'

'What if she doesn't?'

'She will. Trust me.' Secretly pleased her experience was coming in handy, she guided them over. 'Come on, let's go.'

As they approached, the group kindly made room for them to join the conversation.

'Marco!' the ceramicist said. 'How lovely to see you.'

'Good to see you too, Vittoria. I hope business is good?'

'Business is very good, thank you! I've been meaning to call you about an exhibition I have coming up.' Beth grinned at Marco who, politely, kept his eyes on Vittoria. She turned to Signora Cadora. 'Marco runs an excellent PR firm. He always helps get people to my exhibitions.'

'Not that you need any help,' he added to the *signora* and Beth had to hide her smile at the blush creeping up his cheeks. She gently tightened her grip on his arm for reassurance. 'I just wanted to say how much I admire your work, *signora*. I saw your last exhibition and thought the pieces were wonderful.'

Signora Cadora, who was older than Beth had expected, nodded her head benevolently. 'It's very nice to meet you too. What is the name of your agency?'

'It's the Di Rienzo Agency.'

'Your family makes glass does it not?'

His mouth dropped open. 'Yes, yes, that's right. We've been making glass on Murano for hundreds of years. My father is very proud of the family heritage.'

'And so he should be. Do you have a card?'

His hands flew to every pocket, unable to find anything, and Beth's heart rate increased. He hadn't left them at home, had he? Then she realised he was just excited and nervous, like a kid at Christmas. Finally, he found them in his inside jacket pocket and handed one over.

'*Grazie.*'

She didn't say any more and, as she sensed the awkwardness seeping in as Marco stood grinning, Beth leaned forwards. 'Enjoy your evening.' She guided Marco away, who seemed to still be in shock.

Beth pulled Marco to the side of the room. 'That went well, I think.'

'She spoke to me,' Marco said, causing Beth to giggle. 'And she asked for my card.'

His eyes were wide, and he couldn't look more different to the aloof businessman he'd been at the start of their working relationship. 'Thank you, Beth. Thank you. I can't tell you how much this means to me. How much *you* mean to me.' He took her hand and pulled it to his lips and an electric shock prickled her skin. 'We should dance. Come.'

He led her through to another gallery where people were dancing to the small classical ensemble. He put his mask on, tying the ribbon behind his head and, following his lead, she did the same. Marco took her hand, pulling her into the crowd. His fingers tightened around hers while his other hand pressed gently into her lower back. As he drew her closer, she feared the feelings swirling so strongly inside her, and that he'd see her desire for him on her face. The mask gave a sense of protection, confidence even and as they swayed to the music, unspeaking, she felt safe in his arms, happy. It was like this was the only person whose arms were meant to be around her. But what was Marco feeling? Were similar thoughts going through his head? Feeling bold with the coverage of the mask, she lifted her gaze just as he lowered his to look at her.

The air stilled around them, the music fading in her ears. It was just the two of them and this special, wonderful connection that had formed between them.

'Beth,' he said breathily. 'I want you to know how happy I am that we met. That . . . that I am . . .'

'Yes?'

He opened his mouth, but nothing came out, his eyes narrowing slightly as if he was struggling to find the right words. She almost begged him to speak in Italian if that was easier. Who wouldn't want to be told someone was falling in love with them in that beautiful language, if that was what he was going to say? She hoped it was with every fibre of her body. His eyes pinned hers. He'd found the right words and was about to say them when a voice she instantly recognised cut through the blood thumping in her ears.

'I told you you'd look beautiful in that dress! Emilio, doesn't she look absolutely stunning!'

Marco suddenly moved away from her, and Beth turned, confused. It was a moment before she could speak, her eyes drifting to Marco, her brain struggling to regain its equilibrium. 'Cesca?'

What was she doing here?

Beneath a plain white half-mask decorated with black diamonds on the cheeks, Cesca grinned. 'Surprise!'

'What are you doing here?' Icy air flooded the gap where Marco had been, and she could feel the void as though an iceberg had replaced him.

Emilio appeared at Cesca's side, smiling. They were in matching colours. His dark, navy suit virtually the same shade as Cesca's midnight satin dress.

'Emilio invited me.' Cesca glanced at her brother as she replied, and Beth suddenly felt the heavy weight of Cesca's secret as though it were pressing down on her chest. 'He was invited as our local sports hero.'

'You didn't say anything,' Marco replied, coolly, removing his mask. With the moment well and truly gone, Beth removed her own mask as Cesca's face hardened.

'He wasn't sure if he'd be here,' she replied before Emilio had a chance.

'Shall we go and get some drinks?' Emilio said, trying to gently move Cesca away, but there seemed to be some kind of showdown between brother and sister that Beth and Emilio could do nothing about. When Marco didn't move, but his ice-cold gaze flicked between Emilio and Cesca, zeroing in on Emilio's hand wrapped around her waist, Beth tugged at him gently.

'Marco, let's get a drink. People are starting to stare.'

At this he came to, and they all moved to the side of the room, grabbed drinks from a passing waiter and pretended to smile at passers-by. Cesca moved to Beth, her good humour returning instantly.

'You look absolutely beautiful.'

'So do you. But why didn't you tell me you might be here?'

Cesca angled them away from her brother and Emilio, who were having their own tense conversation in Italian. Beth couldn't hear their words completely but could make out Marco hissing, 'Yes, but why ask my *sister*? You have hundreds of women you could invite.'

'Emilio honestly didn't know if he'd be here, so he didn't want to get my hopes up.'

Behind them, Emilio said something, his voice soft and placating, but Marco wasn't impressed and again hissed, 'You're leading her on, Emilio, and I won't have it.'

Cesca turned around and Beth's stomach dropped. 'Marco, stop it—'

This was it. This was Cesca's perfect opportunity to explain what was going on between her and Emilio. For Marco to see how much they cared for each other and that his sister was grown up and able to make her own choices. Her breath stuck in her lungs as Cesca continued.

'Emilio asked me because he's only here for one night and he knows I won't read anything into it.'

No! Beth thought and she glared at Cesca, imploring her to tell the truth not make things worse.

'I don't need your protection,' Cesca whispered to her brother through clenched teeth. 'There's nothing going on between Emilio and me.'

Slowly, Beth closed her eyes and took a deep breath. Now Cesca had made everything worse, and she cringed at the lies Cesca was piling on. It would be even worse now when the truth finally did come out.

'Good,' Marco muttered. He turned to Emilio. 'Keep it that way.'

Emilio, not looking at his friend, left with Cesca. In the awkward silence, they sipped their drinks. She couldn't believe that only moments before they'd been so close, so together. In a moment made just for them.

'Did you know they were going to be here?' Marco asked and Beth stiffened.

'No. I was as shocked to see Cesca as you were.'

His voice softened a little, but hurt still cut through her. 'She didn't say anything at all about coming?'

'Not to me.'

He searched the crowd for them, and when he didn't spot them, turned back to her. 'Do you think there's something going on between them?'

Ice trickled down Beth's spine. She'd kept Cesca's secret, but now . . . now she was going to have to lie directly to his face and she hated herself for it. She wasn't too fond of Cesca in that moment either. So far, she'd been able to skirt around the issue as he'd never once asked her an open question about it. But now . . . 'I—'

People had already started staring at them once this evening. If she told him the truth he'd march over to his sister and make a scene that wouldn't do either of them any good. As much as it pained her to lie to him, tonight wasn't the night, and this wasn't the place to be honest. As she opened her mouth to speak, it was like a wall had been built between them. A literal barrier that she wasn't sure they could overcome.

His eyes bored into hers and she stumbled for a sentence that meant she wasn't lying and didn't drop Cesca in it. 'I'm sure if there is, Cesca will tell you.' She kept her eyes on her glass, unable to meet his gaze. She'd never felt so sick, or so deceitful.

His shoulders relaxed. 'I'm sure you're right.'

But though Beth tried, the magic of the night was ruined. From then on, Marco was distracted and though Beth tried to move the conversation on and to return to the moment they were having right before Cesca turned up, there was no going back. The evening was over as they didn't dance and he didn't kiss her again. Instead he searched for his sister and Emilio, barely speaking to her. Unable to take it any longer, with the clock nearing midnight, she said her goodbyes.

'You want to leave?' He seemed surprised and she almost laughed, grabbing her hand as she turned to walk away. 'Shall I walk you home?'

Beth shook her head. 'It's fine. You should stay and find Cesca and Emilio.'

'I'm sorry,' he replied, scrunching the hair at the back of his head. 'I've been looking out for them and not giving you my full attention.'

'I'm not a puppy,' Beth snapped, the hurt of the night finally getting to her. 'I don't *need* your attention. I just thought we were . . . you were going to say . . .' She couldn't finish. What if she were wrong and he hadn't been about to say that at all? After all, they'd barely started seeing each other.

'What?' Had he forgotten where they'd been before Cesca arrived?

'Nothing.'

'Beth—'

Frustration, anger and a little bit of embarrassment at her own thoughts and feelings burned at her. 'Your sister is old enough to run her own life, Marco. She can make her own choices for good or bad. She isn't yours to control.'

'I don't want to control her,' he snapped. 'I just don't want her to get hurt.'

'That's life I'm afraid, someone should have told you that by now.'

'She's my family and Emilio—'

'Emilio might have grown up. Don't you think you've changed over time? People do. Maybe you should give him a chance.' He opened his mouth, just like he had earlier when he was about to say something important, but he didn't speak and she couldn't stand to be there anymore. 'Goodnight, Marco. Please say goodbye to Cesca and Emilio for me.'

His mouth hung open as she strode away through the crowd and out into the cold night air. It had begun to drizzle, and the chill rain prickled her skin sending goose bumps over her bare shoulders. It cooled her anger and her hot cheeks though her temper remained high. Even in the dark Venice was beautiful, the lagoon a pool of black surrounding the floating city, the buildings lit with orange lights that highlighted the age of the city, making her feel like she was in the Renaissance and not the twenty-first century. Her beautiful mask was getting wet, and she almost turned her ankle on the uneven cobbles as she struggled home in heels that had suddenly started hurting.

The night was over, and she had a feeling that whatever had been starting between her and Marco – the special, growing connection between them – was over too.

Chapter 21

Beth's head, and heart, ached as she approached the rowing club on Sunday morning, eager to work the emotion of the night before out of her body. Coming home to Polo had provided some comfort. The cat had purred and padded her lap before settling into bed with her, curling up at her feet. She'd never been more grateful to Signor Balbo for making her take him, and she'd stroked his fur as she'd stared at the beamed ceiling and listened to the water of the canal gently run against the side of the building. But all through the night, as angry as she was with Marco for being so preoccupied with his sister and Emilio, she couldn't shake the memory of that moment on the dance floor. Her heart had pounded like a marching band. She hadn't felt this way about anyone in a long, long time, if ever really. Her feelings for Marco were real and powerful, and she'd thought his were becoming the same for her, but then it had all gone wrong.

As she approached the boathouse, the fresh air blew the night's dullness from her mind. She pulled out a one-person boat and was just hauling it onto her shoulder when he appeared out of the morning mist as if she'd somehow summoned him just by thinking about him. She huffed out a breath, unsure if she wanted to see him or not. The guilt was growing heavier, and seeing how much he was worried for his sister last night, she felt trapped by Cesca's lies. His hair was ruffled, falling in all directions, and he hadn't shaved the night's stubble from his jaw. Her unhelpful heart twinged, and she wished it would stop making her feel things for him. Life was far easier when she stayed focused on her goals and didn't allow handsome men to distract her.

'Beth,' he called, jogging towards her. She thought of ignoring him, but they had to work together, and she couldn't be childish.

'Beth!' Marco called again, waving this time as he moved closer to her.

She slowed her pace and came to a stop, the boat awkward on her shoulder.

'You're going for a row?' He pushed his hair back nervously and her heart gave an involuntary spin. 'Of course you are. Sorry. I – I was hoping to see you. I thought maybe we could go together? It's a beautiful morning,' he added sheepishly, signalling to the pale morning sky.

The sun was creeping up slowly, washing the city in

pale yellow light. The water reflected the golden tones, and banks of white cloud rolled in from the east.

'Okay.'

His smile made her stomach flip and she told herself that until he apologised she was going to be mad. 'Great. I'll take that and grab a two-man. Can you get the oars?'

He took the boat from her shoulder and before long they were out on the water again. The tension drained from her body as her arms and legs worked, her muscles burning and her heart rate increasing. Endorphins flooded her system as she looked at the pale peach of the dawn sky and listened to the movement of the water. The world was quiet and calm, her mind focused on the next stroke, on the pull of the oars and the push of her legs, on breathing in and out.

'Beth,' Marco said, panting slightly at the physical effort. As usual, he was behind her, so she couldn't see his face, but his tone was soft.

'Yes?'

'I – I'm sorry about last night. I was a terrible date.'

All Beth's senses suddenly heightened, like her hair was standing on end. First of all, he'd said date, and she loved that. And secondly, she appreciated that he'd come out and apologised and not tried to justify his actions.

A tremor underlined his words, and she listened intently as he spoke. 'After I saw Cesca, I was so worried about her and Emilio that I ruined our evening and I – I was having a wonderful time with you. I'm sorry I threw it away.'

Beth felt herself softening, her anger fading. 'I get you

don't want her to get hurt, Marco, but would it really be so bad? I thought Emilio was your best friend?'

'He is.'

'So why would it be so awful if they were dating? I know he's had a reputation in the past; Cesca told me. But maybe he's given all that up. Maybe he's in love.'

The word *love* floated in the air between them. She knew she was falling for him, and had hoped last night he was going to say the same. Would he now?

A silence settled between them, heavy and expectant, different to the ones they'd enjoyed together rowing. 'I hope Emilio has grown up,' he said eventually, 'and is ready to make a life with someone; I really do. Just not with my sister. She's always liked him, and I don't want her to get her heart broken. She acts tough but she's really very sensitive. It would hurt her too much.'

'Surely that's her decision to make?' She spoke softly, not wanting to labour the point but hoping she could make him see.

'She's been hurt enough already.'

'Are you talking about the accident?' He didn't answer and she knew she was right. 'Marco, that was a long time ago and you were both teenagers. It wasn't your fault. Accidents happen all the time. You didn't deliberately hurt your sister.'

'I'm supposed to protect her.'

'But you can't do that forever. She's a woman now. The best way to support her is to be there for her if and when she needs you.'

Marco didn't speak but his breathing increased as they sped up, the water resisting deliciously against the oars. She hoped he would believe what she said. Cesca didn't blame him for the accident, and it was time he stopped blaming himself.

'Anyway,' he said after a moment. 'I'm sorry I ruined our night. I – I was enjoying it before they interrupted us.'

Although Beth was already hot and sweaty from the rowing, heat rose up her spine. 'I was too.'

'I have another artist for us to see this afternoon, when you finish work, if that's okay.'

'Yes, yes of course.'

'Good.'

They continued rowing in silence, but it wasn't uncomfortable. Despite their difficult conversation she appreciated his apology and as they lapsed into companionable and easy quiet, she watched the sky lighten, the last remnants of night's darker colours drifting away to reveal a bright day. The red roof tiles of the buildings and the pale grey lead of the domes of St Mark's Basilica shone brighter in the shafts of light punctuating the cloud. As they slowed, she took deep, steady breaths of the salty air.

They returned to the dock and washed down the boat and oars.

'So I'll see you at, say, five?' Marco asked tentatively.

Beth nodded. 'What are you up to today?'

'I'm working on the family business,' he added. 'We need sales to pick up and I'm hoping I can convince Papa to let me try some advertising or at least contacting some local galleries to see if they'll stock some pieces.'

'I hope he agrees.'

'After your analogy, I'm hoping he'll see it – and me – differently. I wished I'd thought of it earlier.' He stepped forwards and placed a kiss on her sweaty cheek.

'That can't have been nice,' she replied, smiling.

'I wouldn't have done it if I didn't think it would be.'

With a flash of his devastating smile, he walked towards the gym and, wishing once more they hadn't been interrupted the night before, Beth followed. She might even need a cold shower this morning, if her tingling body was anything to go by.

***

As she opened *La Libreria delle Parole*, Polo leaping from his carry case and deciding to stroll around on the *fondamenta* before taking himself off, Beth breathed in the lingering smell of fresh paint and admired the neat and tidy bookstore she and Cesca had created. Yes, there was still work to do outside, but for now, she'd bask in the glory of accomplishing so much in such a short timescale.

Lolanda and Galvano were next door again and the two performers were back down the street. She wondered if their repertoire would be the same or if she'd have something new to watch today. This being her own boss was proving wonderful, and she was even enjoying making conversation with customers, seeking them out to find out if she could help and talk about the books they'd enjoyed. She could feel herself growing, like the bud of a flower opening up so its petals can feel the sun. From her chats with customers she discovered she lacked a bit of literary fiction and made a mental note to order some.

The day flew by, and she closed up the book barge as soon as she saw Marco, grabbing her coat to meet him on the bank. They would drop Polo off on the way. 'So where are we off to then?'

'Are you wearing clothes that can get dirty?'

'Ummm, yes.' She was in her usual uniform of trousers and a jumper, but as she had so many, it wouldn't matter if these got dirty. Her interest, and nerves, were piqued. 'Why?'

Marco held out his hand. 'You'll see.'

She slipped her chill fingers into the warmth of his and followed his lead as they moved through the city. They were walking towards Dorsoduro and stopped outside a pretty pottery shop. Through the window she could see pale wooden shelves lined with plates, mugs, vases and jugs. Some were plain, others brightly coloured or intricately patterned. The sign on the door said *closed* and Beth turned to Marco in alarm.

'Did we miss the appointment?' She checked the time on her phone.

'Don't worry.' He knocked, giving three loud taps on the glass of the door. Before the last one had even finished echoing through the shop, a young man appeared wearing a clay-covered apron. He had a tidy goatee and a messy man bun, and his dark brown eyes crinkled at the corners as he opened the door.

'Marco!' They did some kind of handshake-into-a-hug move and then Marco introduced Beth.

'It's lovely to meet you,' she said, following them both inside.

'I'm so pleased you've come for the class.'

'Class?' She turned to Marco who was grinning.

'When I spoke to Fabrizio about possibly selling through the book barge, he offered us a class to make something ourselves. I thought you might enjoy it and then you'd have something special of your own in case you ever return to England.'

'Oh, right. I don't plan to go back but . . . thank you!' Marco's eyes widened a little as she said this and something passed across his eyes she couldn't read. She turned to Fabrizio. 'I don't know if I'm any good at pottery but I'm happy to give it a go.'

Fabrizio smiled. 'Come through to the workshop and I'll get you both an apron.'

The apron was almost as big as Beth was, but she wrapped it tightly around her and sat at her wheel. Marco did the same, with a few other people who were there for the class.

Fabrizio dropped a lump of clay in front of her and said, 'Would you prefer me to speak in English?'

'No, Italian's fine! If everyone else is Italian, then please speak that. I'm pretty fluent and I can always ask Marco if there's a term I don't understand.'

'*Grazie*. It will be easier for my other students whose English is not so good.'

From then the class was conducted in Italian. Fabrizio sat at his own wheel showing them how to mould the clay into a basic cup shape and how to add ridges. Marco took to it quickly, the artistic tradition of his family making it easy for him. Beth, however, struggled. Her cup wasn't round; it was more of a lump with a shallow bit in the middle and the sides were thick and uneven. She wasn't going to be able to drink out of it anytime soon; that was for sure.

'Psst, Marco!'

He looked over, eyes twinkling with amusement. 'What?'

'Help me!' she mouthed, not wanting to draw attention to herself.

He manoeuvred his stool so he was sat behind her, and she felt his strong arms either side of her body. He was so close she could smell his aftershave and feel the heat of his torso. Goose bumps flew over her skin as his hands folded on top of hers, guiding her fingers to form the clay. She could see why the movie *Ghost* was famous for its clay scene. She hadn't imagined anything like this would ever happen to her and as Marco's breath brushed the back of her neck, her mind flew to what it would be like if his wonderful kisses began at the sensitive skin under her ear, reaching down her neck and shoulders to . . . Her body began to tingle, and she exhaled a shuddering breath.

She didn't know if Marco could feel it too, but his fingers trembled.

Beth glanced around, relieved to see the other students intent on their own work.

Marco spoke in a low, husky voice as though he too were struggling to control his breathing. 'There, you see. Cupping the hands gently and drawing them up gives the shape.'

His head rested against the side of hers and she mumbled, 'When did you get so good at this?'

'I don't know. Maybe it's just in my blood.'

'Right,' Fabrizio announced, eyeing Marco and Beth with a sly grin. 'Time to make the handle.'

Marco moved back to his wheel and again Beth missed the weight and warmth of him behind her. Her body sizzled from the contact. She desperately wanted this romance between them to be her future, but not only was there Cesca's secret creating a wall between them, what if he wanted children? He already knew how she felt about it but hadn't given any indication of his own feelings, and seeing him with his nieces and nephews made her wonder if he would be okay with the idea of never having a family of his own.

As they went about throwing the clay for the handle, Beth felt the barrier grow between them. The foundations had already been laid by Cesca, and now, bricks were stacking on top, pushing it ever higher.

'What are you doing tomorrow evening?' Marco asked.

'Nothing. Why?'

'I have someone else I want you to meet.'
'Another artist?'
'Yes. Can you meet me at Campo San Barnaba at seven?'
'Sure. I'll be there.'

He smiled and turned his attention to his cup. Beth's handle almost flew off, onto the person next to her and she managed to squash it before it left her wheel. She swore in English and Marco chuckled. She should really stick to selling books.

Chapter 22

The Venetian dawn was growing brighter as the seasons changed and spring grew closer. The delicate pink and blue of the sky reflected in the waters of the lagoon, gulls calling even at this early hour. The slight tang of salt and seaweed, and of damp timber carried on the air. It wouldn't be long till Easter came and the tourists began to flock to the city, the streets growing busy until they were crammed full of people. Buds were beginning to form on the trees, tiny green shoots and leaves opening up so the city would soon be blooming with wisteria blossoming and colourful flowers too. As the cafés came to life, the sweet smell of pastry and the rich aroma of coffee took over, making her mouth water, and Beth decided to stop by Giambattista's on her way back towards the book barge.

'*Ciao*, Beth,' he replied warmly as she greeted him. 'I haven't seen you for a while.'

'No, life's been . . . well it's been busy!'

'I've heard. Signor Sanna keeps me updated when he comes by. He said you were at the masquerade ball and told me the book barge is doing well. I think Signor Balbo would be very pleased.'

'Would he? I was worried he'd be upset that I've . . . decluttered so much.'

Giambattista shook his head. 'No, no, no. He always knew he had too many books. He just wasn't really a very good businessman. He is very happy now. Enjoying his retirement.'

'Does he come in here sometimes?'

'Now he has time, yes. And he travels to see his children. He is very, very happy.'

'I'm so pleased.' Beth felt a warm glow inside. Not only did she feel she would be making Signor Balbo proud with what she was doing with the book barge, but she was happy he was seeing his family and building those bridges. He had seemed so sad when they discussed it that day.

'So when can we actually celebrate the opening of your bookshop?'

'What do you mean?'

'We need a party, a celebration! A grand reopening.'

The idea hadn't occurred to Beth, and she chided herself. If she'd planned this from the beginning she would have thought of all these things, but going with the flow, while freeing, also meant losing track, it seemed. 'Do you think I should? Wouldn't it be weird as I'm already open?'

'Of course you must! You need an official opening, something people can come to.'

'That's a good idea,' she said, inhaling her coffee as her mind began to work. 'Leave it with me and I'll let you know when it is.'

She could tie it in with Easter and the start of the tourist season, maybe? She'd give it some thought.

After catching up on all Giambattista's news and listening to him rave about his new tables again, Beth grabbed two coffees and made her way to the book barge, eager to speak to Cesca. There was a lot to discuss.

'So,' Cesca said when she arrived to begin work on the upper deck. The lower deck was done, fully painted and with new shelves so they could now concentrate on the Parisian-style cabinets lining the outside. 'What are you thinking? You want an event space don't you?' She climbed up onto the deck, manoeuvring around broken wooden cabinets and dead pot plants. 'So why don't I build a stage here? Nothing fancy, just a small, raised platform where someone can give a talk or you can do an interview or something? We might be able to create more room, but I'll need to work on those cabinets on the front first to ensure people can walk around up here without tripping over and falling in the water.'

As much as she wanted to dive in and talk about her new plan for a grand reopening, there was something equally important to discuss. 'Cesca,' Beth said firmly. 'Can we talk about this later? I need to speak to you.'

Beth turned and walked inside, and Cesca followed. Beth closed the door behind her and turned the sign to *Chiuso* – closed.

'What is it?' Cesca asked nervously.

Sensing the atmosphere, Polo leapt through a small open window and disappeared for a walk. Beth motioned to the armchairs and two waiting coffees she'd purchased from Giambattista's. The fire was lit, sending a golden glow and fierce warmth through the floating bookshop, but this wasn't to be a cosy chat.

Beth took her coffee, cradling it in her lap.

Cesca lowered herself into her seat, her olive skin turning pale. 'What is it? Are you not happy with my work? Have I done something wrong? If I have I can fix it. I—'

An iciness shot down her spine. She hadn't meant to scare her friend and quickly put her mind at ease on that at least. 'No! Your work is amazing; you know I love it! I'm sorry, I didn't mean to make you think that. I – I need to talk to you about Marco and Emilio and you two.' She took a deep breath as Cesca grabbed her coffee, wrapping her fingers around the cardboard cup. She looked up to meet Cesca's deep brown eyes. 'I can't keep your secret anymore, Cesca. Marco and I, we're . . .'

'Are you dating?' she asked excitedly.

Beth nodded. 'Yes. It's very early stages but I really like him and I want to see where this goes.'

Cesca immediately leapt up and hugged her. 'I'm so happy for you!'

'I can't see him and keep this secret, Cesca. It's dishonest and as soon as he finds out he's going to hate me for lying to him.'

'You haven't lied,' she replied, dropping her eyes. 'You just haven't told the truth.'

'I've lied,' she said, firmly. 'The other night, at the masquerade ball, when you showed up, I had to parrot back what you'd said when he quizzed me about it. I might have tried not to out-and-out lie, but I have as good as and I feel terrible about it.'

'Oh.' Her eyes fell to her hands. 'I'm sorry. I didn't mean to put you in that position.'

'I know you didn't,' Beth replied, gently. 'But now you need to fix this. You have to tell him the truth. He might be angry for a while, but he also might be fine about it.'

Cesca scoffed. 'He won't. You saw his reaction at the ball. He's always been protective of me, especially since the accident.'

'He told me.'

'He did? Then he really must be in love with you.'

Beth's heart tingled. 'Either you or Emilio need to talk to him. Maybe Emilio can make it clear he's changed. You have to tell him soon, Cesca, or I will.'

She looked up to see Beth's steeliest gaze. After a second, she nodded. 'I will. I promise.'

'When? By the end of this week?'

She nodded. 'I promise. I want you to be happy too, Beth. And my brother. You both deserve it and I'm sorry if I've got in the way. I haven't meant to.' Beth hugged her friend, wishing they hadn't had to have this conversation at all. A small smile played on Cesca's lips as they made their way to the door. 'So . . . you and Marco . . . ?'

'I'm not talking about this with you. You're his sister,' Beth teased.

'It was the dress,' Cesca announced, sipping her coffee. 'I knew it would do the trick.'

Beth smiled. 'It was a great dress. So, when will this all be finished, do you think, Cesca?'

'Oh, a couple of weeks, maybe less.'

'Great.'

'Why's that?'

'Because I was thinking of planning an official opening of the Library of Words for about three weeks' time. Just in time for Easter and the start of the tourist season.'

'That's a wonderful idea! I love it! Yes, I'll definitely be done for then. Have you told Marco?'

'No, I only decided this morning!' She really was learning to go with the flow, she thought proudly. 'I just feel like I need to mark my official opening somehow.'

'You definitely should, but look, we better get moving. You've got customers waiting.'

Cesca nodded towards the window and Beth followed her gaze to see people loitering outside. Beth rushed to the door and welcomed them in. A feeling of being home, of being in the right place, wrapped around her and she added another log to the fire before heading into another conversation with a customer about the latest book they were reading and what they planned on reading next.

***

When Beth arrived at Campo San Barnaba, she'd figured they were meeting someone to do with the church. It was another famous tourist attraction in Venice known the world over. Perhaps the artist was a stained-glass artist or a candle maker. Beth suddenly decided that, at some point, she'd have a piece of glass made to replace a window in the boat: something beautiful with books and the name of the book barge. Something to really make the place special.

The evening sky was a light blue velvet, free from clouds, but as spring drew closer, the day had been warmer and that meant the evening was too, the breeze cooling but delightful after a busy day working with Cesca and serving her customers. The famous church was another landmark she hadn't been in before, too busy with work, and she stared at the beautiful white neoclassical façade, charming and elegant in the light from the street lamps. She stood next to one of the classical columns on the front of the building as Marco appeared as ruffled as he had been the other morning.

'*Mi scusi*, Beth. I'm so sorry. I got caught in a meeting that wouldn't end. Signora Cadora wants to meet me!'

'Really? That's wonderful!'

'I'm very excited.' He was smiling like a kid in front of an ice-cream shop.

'You should be. I'm so happy she got in touch.'

'Yes, and it's thanks to you.'

'No.' Beth shook her head. 'It isn't. I didn't do anything.'

He kissed her and butterflies took flight in her chest. 'It definitely is. Now, shall we go?'

'It looks closed though.'

Marco furrowed his brow in confusion. 'What does?'

She motioned behind her. 'The church?'

Marco smiled that mischievous smile of his and shook his head. 'We're not going in there. We're going over here.'

He held out his hand and she took it, the warmth of his body filtering into her fingers. He led her around the side of the church where a grizzled old man was stooped over a gondola. When he saw Marco, he rose slowly, his body unfurling as he pushed himself up using his thighs for support. His voice was gravelly and hoarse as he spoke in rapid Italian, greeting Marco.

'Beth, this is Signor Uttini, he is a gondola maker.'

'A gondola maker?' Of course she knew gondola makers existed, but she wasn't sure why Marco was introducing her to one. It wasn't as if she could display them on the book barge. They were the same size as her little floating bookshop.

'It's lovely to meet you,' she continued, but she wasn't sure how to continue the conversation and turned to Marco as a young man drew up on a gondola and pulled in next to them.

Signor Uttini motioned to the tiny boat and Marco moved towards it, holding out his hand. He was taking her on a gondola ride! Beth laughed, her excitement escaping. She'd always wanted to do this but had been waiting for the right person to do it with. And now, she'd found him.

Marco climbed into the boat confidently and Beth followed. The seating was snug, and their bodies pressed close together. Marco lifted his arm and draped it around her shoulders.

The young man handed her a blanket to place around her legs. It went over both her and Marco and, with him close to her, she felt snug and warm, leaning into his strong body.

'I thought, as you'd never had a gondola ride, you should experience one. And it is nicer when it's quiet. A gondola ride in summer is special but when you're the only people on the canal, it feels like Venice is yours alone.'

'It's a wonderful idea.'

'You're not cold?'

She shook her head. 'It's perfect.'

The gondolier popped open a bottle of prosecco and handed them both a glass. Beth sipped hers, enjoying the delicious tingle of the bubbles on her tongue. As the stars began to shine, glittering in the soft evening sky, the gondola crept peacefully and serenely through the Venice canals. They passed familiar sights and wound their way along the narrow water lanes, between houses. Beth even noticed the gondolier use his foot to steer them away from the sides rather than the oar, but he knew his craft and she felt safe and at ease, especially with Marco next to her.

'How did it go with your dad?' she asked. 'Has his attitude changed at all?'

'You know, I think it has a little. He won't admit it, but he was at least happy to listen to some of my ideas and given a few more days he might even agree.'

'That's wonderful! I'm so glad. For both of you.'

Marco tapped his glass against hers and they drank in cheers.

'My mother wants you to come for dinner again. We always have another big family meal at the end of Carnevale. I think she has a soft spot for you, especially after you charmed my papa.'

'Charmed him? I thought he wanted to kick me out.'

'He has a grumpy face. He doesn't always mean to look like that. He liked you. And she did too.'

'They're very kind to invite me.'

'Will you come?' His voice shook a little and she nodded.

Beth told him about her plans for a grand reopening. 'Perhaps some of the artists could attend and display their work and talk to people?'

'It sounds a wonderful idea.'

After a moment's silence, Marco spoke again, his voice more tremulous than before. 'Are you glad you stayed here in Venice?'

'Very.' She turned to him. 'It was a big change for me. I don't do things spontaneously. I never have. But this . . . staying here . . . it just felt right. And I'm glad I trusted my instincts for once. Nowhere has felt as home as Venice does.'

'Good. I'm glad you stayed too. I . . . I like you, Beth. Very much, but you already know that.'

The boat passed under the *Pont des Amours*, the Bridge of Lovers, and it was almost as if the world was sending her a sign, just like it had when she had lost her placement and heard the book barge was for sale. The beautiful, iconic bridge of Venice seemed to speak to her, to prompt her into taking the next step, grabbing this moment with both hands before it could fade away as it had at the masquerade ball. That same feeling of impetuosity began to fizzle in the pit of her stomach, and she turned to look at him. She felt his arm tighten around her, and she leaned forwards and pressed her lips to Marco's.

His mouth moved with hers and his hand threaded into her hair. A feeling of complete bliss washed over her, calming her nerves whilst exciting her at the same time. The kiss deepened and lingered until a moment later, they stared into each other's eyes.

Marco stroked her cheek. 'I was not expecting you to do that, but I'm very glad you did. I – I think I'm falling in love with you, Beth.'

Her breath hitched as she took in the words she'd longed to hear. 'Really?' she whispered. 'I'm falling in love with you too.'

He kissed her again and she closed her eyes, melting into the moment. She had no idea how long they stayed like that, enjoying the feel of his lips on hers, of his warm breath mixing with her own, but eventually, they returned to watching the beautiful city pass them by, drinking prosecco. Francesca would soon tell him about her and Emilio, and without that weight on her shoulders, their relationship would flourish. A voice threatened to ask about children, but she ignored it. His arm pulled her close, and she let her thoughts glide away behind her as the gondola slicked its way through the water. Tonight, there was nothing but her and Marco and the city.

Chapter 23

Beth was even more nervous as she approached Marco's parents' house. The first time she'd been here it was as Cesca's friend, and now she was going as Marco's girlfriend, even though it was still in the very early stages. On the water bus over, she'd cuddled into Marco's side, and he'd reassured her that everyone would be excited for the two of them. She desperately hoped that was the case, and though she felt a little more confident in the stylish clothes she'd finally treated herself to, something that didn't make her look older than her years, her lungs tingled with anxiety.

They were welcomed at the door by Paola, who hugged them both tightly. As before children flew out from behind her legs, wrapping themselves around Marco and tugging on his hands. Beth's worries of the other night flew straight back into her mind. Under Paola's gaze, she kept her smile firmly intact and refused to let her worries bother her this evening.

'You didn't need to bring me flowers again,' said Paola, holding her hands out for the bouquet Beth had brought with her. 'But what's this?' She pulled out a wrapped book from amongst the flowers.

'It's a book bouquet. I wanted to say thank you for your hospitality. You've been so generous inviting me again.'

Marco held out his free hand for Beth while three children pulled his other, leading him inside the house. 'I'm coming, I'm coming!' he joked, and Beth couldn't help but smile as a wide grin lifted his cheeks.

As soon as they stepped into the living room amongst the din of his brothers and sisters, and all the children, Elio moved to Beth, kissing her on both cheeks.

'Marco says you are dating now?'

'Umm, yes, that's right.'

He smiled and it transformed his features, making them softer and gentler. 'I am so pleased. I knew as soon as I saw you that you would make a good couple. It's about time he found someone.'

'Marco hasn't dated much,' Paola said, and Marco spun, his face beetroot with embarrassment.

'Mamma!'

'What? It is true!' She turned back to Beth. 'There was a girl when he was sixteen but that didn't last and then another woman – oh, three years ago?' She turned to Elio who nodded his agreement.

'Mamma!' Marco begged again, pinching the bridge of his nose.

Beth repressed a giggle.

'And what about you?' Paola asked Beth and she laughed even harder at her bluntness.

'Nothing to report, I'm afraid. I was with someone at university, but then I focused on my career and there hasn't really been anyone since.' She glanced at Marco who smiled fondly.

Discussion about exes was normally a third or fourth date thing, she'd thought. She definitely hadn't expected the inquisition from his family on only the second occasion she'd met them, but Italian families looked out for each other and she loved that about them.

There was a knock at the door and Paola bustled to get it, returning a moment later with Emilio by her side.

'We have someone else joining us today. Come in, Emilio! Get yourself a drink. And one for Beth please, as Marco is being so rude.'

Marco was currently wrestling one child off his back while another gripped his shin. He began walking, dragging the leg with the child attached and tiny giggles filled the room. He made his way to Emilio and shook his hand. 'What are you doing here?'

'Cesca invited me.' Marco didn't seem to notice the loaded glance he sent Francesca's way, or the way her eyes melted in return. 'I'm due on the road again soon and Paola makes the best *frittelle* in Murano.'

Paola tsked but swiped her tea towel at him teasingly, pleased with the comment.

Cesca joined Beth as Marco and Emilio caught up, all the while play-fighting the children with scatter cushions.

'I'm pleased you two are here, together,' Cesca said. 'We all are. I've never seen him this happy. For once his professional and personal life are going well at the same time.'

'Same for me,' Beth replied. 'And you?' she asked tentatively.

Cesca glanced at Emilio, love clear in her expression. 'I am going to tell Marco, I promise. I'm just waiting for the right time. But I will do it, maybe after dinner when he is relaxed. I know you hate keeping this secret from him. It will be done soon.'

Beth nodded and hugged Cesca. 'It'll be all right. I know it will.'

Cesca smiled as Paola bustled off back to the kitchen telling them dinner would be in fifteen minutes. A moment later, Emilio and Marco joined them.

'Shall we step outside for some air?' Marco asked Beth. 'It's hot in here.'

'I think it's all that rolling around on the floor you've been doing.'

He opened the door onto the garden and took a breath of the cold, clean air.

The di Rienzo gardens were gorgeous as spring grew closer, the garden bursting into life with green buds and flashes of colour. Birds were singing in the hedgerows and shrubs, and she could just imagine it in summer bursting with flowers, bees buzzing to and fro and the children playing on the grass.

Her fears and doubts erupted inside her like a volcano. She'd been able to ignore them indoors, focusing on Paola and Elio and making a good impression, but as she stood shoulder to shoulder with Marco, his fingers entwining with hers, she knew she had to speak before she fell even more in love with him. Before goodbye became too painful to even contemplate.

'Marco,' she said tentatively, glancing behind her to ensure the door was shut. No children were blowing raspberries on the glass or making faces this time. 'There's something I need to ask you and it's serious.'

He frowned as he turned to her. 'What is it?'

She took a deep breath. 'You remember when we first rowed together. That I was upset and trying to understand how I felt about having children.'

'I remember.' His eyes didn't move from hers and his face was so full of concern she wasn't sure she'd be able to finish.

'I've been thinking about it a lot and with my fertility issues and being asked to be godmother to Daisy and Elsa's baby, I – I think that's enough for me, you know. I don't think I see children in my future, and I need to know if that's going to be enough for you too. I see you with your nieces and nephews, and I can tell how much you love playing with them, and I don't want to start something with you knowing it might never work out because we don't want the same things.'

Stepping closer, he took her hands in his. 'I do love my nieces and nephews. I am always happy to play with them and when I find out another baby will soon join the family, I am ecstatic with excitement.'

Beth swallowed and it was heavy and hard, as if all her hopes had turned to stone and she was pushing them down into her stomach.

'But I think I am like you, really. I love being around them all for a while, but I don't think I see children in my future either.'

Beth's head shot up, tears stinging her nose and eyes. 'Really? You mustn't lie to me, Marco, to try and make me feel better. I want you to have the future you want and if that involves children then you should go and have that. Even if that's without me.'

'The only future I want is one with you in it; that's all I know right now. I like my brothers' children, but I have no wish to have my own. There is so much I want to do still, a whole world to see and explore. My heart doesn't . . . what do you say? Twinge?'

The way he said it made her giggle.

'I don't have a yearning for children. All I want is for you and me to be happy and be together.'

Relief flooded Beth's system, and she quickly wiped the tears from her cheeks as Marco engulfed her in a hug. She looked into his beautiful ice-blue eyes and kissed him. She knew it was strange to have such a serious conversation so early in a relationship, but she couldn't deny how much better she felt. She could throw herself into this thing with her whole heart. There was no need to hold any part of herself back.

The door suddenly flew open, and Paola stared sternly at Marco. 'Did you make her cry? What have you said? Apologise at once.'

Beth laughed. 'I'm fine, Paola. It was just the wind making my eyes water.'

Paola scowled, unconvinced but instead, she encouraged them inside. 'It's time for dinner.'

Marco kissed her again as they moved to the dining room and sat down next to each other. As before the table was laid with more food than they could eat. Some dishes were repeated, but this time, instead of lamb, there were two roast chickens, and Beth couldn't wait to dive in. The various vegetable and pasta accompaniments were there too and it was even harder to decide where to start: with the beautifully seasoned and roasted vegetables, or the delicately flavoured risotto and pastas. Beth loaded her plate as much as she could without seeming greedy and tucked in.

Conversation was mostly in Italian and Beth enjoyed being surrounded by such a wonderful, loving family.

'So, Emilio,' Elio said. 'When are you back on the road?'

'From tomorrow.'

Beth noticed him glance at Cesca, who kept her eyes

down. The sadness in her posture made her want to reach out and comfort her friend.

'We will miss seeing you.'

Paola nodded her agreement.

'Behave yourself, won't you?' teased Marco, and Cesca's head shot up.

'I will.'

'I'll believe that when I see it.'

Seeing Cesca's eyes narrow and her mouth set in a tight line, Beth's stomach sank. *Not here,* she begged. *Please not here. After dinner. Not now.* But before she could send any mental signals or flash any warning signs with her eyes, Cesca had opened her mouth.

'Actually, there's something I wanted to tell you. Emilio and I are together.'

The delicious food Beth had wolfed down turned to ash in her stomach and her mouth dried. She widened her eyes at Cesca, but she was too busy looking at the numerous faces of her family gathered around the enormous dining table.

The table fell instantly silent.

'What do you mean?' Marco asked, his teeth gritted, his jaw tight.

Emilio wouldn't meet his friend's eye, and it was Cesca who continued. 'I mean that we're dating. And . . . we have been *exclusive* for a while now.'

Cesca glanced at Beth and Marco followed her gaze, lines appearing on his forehead as he frowned. Her heart stopped beating as she worried what he'd say but he turned his attention to his best friend.

'How can you do this, Emilio? You don't – you don't want relationships.'

'I didn't before,' Emilio said, his neck red and blotchy with embarrassment, his eyes darting around the table. 'But I do now. Cesca is an amazing woman.'

She had to admire his honesty and the sincerity with which he spoke. She just hoped Marco and his family would feel the same way. Paola and Elio's gazes softened, but Marco remained cold. His face a frozen mark of disdain.

'Emilio,' Paola said gently. 'Do you promise me that you love my daughter?'

'I do, Paola. With all my heart. I know I used to think of her as Marco's annoying little sister when we were growing up, but since I've come back I see what a clever, beautiful, amazing, talented woman she is. She makes me laugh, she makes me feel like a better person when we're together, and I want to be a better person for her. There is no one else for me but her.'

Beth's heart melted. The speech had hit the mark for Paola and Elio who looked at each other and then nodded. 'Then you can see Cesca. We will allow it,' Paola said.

'But if you hurt her—' Elio began.

'I won't. I promise. I'm not – I'm not like that anymore. I was young and stupid. Now I realise what love is.'

All the air seemed to escape from Beth's lungs in a huge exhalation that she felt deep down in her belly. Everyone turned to Marco, knowing his opinion mattered just as much. The silence was deafening and Beth felt dread press down on her lungs.

When Marco spoke, his words were hard and unflinching. 'You have slept with more women than I can count. Women in every city, in every region. You used to boast about it to me. How do you think you're good enough for my baby sister?'

'She knows about my past – about how stupid I've been – but I'm not like that anymore. I was too full of my own importance and now I know that I'm lucky to have found someone as good as she is. I won't hurt her, Marco, I promise. I will never betray her in any way. We are honest with each other.'

'But not honest with me?'

'How could we be honest with you?' Cesca cut in. 'You never forgive people for their mistakes. You never forgive yourself for your mistakes. The accident was so long ago, Marco; it's fine.'

'It's not just about that and you know it.'

Beth felt that she'd missed something. What else could Marco be talking about?

'Marco, no one is perfect. We didn't keep this from you to hurt you. We just knew you wouldn't understand.'

'I don't understand,' he shouted, standing from the table. 'You know what he's like, Cesca. He's incapable of being faithful.'

'I am not,' Emilio replied. His tone was firm but not

aggressive, determined to defend himself but not argue. 'Not anymore. I know I will have to prove it to you, but please give me the chance. Your parents have given me their blessing. Can't you—'

'No, I can't.'

'See!' Cesca said, staring straight at Beth. 'I told you he wouldn't understand.'

Beth heard Marco's sharp inhalation, and all the blood flew from her face. Her breathing quickened as the adrenalin pushed its way into her bloodstream and the flight-or-fight instinct kicked in. She wanted to run from the table, from Marco's fearful, hurt expression. Every feature on his beautiful face screamed of the pain he was feeling. Pain she'd inflicted, even though she hadn't ever wanted to. She felt sick, the wonderful dinner roiling around inside her and turning to stinging, bitter bile.

'You knew?' The words came out as a mumbled whisper, as though his inability to believe meant he couldn't form the words.

'I—'

'I needed to confide in someone,' Cesca said. 'Beth told me to tell you straight away, but I refused because I knew you'd be like this.' Tears fell down Cesca's cheeks, and both Emilio and Paola went to comfort her.

Marco's sisters-in-law stood and began shuffling the children away from the table, their husbands following.

Cesca continued to try and save Beth, but she could see

from his face it was hopeless. 'I asked her to keep this a secret before you got together; you cannot blame her for this.'

'That's exactly how it was,' Beth said almost pleadingly. 'I didn't want to keep anything from you.'

'At the masquerade ball, did you know?' Marco's ice-blue eyes pinned on her and she couldn't lie. He deserved the truth, however bad it made her look and feel.

'Yes. I'm sorry.'

'You lied to me.'

'Son—' Elio said.

'You lied to me! How many times could you have told me, and you didn't? You knew how I felt about them. How I worried for Cesca, but you didn't say anything.'

'It wasn't my place to say anything, and as soon as we started . . . this . . . I told Cesca if she didn't tell you soon, then I would.'

'So you decided today? In front of my family? You decided to embarrass me.'

Cesca poked her head out from between her mother and Emilio's arms. 'She didn't know I would do it today. I didn't know I would do it today. I thought maybe after dinner I'd speak to you calmly but—'

'I told you I . . .' He swallowed heavily and stared at Beth. 'I think you should go.' His mum and sister gasped.

'No!' Paola cut in. 'She is our guest.'

'Then I will go.'

Before Beth could move he stormed out and slammed

the front door behind him. The burn of humiliation flew up Beth's spine, like her blood was on fire.

'I'm so sorry,' Cesca cried, tears falling down her face. 'I'm so sorry, Beth.'

Beth swallowed hard and tried to gather what remained of her dignity. Paola bustled over and embraced her. 'My son is a stubborn, stupid man sometimes. He will soon come round and apologise. I'm sorry for this. Truly. This is not how we normally behave.'

'No, I'm sorry. I—' Beth tried to breathe but she could feel the tears stinging the back of her nose, growing in her eyes. She had to get out. 'I should go. I'm so sorry.'

Numbly she gathered her coat and bag, and despite his family asking her to stay and apologising again and again for Marco's behaviour, she stumbled outside, towards the *vaporetto* and home.

Chapter 24

The tears came as soon as Beth had made it inside her beautiful flat: the one Marco had helped her secure. Great heaving sobs escaped as she poured herself a glass of wine in her small, sweet kitchen, and changed into her pyjamas in her wonderful, beamed bedroom. The waters of the canal splashed against the building as she pulled her pyjamas over her head and wrapped herself in her fluffy dressing gown. As she grabbed a book from the shelf, eager to slide into its pages and forget the world she was currently in, Polo followed her everywhere she went, knowing something was desperately wrong.

How could they have gone from knowing they were so right for each other to this in a matter of hours? The worst thing was, while she hated the way Marco had reacted, she knew that in some ways he was right. She'd had opportunities to tell him the truth, and she hadn't taken them. He had every right to feel betrayed, and if the situation were reversed she'd feel the same way.

As she slumped on the sofa and pulled a blanket over her, there was only one thing to do: call her best friends.

Beth tried to get herself together as it rang but as soon as their happy faces popped up on the screen she dissolved into tears again.

'Oh my God!' Elsa screeched. 'What's happened?'

'What's going on?' Daisy echoed. 'Who do I need to punch?'

Considering Daisy was normally the gentle, calm one, Beth laughed. The pregnancy hormones were clearly kicking in already.

'That's better,' Daisy added. 'Take a deep breath. Now, what's up, Bethy?'

'It's Marco.'

'The guy who we said was into you, but you were sure wasn't?'

She nodded.

Elsa's angry face filled the screen. 'Has he done something?'

Beth wiped her nose. 'We were just . . . something was starting between us. He took me on a gondola ride, and we kissed, and I went to meet his family and then everything exploded.'

'What do you mean?'

Polo curled into a ball next to her, leaning his body against her legs and she pushed her fingers into his soft grey fur. She told them everything about Cesca and Emilio and how she'd been keeping their secret, how it had all come out at the family dinner. 'And now Marco feels I've betrayed him and said I should leave.'

'Well that's a bit bloody rude,' Daisy said, her face lined through scowling. 'Honestly, if I had his number I'd ring him and tell him to never speak to you again. Bloody cheek—'

'Daisy—' Elsa said, but was ignored,

'It's not your fault *his* sister put you in a difficult position and, to be honest, you were friends with *her* first—'

Elsa tried again. 'Daisy—'

'Of course your loyalty is going to be to her and not just some random man you've only just met.'

Even though they'd been flirting with the L word.

Elsa shoved a glass of water at Daisy who took it. 'Calm down. You've gone all red.'

'How can I calm down when he's made our friend cry like that?' She pointed to the screen.

Daisy was right, and whilst she understood Marco being annoyed and upset that she'd known, he hadn't even let her explain. Anger began to grow inside her, drying her tears.

'I can't believe I'm normally the one getting worked up,' Elsa said, 'and this time it's you.'

'Sorry, it's the hormones.'

'But I do agree with everything Daisy's said. It's fair enough he's upset but he should have given you the chance to explain. What happened when he asked you to leave his house? What were his family like?'

'They were shocked, but so nice to me. His mum gave me a hug and told me she was on my side. But—'

'But it doesn't make you feel any better?'

She shook her head. Marco and Cesca had hinted at something else being responsible for his feelings, something she didn't know about, and though she wondered what that could be, it didn't stop the pain shooting through her chest. 'I've never been heartbroken before,' she sobbed.

'No, you haven't really, have you? Sucks, doesn't it, Bethy? Do you want us to come out?'

'No! I don't think Daisy's supposed to fly. Are you?'

'I don't care what they say, I'll do what I need to do for my friend, thank you very much.'

Elsa's eyes goggled. 'Okay. You need to take a minute.'

Everyone erupted into laughter and Beth continued. 'You're not flying out. I'm pretty sure you're not supposed to fly when pregnant and especially not with IVF and everything you've gone through. I'll be fine. I just—' She swallowed down the lump in her throat. 'I just need some time to get over this.'

'If you're sure. You're not thinking of coming home are you?'

She was home already. Venice was home with its winding streets, historic buildings, canals and salty air. This gorgeous little apartment had felt more like a home than anywhere she'd ever been before. She loved that she could dip her fingers into the canal from her bedroom window, that she sometimes ducked to avoid the beams even though she was nowhere near hitting them, that Polo was here snuggled up to her. She loved her book barge: the Library of Words and this new career she was carving for herself. One she'd never imagined in a million years. She had a new wardrobe, a new outlook, she was growing, and she wasn't finished yet.

Beth shook her head. 'No, I don't want to leave Venice. I – I feel like my soul is here, in its history and its culture. I think if I left, I'd feel like a part of me was missing. I've never felt so connected with anywhere.'

Or anyone, her brain added.

'And I was just planning a grand reopening of the book barge. I'm not throwing away everything I've achieved here.'

'Good. And there are other fish in the sea,' Elsa added. 'Venice must be full of gorgeous Italian men. It is in the movies anyway. All of Italy is full of gorgeous Italian men. You'll find another one.'

The problem was she didn't want another one. She wanted Marco and he was gone.

'Time will fix this,' Daisy said calmly.

'I hope so,' Beth replied, but the heroes in her novels had nothing on Marco and she was sure most real men wouldn't either. As Marco's smiling face, his ice-blue eyes, strong jaw and dark hair appeared in her mind's eye, she wasn't convinced at all that time could do anything other than cause her pain.

Chapter 25

In an attempt to distract herself from her heartbreak and the aching in her spirit, Beth concentrated on nothing but the book barge and her reopening celebrations for the next few days. Saturday morning dawned and Lolanda and Galvano were back next to her, the fruit and veg seller on the other side. They all greeted each other warmly and she allowed herself to be comforted by the sense of community around her. Her heart hurt whenever she thought of Marco and seemed to be tender the rest of the time, even when she wasn't actively thinking of him, but she focused on her work and each day hoped the pain would lessen.

Cesca hadn't been round either, and Beth was unsure what to make of that. Was it guilt or embarrassment keeping her away? Beth hoped it wasn't either. While she was still a little annoyed at the way Cesca had gone about telling everyone, she wanted to be there to support her friend and had written several messages, only to delete them because she didn't know if it was too soon or what exactly to say. She'd resolved that if she'd heard nothing by the end of the day, she'd contact her this evening and make sure she was okay. Maybe invite her for coffee or for lunch at her apartment. They didn't even have to talk about Marco, though she was itching to know how he was and if he was missing her as much as she was missing him.

The smell of Lolanda's rich coffee drifted on the air towards her, and she could already taste it as she went to grab a cup before opening the bookshop. The day was bright and sunny, warmer than any they'd had so far, and the sunshine lifted her spirits. With Carnevale over, Beth had wondered if it would be quiet, but Lolanda, who clearly had more experience than her, was convinced it would still be busy.

'It will be a good day,' Lolanda said, passing over the takeaway cup and eyeing the sky. 'But you should enjoy this time of year. Only a month to go and then it is busy, busy, busy until the end of the summer. You will long for days like today then.'

'I'm sure I will,' Beth replied.

Venice in summer was spectacular, even if it was packed so full it was hard to move. But the idea of being at the book barge through the busiest months, with the sun beating down on her as she flitted in and out, speaking to customers both outside and in, sent a bolt of excitement through her, which for the first time in days actually lifted her mood. For a second, she forgot the ache in her heart, the pain, like a stitch, that wouldn't go away as she pictured locking the door and heading back to her apartment. Maybe stopping at a restaurant on the way home before lounging on her sofa, examining the age-old beams overhead before choosing something to watch on TV. It seemed perfect. But was missing a key piece: Marco.

She sipped her coffee, focusing on the flavour and wishing for the respite she'd had of moments before as her chest constricted and her heart squeezed.

'Do you hire extra help in the summer?' she asked, eager to think about something else.

'Sometimes,' Lolanda nodded. 'We have a daughter. She comes home from university and helps, but not always. Students . . . they are lazy!'

Beth laughed. 'I'll look forward to meeting her then.'

She moved back to her barge and double-checked all the stock she had was available and on display. She'd have to buy some more commercial fiction soon, she thought happily, and might even perhaps think of something to do with the remaining non-fiction she'd inherited. Despite the brighter day, the barge was still a little dark in places and Beth turned on the lamps and lit the fire. Polo had already curled up on the armchair and was happily asleep after devouring his breakfast.

As Lolanda had forecast, it was busy as the sunny weather drew more and more people from their homes.

With the sun and breeze warmer, Beth didn't need to light the fire and enjoyed a few moments on the canal side to breathe in the cool, fresh air. The day passed quickly with lots of book sales and faces she recognised. It seemed that the local community, as much as the tourists, liked what she was stocking, and she loved catching up with people and asking what they wanted to read next.

At the end of the day, she'd just finished counting the takings and getting ready to leave when there was a knock on the door. Beth stood up and opened it, surprised to see Cesca, and for a moment they stared at each other, then Beth realised she was being rude.

'Hi! Umm . . . come in.' She backed down the set of stairs and put Polo's carry case down on the floor. He meowed but soon settled again, having got used to their strange routine. She slipped off her coat.

'I can come back tomorrow if you were just going home,' Cesca replied, toying with her hands.

'No, no, that's fine. How are you?'

Cesca's lip wobbled. 'Not great. Marco, Emilio, the family . . . things are . . . strained and I didn't want to lose your friendship too.' She quickly swiped a tear from her cheek and Beth rushed to her friend and engulfed her in a hug.

'You won't! I'm sorry I haven't texted. I didn't know what to say and then I thought, right, I'll message her tonight if I haven't heard anything—'

'I'm the one who should be sorry. It was stupid of

me to say something at dinner. I really did mean to do it afterwards. I should have kept my mouth shut and spoken to Marco alone but—'

'What's done is done.' Beth tried to keep the wobble from her voice but failed and Cesca raised her head. Seeing her friend's concerned gaze sent tears into Beth's eyes and she turned away, refusing to let them fall.

'Do you – do you fancy a drink? I can go and get some wine.'

'That sounds like a good idea. We need to talk this through.'

Cesca went off, and Beth opened Polo's case so he could roam around, but not wanting him to escape for hours on end, she made sure the doors and windows stayed closed. After a few minutes, Cesca returned with two bottles of wine and had even stopped in at a deli, grabbing some bags of food to snack on. Beth found two mugs and Cesca poured them both a drink. With the bread, breadsticks, meats and dips between them, they relaxed back into the armchairs, the setting sun sending golden sunlight through the windows.

Knowing there was no easy way to start the conversation, Beth said, 'So . . . ?' and waited for Cesca to begin wherever she felt comfortable.

'So . . . as you can imagine it all went mad after you left – which I'm so sorry for. Marco shouldn't have done that.'

'No, he shouldn't. But I understand why he did. He felt betrayed and I was in his home.'

'No. That is not the Italian hospitality we're proud of here. Mamma was so angry with him. She hit him with her tea towel after you'd left.'

'So he came back?'

Cesca nodded. 'About . . . I don't know, fifteen minutes later. He arrived back – I think he might have been looking for you – and the first thing she did was hit him with the tea towel. It hurt him.'

'Good.' Beth managed a smile, but the scene playing out in her head caused her more than a little pain. She could picture his stricken face, feel his hurt even though she hadn't purposely caused it. And she was angry too. Angry that he hadn't heard her out or accepted she'd never wanted to be put in such a difficult position. 'How is he now? And how are things with you and Emilio?'

'Mamma and Papa had a long conversation with Emilio and are convinced he's changed. They see what I see. But Marco . . . he will not accept it. He knows Emilio has had a lot of flings, but he won't believe that he loves me. It is possible that Emilio has fallen in love with me. Why won't he see it?'

'I'm not surprised Emilio loves you. There's nothing not to love. But you know Marco doesn't want you to get hurt. You're his baby sister.'

'Even though I'm in my mid-twenties! I'm not a baby anymore. My life isn't really any of his business.'

'No, it isn't, but it won't stop him caring. Besides, that's not the Italian way, is it.'

Beth thought of what else was said as she and Cesca sipped their wine. It was a rich, delicious red and the smoothness slipped down her throat, instantly relaxing some of the tension from her shoulders. Beth felt herself relax, grateful that she and Cesca were finally able to talk about what happened. But something had been mentioned, something she wasn't aware of, another reason for Marco behaving the way he had. She was just about to ask when Cesca said: 'You need to know though, that I've told Marco that it was all my fault you couldn't say anything. I told him that you'd begged me to tell him so many times and I'd refused. I've tried to explain that he shouldn't be angry with you, but with me instead.'

'And what did he say?'

'I said all this at the family dinner, but he didn't reply. He just looked at Emilio like he wanted to kill him, stood up, and left without saying a word. No one has heard from him since.'

Beth's head shot up. 'No one?'

Cesca shook her head. 'He's come here and got on with his work. He's done this before.'

'When?'

Cesca sipped her drink. 'The reason Marco got so angry – the reason why he struggles with trust and letting people in is not just because of the accident we had when we were children, but because he had a business before this one. It was doing the same sort of thing – PR for local artists – but was with someone else – another friend—'

'Male or female?' Beth asked, unable to stop herself.

'Male. But they left, leaving him with debt they'd racked up without him knowing and he had to face the consequences. That business folded and he started a new one on his own. Papa wanted him to come into the family business after the first PR firm fell apart, but Marco wouldn't. I know he began working on the business side rather than blowing the glass because of the accident, but I honestly think he likes it more. He's always wanted to stand on his own two feet and so he tried again. Papa thought it was a bad idea, and they argued over it a lot.' Cesca paused and Beth's mind was a whirlwind of thoughts. 'Since then, he's struggled to open up to anyone. To trust them. And I think that's why he's so angry with Emilio. He feels another friend has betrayed him.'

'And me too,' Beth said as more of Marco's reaction fell into place. She still couldn't forgive him for not letting her explain, but this did at least make his reaction make more sense.

'Why didn't he tell me all this?' Beth asked. Her heart ached as she understood why this situation had hurt him so much.

'He didn't want anyone to know. He didn't want to talk about it. Ever.' She pushed her hand against her forehead. 'I've made such a mess of everything. I knew all this, and I still didn't tell him about me and Emilio. But he shouldn't have taken it out on you. That was wrong of him and all my fault.'

'Not all your fault. He's a grown man responsible for his own actions. But he has hurt me. A lot.'

'Have you tried contacting him?'

Beth shook her head. 'I wouldn't know where to begin. Not yet.'

'I've ruined things for you. I'm so sorry.' Cesca reached out and took Beth's hand. 'I'll do everything I can to make it right, I promise.'

'I'm not sure there's much you can do.'

'Are we . . .' Beth looked up when she didn't finish the sentence and Cesca tried again. 'Are we still friends?'

'Of course we are!'

'We shouldn't let men get in the way again.'

'No. Definitely not.' Beth raised her mug full of wine. 'Let's drink to that.'

'I will speak to Marco again though. Try and make him see he shouldn't be angry with you.'

'It might just be better to let things lie.'

'You're not giving up on him, are you?' Cesca's expression was so pained and panicked Beth felt instantly guilty.

'I don't know,' she admitted. 'But it takes two people to make a relationship work. And if he's not ready, or can't forgive me, I can't make him. And whilst I understand, he's hurt me too by not listening to me. I've done so much this year already – changing my life, making decisions for my future – I refuse to sit around waiting for any man. Even one as handsome as your brother.'

Beth's words were stronger than she felt, but at least

she'd tried her best to believe them. She stared out of the book barge's window, seeing the waters of the canal drift by, splashing the bank and the houses on the other side.

'You will still come to the big race in two weeks, won't you?'

'What big race?'

'Haven't you seen the posters all over the rowing club?'

'Sorry, I've had my head down just getting to the showers or getting out on the water.'

She forced herself not to relive images of her and Marco rowing together, talking as the sun rose.

'It's a local competition between us and a rowing club from Giudecca.'

Giudecca was another local island, even smaller than Murano. Another place Beth knew she should visit.

'I'm not sure I can. I should probably be open as much as possible.' The thought of seeing Marco again was too much.

'Really? I was hoping we could row in the women's race together.'

'Me?'

'Yes! You went out on the water with Marco, didn't you? And you're very good. If nothing else, it could be fun. Please? I haven't got anyone else I can ask, and I would like to do it with my best friend.'

Beth looked up at Cesca's face, so sweet and shy. Whilst she had Daisy and Elsa, Cesca was her best friend here in Venice and she'd loved going shopping for the ball gown and new clothes with her. But this was a lot to ask, especially as it could mean seeing Marco. 'Cesca, I—'

'Pleeeeeese? Emilio goes away again after that, and I won't see him for months. Please come? I know I have no right to ask but I don't want to row with anyone else, and I tell you what, I will not charge as much for renovating the top deck of the book barge if you agree to race with me. And you can leave straight after if Marco is there. I'm not even sure he will be.'

'You're resorting to bribery?' Beth smiled.

'I am. You've left me no choice. Please.'

Beth closed her eyes and exhaled a long, slow breath. With any luck, Cesca would be right and Marco wouldn't attend, and she did quite fancy racing for the first time, especially with her friend. 'Fine.'

Polo jumped onto her lap and pushed his head onto her hand, demanding attention.

What would she do if Marco was there? Beth studied Polo's thick grey fur. She was going to have to speak to him sooner or later and at least this way she had two weeks to compose herself. With any luck her heartache would have faded away entirely by then, but was that even possible? As it stabbed once more, as strongly as one of Polo's claws catching her skin, she knew it wasn't. It wasn't possible in the slightest.

Chapter 26

As she worked at the book barge the next day, this time with Cesca continuing on the upper deck, making a small stage and reshaping some of the Parisian-style cabinets so there was lots of room, a message popped up on Beth's phone from Marco.

She read it with trembling fingers, hoping above all it was an apology. It wasn't and that made her both angry and sad. Instead, Marco asked for her to meet him so he could introduce a new artist. At least he was still honouring their agreement, but nerves fluttered around her stomach at the prospect of seeing him again. She'd have to control her treacherous feelings, both physical and emotional, and she absolutely wouldn't think about that special, earth-moving kiss on the gondola, or that he'd said he was falling in love with her.

'Are you all right?' asked Cesca as Beth stacked shelves, unspeaking.

'Marco wants me to meet him. A new artist.'

'Will you go?'

'I have to. I need to for my business.' She checked her phone. 'It's pretty soon, so I better get going.'

'Good luck,' Cesca called. 'I hope he apologises.'

I do too, she thought, ignoring the slight queasiness rising into her throat.

When she arrived at the location Marco had given, her she frowned. It was an old, battered building, like a warehouse, and given the state of it, she couldn't imagine what kind of artist worked here. Marco stood stiffly, his hands in his pockets, his feet planted. A smattering of stubble clung to his jaw and when his blue eyes spotted her, she was sure, just for a moment, that they softened. He smiled nervously and scuffed his foot along the pavement. Just seeing him made her feel whole, like a broken piece of her had been put back together. She forced herself to smile through the pain and decided to remain professional, as she would have done at the gallery.

'Hi. Thanks for setting up this meeting. Who are we seeing?'

'I thought you might occasionally want something different from the traditional Venetian crafts, so I wanted to introduce you to a new modern artist.'

'Oh. Right.' She wasn't a huge fan of modern art. Give her the classics anytime.

'I know you like classical paintings but trust me.' He

smiled shyly again, and she hated that he knew her so well. 'He makes canvases large and small using spray paints.'

'Spray paints?' she squeaked. 'Like graffiti?'

Marco laughed at her look of disdain, and the glimpse of the man she'd been falling in love with appeared once more. 'I wouldn't pull that face when he shows you his work.'

Her hand went to her mouth. 'Sorry. But I'm really not sure about this.'

'I promise, if you don't like it, you don't have to stock it. I will come up with an excuse.'

'All right then.'

He watched her for a second too long, but then tiny frown lines appeared on his forehead and he seemed to gather himself, the softness of moments before fading. He cleared his throat.

'Shall we go in?' she asked, keeping her tone neutral.

'Yes, of course.' He opened the door for her.

The smell of canned spray paint hit her like a fist in the face, and she coughed instantly.

A young man with low-hanging trousers and a thick, long beard, removed a mask from his face. '*Mi scusi*! I open windows.'

He ran to two small windows on the side wall and cast them as wide as they would go, which wasn't actually that wide and did little to remove the dense, pungent smell. Marco went back to the door and wedged it open to allow some more air in, then made the introductions.

'Riccardo, this is Beth.'

'Pleased to meet you,' he replied, wiping his hand down his side before holding it out for her to shake.

Beth took it, secretly charmed by his manners. He was younger than she'd expected, but then she hadn't expected to meet a young man spray painting graffiti onto a canvas today. 'What are you working on?' she asked, eager to put him at his ease.

'Let me show you.' He took her to a large canvas almost the size of the book barge that was propped against the wall. 'It's called *Fear the Pigs*.'

'Right.'

Marco coughed to hide his laugh.

'But for the book barge, I was thinking you'd want something more mainstream? I have these—' This time he moved to the other side of the room and much smaller canvases stacked against the wall. 'They're all dry.' He motioned for her to look, so she did.

These were more like pieces by Cubist artists like Picasso and she could definitely see a place for these on the book barge.

'I like these very much.'

Marco smiled, and as his eyes met hers, she had to look away. 'Shall we talk business then?' he said, and she could feel him pulling away from her once more.

After the discussion, Beth was pleased to escape into the cool afternoon air. She took deep breaths, clearing her lungs of the fumes. The fresh, salt smell from the nearby canal was far nicer mixed with seaweed and brine.

'Right,' Marco said, shuffling awkwardly. 'I will email you a contract and the details, like I have for the others.'

So that was it, she thought as disappointment hit her. Back to business.

'Sure. I'll look out for it in my inbox.'

She felt stupid being so formal when it wasn't long ago they'd kissed under the Lovers Bridge. Unable to bear this strained, difficult atmosphere, she turned to go.

'Beth—' Marco said, and she spun back to see as much turmoil in his eyes as she felt inside.

'Yes?' she asked quietly.

He studied her for a moment, then dropped his eyes.

She didn't know where it came from, but Beth found the words tumbling out of her mouth in an attempt to clear the air. 'Francesca told me about what happened with your business partner. How that betrayal hurt you.'

His face grew stony, his voice harsh. 'She shouldn't have said anything.'

'She was just trying to explain—'

'Explain what?'

'Why you were so upset about her and Emilio keeping their relationship from you.' His eyes met hers, but a shutter had come down over them.

She glanced around, wondering how to continue. The battered workshop, the *paline* mooring posts in the water, this was the city of love and yet, her heart was being ripped apart.

'I just wanted to say,' she continued, 'I understand

why it hurt you so much and – and I will always remain professional no matter what's happened between us.'

'Beth—' His voice softened and shook. He swallowed.

Her heart beat faster as she waited for him to speak.

'I will always be professional too—'

Her heart shattered all over again. So it was definitely over. She turned away, tears in her eyes and her chin wobbling, anger mixing with the pain and grief. This was it. Her last slot filled. With their professional relationship fulfilled there was no reason to see or speak to him again. The pain stabbed even deeper, ripping through her lungs. It took everything she had not to look back.

Chapter 27

When race day came, the pier by the boathouse was busier than Beth had ever seen it. Families of the local rowers had pitched up with chairs and picnics and were welcoming the people from Giudecca. All Cesca's family were there, including her nieces and nephews who were running around, waving little flags and holding balloons. Everyone had come out for the event. Beth watched before approaching, her eyes scanning the crowd for Marco. When she couldn't see him, a mix of both relief and sadness sent her early breakfast roiling around her stomach.

Cesca stood by Emilio, cuddled into his side, and they beckoned Beth over. Cesca's parents bustled over as soon as they saw her and wrapped Beth in an enormous hug as though she were still part of the family. Paola immediately apologised for Marco's behaviour, tutting and rolling her eyes.

'He's closing himself off from everyone again,' she said regretfully. 'He did this after the accident and after his business failed. I wish he wouldn't. Family should rely on each other, but when his friend left him with all that debt, it was very hard for him.'

'He should have come back to the family business and given all the rest of it up,' Elio replied.

Paola flung her arms in the air, speaking in Italian. 'That's what you said then and look how that helped matters.'

To stop them having an argument, Beth turned to Emilio. 'Cesca said you go away again after this?'

His grip on Francesca tightened as sorrow washed his usually cheerful features. 'Yes. I wish I didn't have to, but there are regionals coming up.'

'He needs to prove he should keep his place in the national team,' Cesca added.

'That seems like a lot of pressure.'

'It is, but mostly I will miss Cesca. She is my good luck charm. We're figuring out how we can make it all work and be together as much as possible.'

Beth smiled at the love so evident between them and wished Marco was there to see it too. It might have changed his mind if he had.

Cesca and Emilio both stiffened and she could tell as they looked over her shoulder that Marco had arrived and was walking towards them. Beth thought about scurrying away and getting ready for the race, knowing seeing him again would only hurt, but she didn't want to look like she was avoiding him, even though that was exactly what she would be doing.

'Son!' Paola said to Marco, as his nieces and nephews swarmed around him. Marco smiled and hugged them, then his mum. When his eyes landed on Beth, his face retained its softness, and she found herself smiling, just as he did.

'Beth,' he said, throwing her off by speaking to her first. 'I'm so glad you're here. I've arranged Signor Zambelli and Riccardo to be at your grand opening. They're very excited.'

That he'd done that for her without asking warmed her broken heart. 'Thank you. I appreciate it.'

'Also, there is something I need to say.'

'Yes?' She held her breath, waiting for him to speak, her body tingling with anticipation.

'Beth, I—'

'We have to go!' Cesca shouted as their race was called. She began tugging on Beth's arm, but there was no way Beth could move now. Something was different: she could see it in Marco's eyes, in the set of his mouth and the tilt of his head. She had to hear what he had to say.

'Yes?' she asked Marco imploringly.

'I—'

The announcer called the race again and Beth glanced at Cesca.

'Come on, Beth, or we'll be disqualified.'

'I'll still be here when you get back,' Marco said softly, and she almost melted at the need in his expression.

Cesca pulled her away and before she knew it, she was

following Marco's sister to their boat. As she looked over her shoulder it was to see Marco watching them. He held up his hand, two fingers crossed, wishing her luck, and the love that had been growing for him rushed back stronger than ever.

Focusing on the race, Beth climbed into their boat and took her position on the water. They'd had a few training rows but nerves still sprung up into her throat and she took a moment to breathe deeply and fill her body with oxygen. The water was calm, the day clear and bright. It was perfect spring weather, perfect for her first race.

'We can win this,' Cesca said, pumped with excitement and anticipation. She was in front of Beth, so all Beth saw was the back of her head, her ponytail bobbing as she nodded to her own words. 'We can do this.'

The countdown started and before she knew it they were off, rowing in time, breathing hard, lungs burning, legs aching. Beth gripped the oar and concentrated on breathing in and out with each stroke, pushing on her exhalations, relaxing on her inhalations. They were in the lead, but another boat was creeping up. Beth glanced at it from the corner of her eye. They were falling behind and needed to up their pace.

'Let's go!' Beth cried and though speaking seemed to suck all the air from her lungs, she felt her body move up a gear and find the extra push they needed as exhilaration took over. She struggled to breathe rhythmically, but soon they were moving quicker, edging past the leader by nothing more than an inch.

Cheers resounded as they crossed the finish line, Cesca's

family the loudest of all while other members of the rowing club clapped and whooped. They'd done it. They'd won.

Beth's eyes were drawn to Marco who was joining in with the celebrations. Their eyes met as she stepped out of the boat, and she and Cesca made their way towards them. Though she was red and sweaty, with hair plastered to her head and perspiration falling down her cheeks, it was clear there was something between them once more – that same affection in his gaze she'd seen just before he'd kissed her.

Cesca high-fived her without speaking. Unable to talk as their heart rates dropped and their breathing returned to normal. Beth felt on top of the world, like she could solve any problem, outlast any difficult patch. She was strong, determined, undefeatable.

Cesca's family swamped them as soon as they came close enough. Emilio pulled Cesca into his arms and Marco's nieces and nephews were all hopping up and down, eager to get the next high five from their auntie.

All the while Marco smiled on.

Had his thoughts changed? Did he see now what everyone else saw?

'I'd better go get changed,' Beth said.

'I'll get you a drink for when you're back.'

'Thanks. I won't be long.'

Beth showered and changed quickly, putting on a nice pair of jeans and top she'd recently bought, enjoying the change from the boring tailored trousers and jumpers she normally wore. Her uniform of unflattering black and grey had been replaced by dark blue denim jeans that hugged her hips while the top was a pale pink. Her cheeks were still rosy from the race, and she tied her still slightly damp dark brown hair up in a ponytail.

'Ready?' she asked Cesca who had changed into a pair of skinny jeans and a large, floppy jumper.

Cesca nodded and they made their way back outside as Emilio's race was called. They hurried out and he kissed Cesca on the cheek before running to the pier. Marco scowled, but didn't speak, smiling at Beth as she stopped beside him. She noticed his slight double take as he took in her changed appearance.

'I bought some new clothes,' she said shyly. 'Thought I could do with something less . . . grey.'

'You look beautiful. But you have always looked beautiful. Always.'

As the second *always* floated in the air between them, the starter pistol fired, shocking her out of the moment, and the race began.

Cesca immediately began calling Emilio's name and Marco clapped and mumbled words of encouragement for his friend. Beth smiled, glad that despite everything he still wanted to support him and was growing more hopeful his views on Cesca and Emilio had changed. In fact, as the race continued, he couldn't help himself, and shouted for Emilio to row, calling the pace, encouraging him to move quicker as he fell behind. They all edged further and further to the water, standing on the edge of the pier.

Suddenly, Beth was aware of Marco tensing, stepping forwards and shouting in Italian. She wasn't sure what he was saying at first, but the worried look on his face and the change in his tone told her something was wrong. She followed his gaze and saw for herself his concern: Emilio's was about to collide with someone else. The rower from Giudecca was slipping further and further into the line of Emilio's boat, but they were moving so quickly, and Emilio had nowhere to go, no way to correct his course. The shouts changed from those of encouragement to warning, Marco bellowing louder than everyone. And then, as if in horrifying slow motion, it happened.

The boats crashed together.

Beth's hands flew to her mouth, pressing hard against her lips. Cesca was screaming as loudly as Marco at her side. The rower from Giudecca's boat hit the side of Emilio's. Oars collided and thrashed in the water, Emilio's boat rocked, and he toppled into the water. Suddenly, like a domino effect, boats were everywhere as chaos ensued.

Beth waited for Emilio's head to pop up, for him to float to the surface and gulp the air. But his head didn't break through the water.

The waters of Venice were such a part of the city and its beauty, it was easy to forget how treacherous they could be. It was a horrible reminder that behind the picturesque place were the same dangers that existed anywhere. The idea sent a shiver down her spine and she instinctively wrapped her arm around Cesca.

They waited what felt like minutes but couldn't have been more than twenty seconds, but still Emilio hadn't appeared.

'Where is he?' Cesca asked in shaky, brittle English. 'He hasn't come up yet.'

Beth glanced at Marco who was already throwing off his jacket and shoes and after a short sprint had dived from the side of the pier into the cold, icy water. The crowd were silent around them, everyone clasping hands together, drawing the children away, afraid of what they might see next.

With strong movements, his arms powering through the water, Marco swam to the boat, took a breath of air and dived underneath. The rower from Giudecca who'd fallen in the opposite side, did the same as they searched for Emilio underneath the surface. Beth felt Cesca's body shake and picked up Marco's coat from the ground, wrapping it around her shoulders. Tears were streaming from her eyes as she muttered prayers in Italian.

'Where is he?' she asked, as Paola too wrapped her up. 'He's going to be all right, isn't he?'

'He'll be fine,' Beth responded. 'Marco will get him out.' She spoke in Italian knowing that English would only tax her friend's brain more than needed right now. Emilio must have hit his head on the boat or perhaps one of the oars caught him during the crash. She hoped he wasn't unconscious, but she knew they needed to get him up soon. He needed air and quickly.

Her heart was beating so fast she thought she might pass

out. She had to concentrate on her breathing, telling herself to calm down. Cesca needed her and panic wouldn't help anyone. Her mind began to plan, to think of what needed to happen next.

'Has anyone called an ambulance?' she asked out loud, speaking first in English then repeating it in Italian. When she was met with shocked faces, she knew she couldn't take a chance and pulled out her phone. It was possible the organisers had already called one, but it couldn't hurt to be sure. She dialled 112 and explained what had happened, giving the operator the address.

As the operator was giving her instructions on what to do next, Marco's head popped up from under the water with Emilio in his arms. Marco had angled his head back so it was on his shoulder and was holding it tightly. With the help of the other rowers who had all jumped in to find their friend, they manoeuvred him to the pier where Cesca's father and brothers pulled him out onto the side. He was unconscious, his mouth falling open and head lolling horribly to the side.

Having had first-aid training, Beth fell to her knees and checked for a pulse. Thankfully he was breathing, so didn't need CPR, but in all likelihood he'd inhaled some water.

'Emilio? Can you hear me?' she asked in Italian. His eyelids flickered and she took his shoulder, rolling him into the recovery position.

Cesca knelt down in front of him, taking his pale, shaking hands. 'Emilio? Emilio, please, you have to wake up.'

From somewhere someone handed Beth some blankets and towels and she covered Emilio to try and keep him warm.

'He's breathing,' Beth said to her gently. 'Which is a very good sign. The ambulance is on its way.'

'Emilio, please?' Tears fell from Cesca's eyes as she sobbed, and Beth rubbed her friend's back. She noticed Marco, pale and shivering, looking as though he might cry, and she stood, placing another of the blankets around his broad shoulders. Doing so brought her face incredibly close to his and their eyes met for a second, fear and tears softening the ice-blue to a washed-out paleness.

'Will he be all right?'

'I don't know,' she said quietly. 'But he's alive and he wouldn't be if you hadn't dived in to save him.'

From behind her, Emilio coughed, and she spun back. It was a wet, rattling sound as the water he'd inhaled exited his body. Beth was relieved to see there wasn't much, which meant that though it had seemed a lifetime, he hadn't been under the water long enough to really fill his lungs with liquid. That would have been even more treacherous.

'Emilio!' Cesca cried, kissing his cheek.

'*Ciao, amore mio*,' he mumbled, still coughing with the effort of speaking.

'My love,' Cesca replied in Italian.

Beth found herself tearing up as she stood next to Marco. She felt the weight of his hand on her shoulder and she stepped closer to him. She wanted to press herself against his body, to wrap her arms around his waist. She didn't care that he was wet. She wanted to hold him, to comfort him, to warm him. His teeth were chattering.

'They really love each other, don't they?' he said quietly, his voice gravelly with emotion.

'Yes, I think they do.'

'I've been an idiot haven't I?'

She smiled. 'Maybe a little.' She turned to him, seeing the man she'd known before. The kind, gentle, sweet person who'd helped her find an apartment, who'd helped her business, who had kissed her as no one else had. 'You should go and get dry.'

'Not until I know he's definitely okay.'

The ambulance arrived, the crew bustling over to Emilio where he lay on the ground. He kept trying to sit up, but Cesca wouldn't let him. The paramedics took over, helping him sit up gently and checking his vitals.

'We'd like to take him to the hospital for some further checks and observations. You could have a concussion,' the paramedic said in Italian. 'And there is a risk of secondary drowning.'

'What's that?' Paola asked, as worried as if Emilio was her own child.

'Water inhaled can cause problems hours, sometimes even days later. We'd like to be sure his lungs are clear.'

'I'm coming with you,' Cesca said and as they manoeuvred him onto a stretcher, Emilio held out his hand to her.

'Wait!' Marco suddenly stepped forwards, surprising

them all. He placed his hand on his friend's chest and Emilio gripped it in return. 'I'm sorry.'

'*Mio amico*. It's all right. Bring me some sweets in the hospital. And beer.'

'No beer!' the paramedic replied with a laugh. 'I can see you're going to be trouble.'

'He always is,' Cesca added, following them into the ambulance.

They watched as the doors closed and the ambulance drove away. Other members of the rowing club were clearing the boats from the water, congratulating Marco on his quick reflexes, saying that he'd saved Emilio's life.

'Can we get out of here?' he asked Beth, as soon as he was able to speak just to her.

Shocked, she almost didn't know what to say. 'Of – of course.'

'I don't live far. Will you come? Please? I – I don't really want to sit alone right now.'

'Okay.'

Paola wrapped her son in a hug, telling him how proud she was of him. When she let him go, to everyone's surprise, Elio did the same, patting his son firmly on the back then cupping his cheek.

'Do you want to change here first?' Beth asked.

He shook his head. 'I just want to get out of here.'

Chapter 28

Marco's apartment was only a few streets from the rowing club with views over the lagoon. Two floors up, the high-arched windows let in the bright golden light. The décor was muted creams and soft browns, like an interior designer had devised everything for 'executive living'. The small kitchen had dark, modern units but the space didn't feel bleak; it felt serene and calm, like entering a spa.

Beth suddenly felt like she was seeing a whole new side to Marco. A part of him he kept hidden from most people. There were pictures of his family on shelves in the living room, his nieces and nephews smiling out at her, and it reminded her of the connection she and Marco had had. Something special and strong. There were books too, more than she'd thought he'd have, of all different genres.

'I'm going to take a shower and warm up,' he said, his teeth still chattering after the short walk. People had stared at him in his soggy, dishevelled state, but he'd kept his head down and spoken to no one but her. 'Help yourself to anything you like. You must need a strong coffee after what happened.'

'I definitely could.'

He took a few steps towards his bedroom before pausing and turning back. 'You were magnificent looking after Emilio, knowing exactly what to do.'

'I could say the same about you. You saved him.'

He dropped his eyes shyly. 'I don't know. I'll – I'll be back soon.'

He stepped into the bedroom, closing the door behind him. She heard the sound of the shower and hoped the hot water would revive him. Images of his body flashed across her mind, but as the adrenalin began to subside, she felt worn out, her eyelids heavy. If she sat down he might come out to find her fast asleep on the comfortable-looking sofa. They both needed a large, strong cup of coffee.

While she found cups and coffee, Marco emerged, dressed in clean, dry clothes, towel-drying his dark hair. He'd never looked more handsome, and swoon-worthy and she forced herself to keep a tight hold on her feelings. Her heart still hurt whenever she thought of him asking her to leave his parents' house and the humiliation still burned the back of her neck as the moment replayed. She didn't want to be hurt like that again.

She handed Marco a cup of coffee. 'How are you feeling now?'

'Warmer.' He smiled and she looked away.

'This is a beautiful apartment.'

'It is. I like being here. It's calmer, peaceful. Murano always feels busy and noisy – probably because of my family always being there. But here – this is my refuge.'

He sat and Beth went to the window, eager to see the views of the city. She cupped her hands around her mug, warming her fingers.

'Beth,' Marco said, drawing her attention. 'I need to thank you again for helping Emilio.'

'I didn't do much, Marco. It was you who acted quickly. I just kept him warm and called an ambulance.'

'No, you didn't panic once we got him out. You did everything right and you helped Francesca. I'm forever grateful you were there. And—' He grabbed his still-damp hair at the back of his head and Beth knew he was nervous. 'I'm sorry. I'm sorry for everything that happened at dinner that night. When I found out about Cesca and Emilio, I was angry, and I shouldn't have directed that at you. It wasn't your fault Cesca had made you keep a secret.'

So they were finally going to have a conversation about it.

'I was friends with her before I even met you. When she told me, I didn't know what to do. I couldn't do anything without betraying my friend and as we . . . grew closer, I did everything I could to get her to tell you, but it wasn't my secret to share.'

'I know. I was wrong. I'm so sorry. You said Francesca told you about my first business partner?' She nodded, drawing her eyes back to him. 'I shouldn't have trusted him and since then, I try not to trust people at all.'

'That's not very healthy, you know.'

'I know. But I felt like Emilio and Cesca had betrayed me. They could have just told me.'

'And you'd have listened?' There was a teasing edge to her voice, but she felt it was a point she had to make.

Marco sipped his coffee, glancing at her over the rim. 'I know I wouldn't have taken it well no matter when I was told, and I shouldn't have blamed you for that. I'm sorry. Today I saw how much Emilio and Cesca really care for each other. And I – I'd already realised how much I want you in my life. How much I love you.'

The words reverberated around the silent apartment, ricocheting in her head, bouncing from one side of her skull to another. He'd said it before but hearing it now, after everything had happened that day, it was like he was speaking a foreign language. One she wasn't fluent in. 'You love me?'

'I do.' He stood, placing his cup down and moving towards her.

Beth's hands and legs began to shake, and she leaned against the wall for support. He cupped her cheek, his thumb brushing her skin softly. He dipped his head to kiss her and though she wanted this more than anything, pain and anger shot up inside her. Hurt rippled through her body that it had taken a near-death experience for him to realise it wasn't her fault when he could have just spoken to her, but instead, he'd closed himself off and returned to the distant businessman she'd first met. She stepped backwards.

'What is it?' Hurt flashed across his features and suddenly anger burned inside her.

'Marco, we can't just go back to where we were before.'

'But . . . why? I've apologised. I am truly sorry for what happened, and I promise you it won't ever happen again. And I want the same as you. I want us, not necessarily a family – children, but us.'

That he wanted the same things as her almost swayed her, but she needed to say what was on her mind. If she didn't, what sort of future would they have anyway?

'I believe your apology, but do you not understand how hurt and humiliated I was? You made me leave your house, in front of all your family.' He dropped his eyes, stepping away from her and swallowing. 'And then you just went to ground, causing everyone to worry about you. Cesca was beside herself. She felt she was to blame for everything. So did I.'

'I just needed some space to think. I love you, Beth. I'm sorry for the way I behaved. I didn't mean to humiliate you. I – I wasn't thinking.'

'I understand you needed space, Marco, and that things have happened to you that have caused wounds, but you pushed me away so fiercely and now, now you've decided you're over it you want to just start again?' She took a deep breath.

'Beth—'

'I was falling in love with you too and you just shut me out.'

His head snapped up, hope flashing across his features.

'I just . . . I think I need some time too. Because if this is how you react to things, if you're going to always shut me out when something goes wrong, or when you're upset, I don't think I can deal with that. I need someone who's going to talk to me, who wants to fix things together.'

He took another step back and spoke softly, defeated. 'I understand you're still hurting and I'm sorry. I – I didn't mean to mess everything up. If you need more time, I'll respect that, but please know I won't ever do that to you again. Like you, I've always been focused on my work and relationships . . . I have a lot to learn.'

She wanted to believe him, but pain was still pulsing inside her. It had been such an emotional and terrifying day she didn't think it was the right time to make any decisions at all, let alone one so important. She smiled softly at him and kissed him gently on the cheek, then went to the kitchen and placed her cup on the side before grabbing her coat and closing the door behind her.

In turmoil, she didn't know if she'd made the right or wrong decision and part of her wanted to run back in and throw her arms around him, but another told her she needed to think slowly and logically. She'd spent the whole year so far making off-the-cuff, rash decisions and look where it had led her: with a business she loved but with a heart in tatters. It was time to revert to her old ways. Her careful, practical, safe ways and protect her poor broken heart.

Chapter 29

'You did absolutely the right thing,' Elsa replied, leaning into the screen for extra effect. The only effect though was that Beth had a close-up of her right nostril and part of her right cheek. 'He can't expect you to just open your arms and say, "Oh, you love me? Well, that makes everything all right doesn't it?"'

'But—' Daisy added, her calm tone more evident than it was the last time they'd spoken. 'Love is about forgiveness and admitting and apologising for mistakes.'

'Daisy, don't tell me that!' Beth cried, then screamed into a cushion, which made Polo who'd cuddled into a ball on her lap, look up. 'What am I going to do? Have I done the wrong thing? It's just . . . no one's ever got me like he has.'

'What do you mean?'

Beth stared at their expectant faces and took a deep

breath. It was time for the conversation she'd been putting off, not wanting them to feel guilty or worry about her even more. She should have told them about her decision not to have children long ago, but now it was time. She raised her eyes to the beautiful wooden beams above her head, in her beautiful apartment, now complete with bookshelves rammed with books and pictures of her friends.

'There's something I've been meaning to talk to you about for a while but . . . but I just couldn't ever find the right time and then things changed and now—'

'Bethy,' Elsa said kindly. 'Slow down. What is it you need to tell us?'

She took another deep breath, ready for their questions. They'd wanted a family for so long she wasn't sure they'd understand her decision, but the time had come and as their friendship had weathered so many changes over the years, she hoped it would cope with this one. 'So . . . I've kind of decided that I don't want kids.'

'Right.' Elsa stretched out the word so it sounded like a question.

'Okay,' Daisy added, waiting for more.

Beth's chest tightened at the anticipation coming through the screen, seeping into the room. 'I just . . . I just don't see them in my future. I see your kids in my future,' she added quickly. 'I can't wait to be a godmother and to hold your little baby in my arms and play games with them and hear them giggle. But you know I have PCOS, so the chances of my conceiving are pretty low and I've kind of come to realise that . . . I don't think I want my own kids anyway. I just don't see my life panning out that way. I want to live here and I probably want to travel a bit too and I want to do things and that doesn't mean I don't want to get married, I just don't *feel* maternal. Like—' She'd started now and as the words tumbled out, she couldn't seem to stop. 'Like you always wanted kids at some point, yes?' Daisy and Elsa nodded. 'And that feeling grew as the time for it to happen for you got nearer.' They nodded again. 'Well, I just don't have that yearning. Ever. So . . . I don't think I want children.'

'Fair enough,' Elsa replied with a shrug.

'Yeah,' Daisy said, looking confused. 'It's none of our business.'

The three of them fell silent.

'Oh,' Beth said. 'So, you get it?'

'Of course we do,' Elsa replied. 'Not everyone's the same, Beth. We're all different and want different things out of life.'

'But aren't you disappointed?'

'Why would we be?'

'Because people don't always understand.'

'Bethy,' Elsa said sternly. 'We're a lesbian couple conceiving via IVF and donor sperm. We're not exactly most people.'

She laughed. 'No, I suppose you're not.'

'You live your life how you want, babe! You do you!'

'Yeah,' Daisy added. 'You have to do what makes you happy and if having kids isn't going to make you happy, then don't do it! And it's about time society caught up with that. But what does this have to do with Marco?'

'Well, he knew about my worries about whether to have kids or not – whether it was something I actually wanted, and then, before everything happened with his sister, when we were at that family dinner, he said he felt the same way. That he loves all his nieces and nephews, but he doesn't feel the need to have kids of his own. He just wants me.'

Her voice trailed away as these words, and the *I love you* he'd given her before, rang through her head.

'Oh,' Daisy said. 'That's actually quite sweet.'

Elsa spoke more softly than usual. 'It is, but there'll be other guys who don't want kids, Bethy. That's not a reason to get back with him.'

'That's true. The only reason to get back with him,' Daisy added, 'is because you love him and he made a mistake, but you forgive him for it. Can you? I know you've never really been heartbroken before, but relationships are just like your career, Beth; they're work. Hard work at times. When you've missed out on a job or a journal article hasn't been accepted, you haven't just given up, have you?'

Elsa nodded emphatically. 'She's right. When things go wrong and we make mistakes you have to work through them.'

'Your relationship has never really seemed like hard work,' Beth replied.

Daisy and Elsa both laughed but then looked at each other with such love and admiration, Beth's heart flipped.

'Umm . . .' Elsa cleared her throat. 'Do you not remember when I was supposed to take Daisy out for her twenty-fifth birthday and got caught up at work and was so late to the restaurant they were nearly closing? You and she were drunk as lords, she was crying, and you were so angry with me we didn't speak for a week.'

'Or the time,' Daisy said with a sly smile, 'that I was so caught up in my own problems that I never realised how miserable Elsa was in her old job and we ended up having that huge row where it all came to a head and I came and stayed at yours for a few days?'

'Relationships take lots of work, Bethy. Just like your career did.'

Beth sat back in her chair. She'd completely forgotten all those things. Maybe because they'd always gotten back together and worked through any problems. They always talked eventually and figured out where they'd gone wrong so they could try to avoid it the next time. Communication was key and she and Marco had already discussed so much. He understood the thing she'd feared most – he wanted the same. And he'd promised her he wouldn't ever just close down on her again. They already knew so much about each other – she knew his wounds and the things that hurt him, and he knew her fears and hopes and dreams. He'd accepted her as she was; was she not going to do the same because he'd made one mistake?

Elsa was right that there were other men out there who would feel the same way about children and life, but she didn't want another man.

She wanted Marco.

But was it too late to tell him so?

Chapter 30

Beth hung the last of the bunting on the front of the book barge ready for her grand reopening. She'd written the name in both English and Italian in fancy swirling letters on a chalkboard, and it was stood on the canal side. She stared over and rolled the words around her mouth: Library of Words, *La Libreria delle Parole*. She took a moment to look at the new and improved floating bookshop. Where it had looked dark and full to the brim, it now looked light and airy. Signor Zambelli the portrait artist and Riccardo the spray-painting artist were setting up on the upper deck, manoeuvring around each other, discussing their crafts in a way that excited Beth as she realised she was bringing both her passions to people in a way she'd never expected.

Even with visiting Emilio, Cesca had finished the upper deck, and the Parisian-style cupboards on the front of the barge had been tweaked and painted in light, pastel colours. With the warm orange light glowing inside from the table lamps, the place looked welcoming and homely. Pride swelled within Beth as she looked at everything she'd achieved just by going with the flow. She'd never thought she could do something like this without planning, preparing, mapping and worrying. If she'd learned anything from this year so far, it was that impetuous decisions didn't mean disaster. They could mean new beginnings and different doors opening.

She'd started the day with another morning row. The sun rising slowly as she pulled the oars rhythmically, matching her breathing to the movement. It wasn't a race, and she hadn't rushed. This was simply for the joy of it. For the joy of moving her body, feeling energised and allowing stress to leach from her system. She'd worried no one would turn up to her grand reopening. Daisy and Elsa had begged to come, but Beth wouldn't let them. Flying in early pregnancy was safe for most people, but they'd gone through too much to take any unnecessary risks. Beth had promised to take some videos and that they could come out as soon as the baby was old enough to fly. She'd also promised a trip back to England when the season ended. But with the customers she'd had so far, she was hopeful that at least a few people would turn up, especially Marco.

Since realising her love for him was too good to let go, she'd wanted to speak to him face to face, to tell him how she felt and admit that she wanted a future here in Venice with him. Today, she'd decided, was the day. Emilio was recovering well and there was no reason to wait. She wasn't yet sure what she'd say, or how or when, but she knew for certain he wouldn't leave here today without knowing exactly how she felt.

Lolanda from the coffee barge next door stopped at her side, handing over an extra-large takeaway mug. 'It looks wonderful, Beth. You are the pride of the canal.'

'I wouldn't go that far,' she replied with a giggle. 'Your barge always looks and smells amazing, and the fruit and veg one with all its colours looks like something from a magazine. But I am very proud of it.'

'You should be. I will save you a *bussolá*.' She patted her arm and scurried off to the coffee barge to help Galvano.

Beth went inside and ensured everything was in place and that the fire was lit, even though the breeze had grown warmer as the spring sunshine flooded the city. Easter wasn't far away and though the sun was shining, the warmth everyone associated with Italy was yet to arrive in all its glory.

Voices sounded from the canal path and Beth recognised them immediately. It was Cesca and her family. Her heart jumped into her mouth as she hoped Marco might be with them, but as she climbed out of the book barge, her eyes scanned for his tall frame and ice-blue eyes, her hopes falling like a stone sinking to the bottom of the lagoon. He wasn't there. How could he miss this? He knew how important this day was for her. It was important for him too. His artists were here. Surely he'd come to support them. Still, she plastered on a smile and hid her hurt.

'Paola, Elio! Thank you for coming.'

Paola was carrying a plastic box full of food. She handed it over, kissing Beth on both cheeks. 'This is for you. To keep your strength up.'

'Thank you.' She chuckled.

'The barge is good,' Elio said, in his usual understated way. 'And I like this.' He pointed to the upper deck and the work on display. 'Has Marco asked you to display our glass?'

'Umm . . . no. No, he hasn't. Yet. Maybe he will when I see him.'

Paola shot her husband a stern look. He must have been told not to mention Marco and had put his foot in it. All Marco's nieces and nephews danced around, tugging on her sleeve and asking if there were children's books. Beth replied that there were and told them they could go in and look if they liked. Being allowed in before anyone else seemed like the biggest treat in the world as they fought each other to get through the door first.

Cesca came over to her and gave her a huge hug. Beth knew that Emilio had been home from hospital the day after the accident when they were sure there was no lingering water in his lungs. 'How's he doing?' Beth asked.

'He wants to get back to training already.'

'What?'

'I know. I tried to tell him he shouldn't, but he wanted to, and his coach said it was fine. But congratulations, I'm so happy we got this done by Easter.'

'Yes, you might have kept my business viable.'

'Oh, it's not that,' Cesca said with a grin. Beth stopped. 'I'm going to go away with Emilio. On the road with him. We want to be together, so we're going to do everything we can to make that happen and I don't want to keep waiting for him to return home. I want to go with him, explore Italy. Explore the world.'

She was smiling so widely Beth couldn't help but smile too. 'And does everyone know this?'

Cesca nodded. 'Everyone. No secrets this time. We told them all yesterday after Emilio and I had decided ourselves.'

'What did Marco say?' Saying his name caused a churning feeling inside her.

'He said he was happy for us, and he told me I have to stay in touch or Mamma will get angry. He told Emilio he better take care of me, or he'll be answering for it, but that is Marco. I don't think he was serious. And,' Cesca continued, 'he's been working with Papa.'

'What do you mean?'

'I don't know what on. Something secret. They keep running off to the workshop together and not coming back for hours. Marco hasn't stepped foot in there for years. It's all very confusing. They've been getting on really well too. Ever since Marco jumped in and saved Emilio, they've been talking and listening to each other. Papa has agreed to some of Marco's plans to promote the business. Nothing too crazy. Just a few exhibitions and hopefully getting a few shops to sell our work. Marco would like an online shop and a website, but I told him to take it slowly with Papa. The strange thing about them going in the workshop though,' she said, circling back, 'is that they won't let anyone else come in when they're working. Papa is always careful because of the furnace, but they are being even more careful than usual.'

'What could they be up to?'

Cesca shrugged. 'I don't know, but it's Mamma and Papa's wedding anniversary soon, so maybe something for that. Whatever it is, it's top secret.'

'Right. So when do you leave?' Beth asked, sad that she was losing her best friend in Venice.

'The day after tomorrow. I don't know how I feel about it. I've always lived in Murano or Venice. I've never really been anywhere else.'

Beth hooked her arm through Cesca's. 'Trust me, as someone who only came here for a year, it'll be an adventure, and you'll learn so many new things about the world and about yourself. And who knows, maybe you and Emilio will come back to Murano or Venice when the time's right.'

Cesca nodded. 'Emilio has already said when he stops rowing professionally he wants to come home and settle here.'

'You know, I'm liking him more and more.'

Her friend grinned. 'So am I.'

'Is—' Beth considered whether to finish the question or not, finally deciding she had to know for sure. 'Is Marco coming today, do you know?'

'Later. I don't know what he's doing, but he said he had something urgent to do first.'

Relief struck hard and fast but was followed quickly

with nerves and anxiety. What if he'd changed his mind and didn't want her anymore?

Before long, crowds began to flock to the canal side. Spring was here, the sun was shining, the waters bluer and calmer, the air filled with birdsong and Venice was lovelier than it ever had been before. All the barges were busy and everyone along the path pointed their customers towards Beth. She couldn't believe how they all supported one another, even those she hadn't had the chance to meet yet. She was busier than she'd ever been, restocking shelves, making lists of requests and orders (something she'd never even thought of with handling everything else on her plate). Her artists sold work and had lots of interesting conversations with new potential customers, the lace bookmarks provided by Marcella were very nearly fought over by two passionate Italian ladies until Beth promised there would be even more coming soon. Even Signor Sanna stopped by from the galleria and bought a book or two, pleased she was staying in Italy and asking if she'd consider doing one or two freelance jobs *if* they came up. She agreed because who knew what the rest of the year held, and a part of her still edged towards caution. She'd realised it always would, but she would choose whether to follow it or take a chance.

When the crowd parted and Signor Balbo arrived, Beth's heart flew up into her throat. He stood in silence, staring at the barge, taking it all in. Polo recognised him and began weaving around his feet. Signor Balbo bent down and petted the cat.

'Ah, his fur is nice and soft. You must be stroking him a lot.'

'I'm definitely enjoying looking after him and I don't think he minds that much either. So what do you think?' she asked tentatively.

He pursed his lips as he scanned every inch of the book barge. Beth, and everyone else who knew him, held their breath. The canal side had become so quiet you could hear a pin drop. 'I like it very much. Now let me see inside.'

He shuffled to the door and a customer helped him down the stairs. Beth followed, glancing at Cesca as she went.

'Yes, very nice. Exactly as it should be. I can go back to see my children in Padua knowing it is in good hands.'

Beth laughed in relief. 'Would you like to sit for a while?' She signalled to the armchair.

'Just a quick rest, I think.'

He snuggled in, Polo immediately jumping onto his lap.

Beth sat with him. 'I've been meaning to thank you, *signor*.'

'Thank me? For what?'

'For selling me the book barge and changing my life.'

'Oh, no!' He waved his hands. 'I didn't change your life, you did. And I'm grateful too. The time had come to pass on the bookshop. And I can see it's in the right hands.'

'Thank you.' Beth kissed his cheeks and went about serving customers.

After a short nap, during which Signor Balbo's snoring filled the barge, he left, promising to stop by more often. Beth returned to the canal side but couldn't help wondering where Marco was. His family were all still there, speaking in whispers at the side of the canal, checking phones and watches. But he still hadn't appeared. She had just grabbed another coffee when everyone seemed to turn, looking further down the canal path where someone was trying to make their way through the crowd carrying a humungous and clearly heavy box. A head of dark hair popped around the side and ice-blue eyes checked the route ahead.

Beth's breath skittered and her heart raced. It was Marco. But what was he carrying? His body was braced, his coat open and the tails drifting behind him as he strode forwards. The crowd parted as his broad form made its way through. He stopped in front of her, placing whatever it was at her feet. As he stood, she could see his chest rise and fall and the closed-off look she'd grown used to was gone, revealing the man underneath. The man she'd been falling in love with.

'I'm sorry I'm late,' he said, motioning down to the giant box at her feet as if that had been to blame.

'That's okay. Thank you for coming. Signor Zambelli and Riccardo are just—'

'I'm not here for them. I'm here for you.'

Beth felt her eyes widen, the skin around them stretching as she gazed at him in wonder. 'For me.'

Marco pushed his hand into his hair, scrunching the back in that way she'd come to know and love. Her heart swelled. 'Beth, I know I was wrong to get angry with you. So wrong. I shouldn't have done that, and I understand if it will take you a while to forgive me.'

She'd already forgiven him, what she was struggling with, was forgiving herself. She'd always been afraid of not being in control and there was nothing more out of control than love. Love did what it wanted when it wanted. It made you act in ways you never thought you would. She wouldn't haven't stayed and made a last-minute decision to buy a book barge if her love for Venice hadn't been strong enough. And now, she knew just how much she was in love with Marco, with his family. Losing him for these few short weeks had been hard enough. She wasn't prepared to lose him again.

'But,' Marco continued, 'I will wait for as long as it takes for you to forgive me. You must know though, Beth, that I have fallen completely in love with you and I will be here ready for whenever you can love me back.'

Beth's eyes misted with tears and as their friends and family gasped, she wasn't sure if she'd be able to speak. She took a deep breath and cleared her throat. 'Marco—'

'Before you say anything,' Marco said, holding his hand up to stop her. 'Please, open this.' He nodded at the box at her feet.

Beth leaned down and opened the top. She reached in and pulled out the layers of bubble wrap hiding whatever was inside. Eventually, she unveiled it, lifting it out to see it in all its glory.

A smile spread over her face as she took in the beautiful glass vase. The colours were of the stunning sunsets she and Marco had seen on their morning rows. A mixture of light and dark pinks with pale and deeper blues. The filigree at the top of the vase made the glass look similar to the water, the way it swirled around the boat as they moved through the lagoon.

'It's beautiful,' she whispered. 'Where did you—'

'I made it.'

Her head snapped up. 'You did? When?'

'I've been working on it for the last few weeks with Papa. He's helped me get it perfect. I needed some teaching as it had been so long.'

A slight blush crept up onto his cheeks and if Beth hadn't been holding the vase she'd have reached out and cupped his cheek, gently brushing the redness with her thumb. She glanced at Elio to see him smiling proudly at his son.

'Marco—' His face fell as her voice had sounded firmer than she'd intended. She had wanted it to be firm as she knew her decision was the right one, but she hadn't meant to alarm him and from the widening of his eyes and his slight step back, she was worried he was about to turn around and run. Cesca stepped forwards and took the vase from her. Elio soon swooped in and grabbed it from her, to keep it safe, clearly as proud of it as Marco was.

'Marco—' she began again. 'I don't need time to forgive you. I already have. And I'm sorry for being too stubborn when you apologised to me before.'

He shook his head. 'No, you were right not to accept my apology straight away.'

'We'll have to agree to disagree. But it made me realise

that I'm not *falling* in love with you, I *am* in love with you. Totally. Already. And I want us to make this work. No one—' She almost stumbled over her words. She didn't want to talk about her decision not to have children in front of everyone simply because she preferred her private life to be private. But she wanted him to know that they were meant to be. 'No one's ever understood me like you do.'

'I feel the same,' he replied with a smile. 'I think we can – we do – fulfil each other. You are the only thing I want, Beth. And I want to build a life together.'

Beth's stomach somersaulted and in the true spirit of going with the flow, she inched towards Marco, lifted her head and kissed him. His strong arms wrapped around her waist, pulling her close.

From around her she was aware of the crowd beginning to cheer and whistle. As they pulled back, from the corner of her eye Beth saw Elio holding the vase tightly, protecting it from his sons and their wives and children who were dancing around and jumping on the spot.

She giggled, but she'd be forever grateful. Just like the paintings she'd always loved, it was a priceless work of art. Her priceless work of art made by the man she loved. In that moment, Beth couldn't have been happier, and she knew without doubt that she'd made the right decision. Venice was the city she loved most and Marco the only man she could ever love just as much.

Epilogue

ONE YEAR LATER

Beth closed up the book barge, dropping the key into the hands of her assistant, Bianca. In Italian, Beth asked her to take good care of the place and to call her if there were any problems.

Bianca who loved practising her English with Beth replied in slightly staccato sentences. 'I promise I will check in every day.'

'Galvano and Lolanda will be next door this weekend if you need any help too.'

The little canal-side community had grown, and Beth now knew nearly all her neighbours. When customers arrived, they always urged them to visit the other shops on the canal and even Signor Sanna and everyone at the *Gallerie dell'Accademia* advised tourists to visit this particular one.

La Libreria delle Parole had been doing well. Books

were flying off the shelves and tourists flocked to her book barge for a holiday read and to purchase unique souvenirs you couldn't find anywhere else. The artist exhibitions were going well and in the summer, when the evenings were long and warm and the sky a blaze of orange and yellow, they gave talks and demonstrations, which were always well attended. She'd been so busy she'd had to hire an assistant. She'd never thought she could get this far without planning every move and triple-checking every decision, but here she was.

'Ready?' Marco asked, adjusting the handle on the suitcase.

'Ready.'

They were headed to the airport as Marco had secured a client in Athens, and they were off to attend their first gallery opening. His PR business was going from strength to strength, as was his family business now Elio was agreeing to a few more exhibitions and outlets. He hadn't quite come round to a website yet, but one of Marco's brothers was working on that while they were away and was pretty confident he'd have agreed by the time they got back.

Cesca and Emilio were still on the road, coming back periodically to see her family and his, and she was still using her carpentry skills, making her own creations. Beth received regular updates from her, and they had dinner together whenever she was in town.

As for Daisy and Elsa, their gorgeous baby boy, Asher, arrived right on time weighing a healthy seven pounds, ten ounces and Beth had flown home immediately to be with them and cuddle the little bundle of joy. She'd loved it, but as she'd left, she'd never been surer of her decision to not have children. She'd looked forward to returning to Marco and the life they were building together.

'Beth,' Marco said, as they made their way to the *vaporetto* – the private water taxi – they'd organised to get them to the airport. 'There was something I wanted to ask you, actually.'

He was always doing this, she thought as her suitcase rumbled over the cobbles. 'If this is about dinner, I thought we could grab something at the airport before the flight and then eat some lovely Greek food when we get to Athens.'

'It's not about food.' He then mumbled, '*Non penso sempre al mio stomaco*.'

Beth giggled. 'I do know you don't always think of your stomach. Just most of the time.'

Marco grinned. 'Why do I forget you speak Italian sometimes?'

They stopped at the pickup spot, and she turned to him. 'What did you want to ask me?'

'I wanted to say that I think we should move in together when we get back from Athens.'

'Move in together?' She'd been wanting this for a while but hadn't been sure how to raise it. 'To your place or mine?'

'Yours. My place is nice, but it isn't—'

'Home,' she answered for him.

Her small apartment had grown to feel more and more

like home – their home – as the year had passed. And while Marco's apartment was nice, some would even say better as it was bigger and in a better part of town, it just didn't have the same feel to it.

'Exactly,' he replied with a grin. 'And it's still close to the rowing club, so convenient for our early mornings. What do you think?' he asked nervously. He raised his hand to scrunch the hair at the back of his head, but Beth reached out and took it, wrapping her fingers tightly around his.

'I can't wait.'

He stepped closer, kissing her gently. 'I love you.'

Her lips were just meeting his again when the *vaporetto* driver shouted Marco's name. Beth swiped a light kiss on his lips. 'I love you too.'

'Do you know how many bookshops Athens has?' she asked as Marco handed the driver the suitcases and they climbed aboard.

'Tell me.'

'Apparently, it has around seven hundred.'

'*Qualcuno mi aiuti.*'

'You don't need help; it'll be fun!'

'Do we have to visit them all?'

'Of course we do.'

'I should have known.'

Beth grabbed his hand as they sat down. 'You know you love it.'

'I do.' Marco kissed her fingers. 'But try to remember the weight limit on the cases this time.'

Beth had absolutely no intention of doing so and Marco knew that perfectly well too. She'd learned that relationships weren't just about compromise but also knowing each other's faults and loving them as much as the good things. Squeezing Marco's hand tighter she sat back and watched the outline of Venice disappear behind them, and though she was looking forward to this trip away, she couldn't wait to get home and make her apartment for one, a home for two.

Acknowledgements

Some books flow from your fingertips and others make you work really, really hard for every sentence, every paragraph and definitely for the happily ever after! *The Floating Venice Bookshop* was one of those, but sometimes those books end up being the ones you love the most and I have to say, I've grown quite fond of Marco, Beth and Polo the cat!

I'd like to send a massive, hug-filled thank you to all the readers and reviewers who have given up their time to read this and my other Annabel French books, who share reviews and post on socials. You might not believe me, but honestly, seeing a picture of your book or a review never, ever gets old. I'm always acutely aware I only get to do this thing I love because of people like you who choose to spend time with my characters. I really hope you enjoy this one and thank you from the bottom of my heart!

A special thanks also goes to Maddie Wilson, my editor, who is kind, intuitive and an absolute joy to work with. She also embodies the positive, uplifting vibes of the Annabel French series and I'm so grateful to have her in my corner. Her edits are always spot on, and she makes my books better than I could ever make them on my own. Sending you a big squidgy hug, Maddie! I'm also sending hugs and thanks to everyone else at the amazing Avon team who work so hard. You've played a blinder so far and I hope we get to keep working together! Special mentions again to my brilliant copyeditor Helena Newton, and the amazingly talented Lindsey Spinks, my illustrator, for the gorgeous covers!

And finally, thanks to my family and friends. I'm so blessed to have you all in my life. I'm grateful for the writing friends who keep me sane when I'm overthinking, and to my family who listen to me moan when my characters aren't playing ball! Thank you! I love you!

PS. Readers, if you haven't signed up to my mailing list yet, get on over there as I'm giving away a free novel! Here's the link: https://bit.ly/3gbqMS0

Loved *The Floating Venice Bookshop*?

Annabel French will be back in Summer 2026 with another gorgeous escapist novel *The Floating Copenhagen Cafe*!

Lose yourself in the latest destination summer romance, perfect for fans of Cressida McLaughlin and Julie Caplin.

Don't miss Annabel's first European set escapist romance *The Floating Amsterdam Flower Shop*!

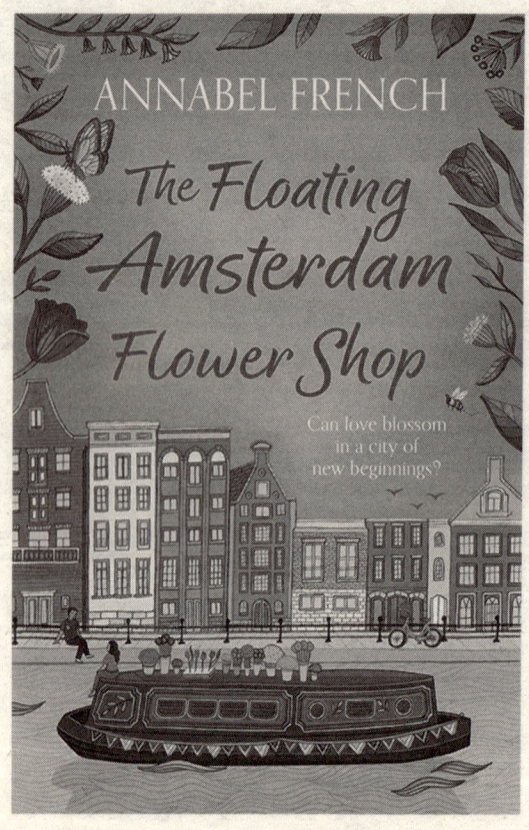

**One fresh start. One unexpected encounter.
Can love bridge the gap?**

Check out the chateau series also by Annabel French!

**A newly single woman. A handsome stranger.
A chateau that keeps bringing them together...**

The perfect feel-good romantic comedy
that will leave you falling head over heels!

Life has gone a little bit downhill for Naomi Winters. . .

Escape to the Swiss Alps with this festive, feel-good novel!

Two friends. One wedding. A love story that's long overdue. . .

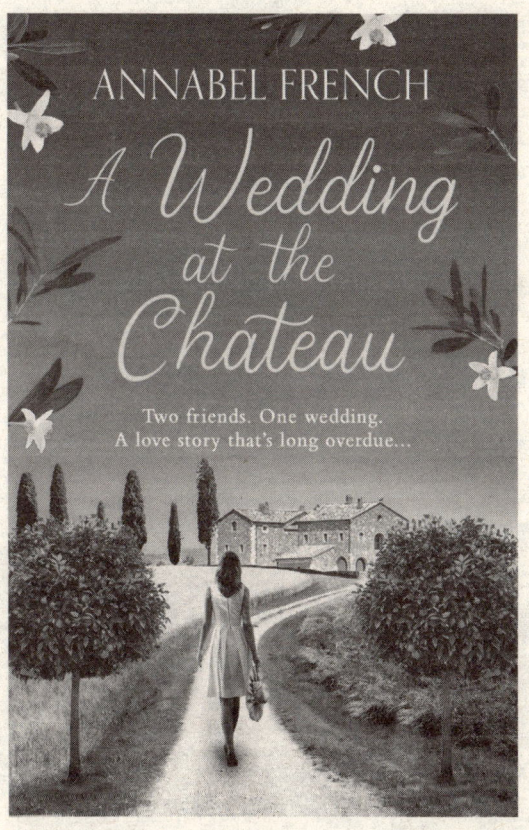

A Wedding at the Chateau is a romantic and heartwarming story, the perfect summer read!